WHATEVER YOU SAY

BY
LEIGH FLEMING

Enjoy!
Leigh Fleming

Published by Envisage Press, LLC

Copyright © 2017 Envisage Press, LLC

Cover by www.spikyshooz.com

ISBN: 978-0-9977351-4-7

This is a work of fiction. All of the characters, names, incidents, organizations, and dialogue in this novel are either the products of the author's imagination or are used fictitiously.

For Tom and Liza

Also by Leigh Fleming

Precious Words
Whatever You Call Me

ONE

The moment her boss threw down the gauntlet, challenging the junior associates at Bell, Goldman, and Greenburg to "show me what you're made of," Kate knew she'd have everything she ever wanted, ever worked for. Patrick Stone had made them a promise: one of them would get fast-tracked to senior associate, with the possibility of early partnership. All they had to do was prove they deserved it.

Dropping into her leather desk chair, Kate had rushed from the meeting and logged in to get a jump on the competition. She glanced over at the framed photo of the young sailor—her dad—when he was but eighteen. She tapped a kiss on her index finger and touched it to the glass.

"We got this, Dad." He'd always told her to do her best or be the best—she could never remember his exact words—but being the best was something she'd always strived for. She knew she was a shoe-in for the promotion and liked to think her peers knew it too; even so, she vowed to step up her game and increase her billable hours.

Her team had just won a guilty verdict in a high-profile hospital negligence suit—a case she had worked endless hours on, had even questioned a few witnesses in court. Now she was assisting in a medical malpractice case sure to bring in the same verdict, all but locking down her promotion. Just another hour reviewing the doctor's deposition followed by a concise summary placed neatly on Patrick's desk, and she could be home by midnight, in time to catch a few hours sleep before coming back at seven.

Two hours later, Kate clicked her laptop off and shoved some loose documents back into their folders. Before heading out her office door, she stuffed a handful of nuts in her mouth to quell her grumbling stomach while tapping a car service app on her phone for a ride back to her DuPont Circle apartment. Tomorrow's agenda was already scrolling through her mind.

The next morning Kate arrived at her office at ten minutes to seven. As soon as she hung her coat on the back of the door, one of the paralegals popped her head in. "Getting an early start, aren't you?"

"I could say the same about you."

"Well, considering you piled several files on my desk yesterday evening, I thought I'd better get at them."

"Thanks, Rebecca. I appreciate you staying on top of things."

Kate walked to the break room and filled her mug with black coffee. A small smile played across her lips as she thought about yesterday's verdict. *Partnership might be closer than you think.* When she returned to her office, Grant Goldman—grandson of *the* Mr. Goldman for which the firm was named—was studying the diplomas displayed behind her desk.

"Good morning, sir."

"Good morning, Kate." He gestured at the frames. "Impressive."

"Thank you."

Mr. Goldman took a seat across from her and brushed an imaginary fleck from his sleeve.

"The partners had a meeting late yesterday afternoon. You and Patrick, the whole team, should be very proud of yourselves for the work you did."

"Thank you. I'm just happy the jury got it right."

"They wouldn't have if it weren't for your due diligence and determination. I hear you're quite a pit bull on cross." He cocked a crooked grin and settled back in his chair.

A pit bull? She squared her shoulders and forced herself to remain stoic, fighting the urge to pat herself on the back. "I appreciated Patrick letting me have a crack at that hospital administrator who tried to turn the blame on our client."

"Obviously, you were effective." He stood and walked behind the chair before he continued. "It isn't often an associate dedicates herself to a case the way you did. Your efforts were instrumental in bringing in a very large award for our client. Twenty million for the negligence and fifty million in punitive damages—that's impressive. Thanks to you and your team, BGG brought in nearly twenty-five million. We want to reward you for that."

"Thank you."

"Because of your hard work, we're giving you a substantial raise."

"I appreciate that. It was an—"

"Look, Kate, I think we can be frank with one another." After straightening his tie, he looked down at her and clasped his hands. "Patrick announced the…competition, if you will, but we both know who the shining stars are around here."

"Oh?"

"All the associates on your team are in the running, but I believe there are only two viable candidates." She held her breath, hoping he would acknowledge her as a front-runner. "If this malpractice case goes the way of the last one, and you prove yourself again, it won't be a contest."

With a heavy sigh, Kate settled into her chair and folded her hands in her lap. "I'm determined to get our verdict."

He gripped the back of the chair and leaned forward, his dark eyes smiling. "I'm counting on it." He patted the upholstered chair and turned to go. "I won't keep you."

"Thank you, Mr. Goldman," Kate said as he strode out the door. She pressed her head against the back of her chair and spun around, lifting her feet off the floor. Only one nay-saying thought managed to creep up from her subconscious: He practically told her the promotion was hers—so why not give it to her now? She dropped her feet to the floor, stopping the chair's rotation, woke up her laptop, and got to work.

Several hours later, Kate threw open her door. "Rebecca, I've got to go out for a few minutes." She swept past the paralegal's desk, dropping a stack of files in her wake. She needed to get out of the office and get some air—and a venti caramel macchiato with an extra espresso shot—for a much-needed mid-day energy boost. Hard at it since seven, she still had several items on her to-do list before the sun went down.

As soon as she stepped onto the sidewalk, a massive black cloud swallowed the late afternoon sun and a sharp breeze blew open her jacket. She pulled the wool around her and leaned into the strong wind attempting to hold her back from the coffee she so desperately needed. Once inside, she tucked into in a dimly lit corner and scrolled through her cell phone log.

There were two calls from a number she didn't recognize with a West Virginia area code. Maybe her grandmother had finally purchased a new cell phone, something Kate had encouraged her to do. Gram was seventy-nine years old, living on her own, still driving her old Buick, and Kate worried she'd break down and get stranded somewhere with no way to call for help. She would call her when she got home this evening.

Once fully caffeinated, she walked back to the office, mentally reviewing her checklist of items still to be completed. It was Thursday trivia night, the only day she allowed herself to leave the office at five to join her friends. If she wanted to get out on time, she had better pick up her pace back to the office. She waited on the corner for the light to change, but before she could step around the puddle of stagnant water gathered in front of the crosswalk, a taxi came along and sent a plume of it in her direction, soaking her pants and shoes. She cursed—loudly—and wondered less audibly if cab drivers did that sort of thing for sport. She shook off the notion and continued toward the office. Not even a good drenching could ruin her day.

Back in her office, Kate used a clump of paper towels she'd nabbed from the bathroom to soak up as much water from her pants as possible and changed into another pair of shoes she kept stashed in her office. When her cell phone vibrated, she looked down to see the unknown West Virginia number and decided she'd better take the call.

"This is Kate McNamara."

"Hi Kate, this is Riley Smith. I live next door to your grandmother and—"

"What's wrong? What happened to Gram?"

"She, um, had a fall this morning on her porch steps and she's been taken to the hospital. I'm not family so they wouldn't tell me what her condition is. I found your number on the little bulletin board she has hanging in her kitchen."

She could barely squeeze out the words around the terror clogging her throat. "Oh my god, which hospital?"

"St. Barts, here in Highland Springs. I can give you the phone number."

She grabbed a pen and scribbled the number on a Post-It, her shaking hand making the digits almost illegible. As soon as she hung up, she called the hospital only to be told her grandmother was in surgery for a fractured femur. Tears threatened as she thought of her sweet Gram all alone, in pain, and most likely frightened. She looked at the legal memo on her computer screen and sighed heavily. Damn it, this couldn't have come at a worse time.

She rushed out the door toward Patrick's office, rehearsing what she'd tell him. She probably only needed a week or two off and there was no reason she couldn't work from Highland Springs. Rebecca could email her any necessary documents and Kate could access the legal database with Wi-Fi. Thank god for technology.

"Excuse me, Patrick?" She rapped her knuckles on his door and stepped into his office. "Could I speak with you for a moment?"

"Absolutely." He waved toward an empty chair across from his desk and she perched on the edge.

"I had a call a few minutes ago that my grandmother fell and broke her leg."

"I'm sorry to hear that."

"Thanks, but you see…" She fingered a stray hair behind her ear and cleared her throat. "The thing is, I'm my grandmother's only relative. My dad was an only child and I'm an only child. She lives in West Virginia and has no one to take care of her."

"And you need to go be with her." He stood and tucked his hands in his pants pockets. "Any idea how long you'll be gone?"

"I'm not sure—but not long." She popped to her feet and leaned across the desk. "I know I can keep up with my billables from there. That won't be a problem. I'll keep my same schedule as here, stay in close contact. You won't even know I'm gone."

He chuckled and shook his head. "I don't doubt it for a minute. Go take care of your grandmother. We can handle things while you're away."

She strolled slowly down the hall toward her office, echoes of *we can handle things* ricocheting through her mind. He meant the rest of the team, the other associates—and particularly Jason, the other "shining star" Mr. Goldman had referred to this morning. More than anything, Jason would love to have Kate out of the way so he could get that promotion—*her* promotion. There was no way she'd let him win. Whether in DC or West Virginia, she wouldn't let this opportunity slip away.

Grabbing one more sweater and a pair of black jeans, Kate had finished packing for Highland Springs. She wasn't sure how long she'd be there, but had enough for ten days, including some winter clothes. Today's sudden temperature drop was a good indication winter would be here soon; if it was this cold in Washington in late October, it had to be below freezing in West Virginia. Annie was jiggling her key in the lock as Kate wheeled her luggage to the door.

"Hey, you're home early," Annie said. "Going somewhere?"

"I have to go to Highland Springs. Gram fell and broke her femur." Kate turned toward her bedroom, but Annie grabbed her arm and spun her around.

"What? Is she in the hospital?"

"Yes. Had surgery today. I'm taking the train to Pittsburgh then catching a bus to Highland Springs."

Annie shook her head and grabbed both of Kate's arms, rendering her unable to move. "Stop. Wait. No."

"Annie—"

"You're not taking a train and a bus to Highland Springs. That will take forever. I'll drive you. Just give me a few minutes to pack an overnight bag." Annie released her and nearly jogged to her bedroom. Kate followed close behind.

"Annie, no. I appreciate it, but that's too much to ask."

"You didn't ask."

"But what about Kip? Your job?" Annie was the new chief of staff for her boyfriend, Maryland Congressman Kip Porter.

"Kip will understand and the office can run without me for a couple days. It won't be a problem." Annie wrenched open her closet doors and studied her wardrobe, organized by color and season. "He's going across the bay tonight and has meetings over there all day tomorrow. He's not back at his congressional office until Monday. He can hang out with his brother over the weekend. So it's no big deal."

"Really, you don't have to do this."

"Hush up, sister—we're going on a road trip to see Gram. Now go in the kitchen and warm up that flatbread I made yesterday. We better eat before we hit the road."

Kate looked down at Annie, who was at least six inches shorter than her. Her dear friend had more energy packed inside her diminutive body than people twice her size, and had a big heart to match. They made an odd pair standing side-by-side: Kate, tall and slender, and Annie, petite and curvy in all the right places. Opposites in nearly every way, they'd been close since college and had moved to DC where they now lived in a two-bedroom apartment in DuPont Circle.

Kate laid the leftover pizza on a cookie sheet and popped it in the oven. She poured two glasses of pinot grigio and carried them to Annie's room.

"You pack fast," Kate said, handing Annie a glass of wine. She waved it away as she finished zipping her suitcase.

"I'm driving, remember? I packed enough for a few days and will come back on Sunday. I can drive back down to get you once your grandmother is settled." Annie lifted the suitcase to the floor then snapped her fingers. "Oh, we need to call Derek and tell him we won't be at trivia tonight." As they walked back into the kitchen, Annie tapped out a quick text to their friend. "Let's eat so we can get going. It'll be midnight before we get there as it is."

TWO

A crystalline white blanket covered the idle wheat field, as a fine mist shrouded the colorless vista. Even in its bleakness, the cloud-laden sky hanging over the rolling hills was a comforting sight to Brody. Eight white-tailed deer lumbered single-file across the lower meadow, disappearing into the woods along the river. It was a typical autumn morning in central West Virginia, but the sight never failed to bring him a sense of calm. It had taken ten years and two cities to bring him back to Highland Springs, the only place he felt truly at home.

"Let's go, Loretta," he shouted to his German shorthaired pointer, who was snuffling around the rabbit warrens along the edge of the yard. "Rabbits are gone 'til spring." He patted the side of his thigh and walked the length of the porch that wrapped around the side of his house—the house he'd grown up in, as had several generations before him. He had bought the farmhouse from his parents two years ago when he returned to Highland Springs, which helped them realize their dream of retiring to Florida.

The old farmhouse had been in the Brody family—his mother's maiden name—since the late 1800s. Brodys had farmed the four hundred acres bordered by the Highland River to the south and east and Cash's Holler on the west practically since Highland Springs was founded. To the north, behind his house, was a steep hill with a sheer rock face topped by a flat ledge. As a boy, he and his friends would climb up the side of the hill and set up a fort on the outcropping, pretending to scout Indians off in the distance.

Since moving back home, he'd been clearing tall oaks and hickories to create a wide path that would eventually lead to a deck and pergola covering the cliff. He'd always loved the view of the valley from high atop the bluff and thought it would make a great place to watch July Fourth fireworks, or the green trees turning golden along the river. If nothing else, it would be a sanctuary to think, meditate…and forget.

Loretta sidled up to Brody, occasionally bumping into his leg as they walked across the gravel drive toward the garage housing the tractor, mower, and other machinery.

"Hey, what're you up to?"

Startled, Brody snapped around and saw his sister, Liza, walking up the lane, her purple hair fluttering in the cool breeze. She was wearing a long quilted coat she'd found at a thrift store and green rubber boots. He'd never understood her style, but then again, it was ever changing so what was the point?

"Hey, stranger. Where've you been? Haven't seen you in a week," Brody said.

"Working on a new series of winter landscapes and trying to get my orders finished before the holidays hit." Liza was a talented watercolor artist, successfully selling her art at regional galleries, as well as online. She made one-of-a-kind, custom-ordered Christmas cards from her watercolor designs and was always swamped this time of year. "Plus, I had to work at the bar three nights last week. One of the other bartenders was sick." She'd worked at the Brass Rail since college and couldn't seem to give it up. She claimed it was all that got her out of the house, but Brody thought it was how she kept up with local gossip.

"I'd like to see what you're working on," he said.

"All you have to do is walk down the lane, big brother. This driveway runs both ways." Liza lived in the little house once owned by their grandparents at the edge of the farm.

"Yeah, sorry about that. Been busy clearing the hill and delivering wood."

"I know. Taking care of your little old ladies and just being a good boy scout."

"Yeah." He chuckled and walked into the garage. He picked up a gas can and began filling the tractor's tank, Liza still on his heels.

"Are you working in the field today? I thought that was Tucker's job."

"Tucker's in Oregon buying hops and didn't get it done. I don't have anything to do today, so I'll do the plowing for him." Brody leased out his fields—for zero rent—to his friend Tucker, who had started a local craft beer business. Since the fields had been fallow and Tucker wanted organically grown barley and wheat, Brody offered to let him use his farm in return for partial ownership in the business. Most of the time, Tucker handled the planting and cultivating himself, but Brody stepped in when needed.

"Sure you do. You can get back in your studio and write some music."

Not this again. He shook his head as he kept his back to Liza.

"I know you can hear me. And you know I'm going to harass you until you've written another big hit."

"No pressure, right?" He twisted the cap back on the gas can and walked across the garage to replace the container on a shelf.

"Seriously. You need to get back to it and stop being a creepy recluse, locked away on your farm where you only talk to your dog and yourself."

"I don't talk to myself."

"You keep everyone at arm's length. Refuse to be among the living. Build your cliff-side hideaway instead of going out."

"You're being melodramatic." He turned back toward the tractor but she blocked his path, standing with her fists on her hips.

"I'm not. I know you've got another great song locked in there, dying to get out." She poked him in the chest with her finger.

"I'm not so sure about that." The days of feeling that buzz when a new riff or chord pattern popped into his head were long gone. He hadn't felt that creative rush since New York and doubted it would ever return.

"You've just got writer's block."

He knew it wasn't writer's block. This was different. Not since he'd dropped out of college his sophomore year to pursue a career in Nashville had he felt such a painful lack of creativity, as if his senses were deadened. He used to hear notes in his head, even the accompaniments that would later round out the song. Not so much as a quarter note had come to him since the accident, and he doubted they ever would again.

"Drop it, okay?" He gathered her shoulders in his hands and practically lifted her out of his way.

"I can't drop it. Brody—" Liza shadowed behind him. "It's not your fault. You have to forgive yourself and let it go."

"Easier said than done."

"Fine. I'll drop it…for now. Let's talk about your love life."

"You just don't know when to quit, do you?" He looked over his shoulder to find his sister just inches behind him.

"Have you even tried to meet anyone?"

"Give it a rest." Brody climbed on the tractor and turned the key, hoping the engine would block out her mantra, but she reached up and turned it off.

"I'm serious. You're young, smart, handsome—well, when you're cleaned up."

"I don't think someone with purple hair has the right to comment on my appearance." He lifted the bill of his cap, adjusting it to his liking.

"My hair is a fashion statement."

"A fashion statement, really?" He leaned his elbow on the steering wheel and shot a narrow gaze at her head.

"I just like it, okay?" Liza fluffed her long locks and climbed onto the foot rest. "Let me introduce you to some women I know."

"Not interested. I like my life just as it is. It's uncomplicated, stress-free, simple," he said.

"And boring. You're lonely."

"I'm not lonely; I've got Loretta." The dog's brown face turned at the sound of her name and she trotted over to the tractor, placing her paws on the opposite foot rest. Brody rubbed her ears and patted her head.

"Loretta may keep you warm at night, but she can't take care of other needs." Liza raised and lowered her eyebrows.

"Stop. We're not going there."

"Don't you want to find that special someone?"

"It's not a good time."

"When would be a good time?"

He released a heavy sigh and attempted to turn the key again, but Liza arrested the action by covering his hand with her own. "I'm not sure, okay?"

"Kyle wouldn't want you to live like this. You aren't to blame for what happened. He would want you to go on with your career without him and you know it."

Would he ever get over what had happened? Kyle was his writing partner, a guy he met a few years after he moved to Nashville. Even though they were very different, their styles meshed. Brody was the impatient one, the one who would work all day, not stopping until the song was perfect. Kyle liked to move at a slower pace, let the tune simmer for a day or two before finishing the song. At times their opposite personalities clashed, but more often they were a healthy counterbalance to each other, which resulted in some amazing music. Now, after nearly two years, the sting of Kyle's death had only decreased to a dull ache.

"Just come to the bar Friday night. You can sit down near the waitress station and talk to no one but me if that's what you want. But I'll be surprised if you don't see some people you know and have a good time."

He stared at the tractor's steering wheel, taking deep, steadying breaths as Liza droned on. "It'll be good for you. Have a beer or two, play a little pool—"

"If I come," he lifted his ball cap and replaced it on his head, not making eye contact with her, "will you promise to stop harassing me about my life?"

"Yes." She gave him a hug and a loud smacking kiss on the cheek. "You won't regret it. You'll have a great time, I promise."

"Okay, okay." He peeled her arms from around his neck. "Get off my tractor. I'll see you Friday."

Friday was five days away. Surely by then he'd come up with an excuse not to go.

THREE

"Those are some nice melons."

"Excuse me?" Kate looked to her right, shocked to find a man leaning over her shoulder. He had waist-length, blonde dreadlocks and was wearing a Bob Marley t-shirt. She looked around for store security in case she needed it; the tingling up her spine had her on high alert.

"I said they've got some good melons in today. This time of year it's hard to find a ripe cantaloupe at the market."

"Oh." She dropped a cantaloupe in her cart and moved down the aisle to a display of golden pineapples. The man followed behind her.

"Did you know if you cut off the top of the pineapple and let it dry out for a couple of days, you can plant it in some potting soil? It makes a great house plant."

"Um, no. I didn't know that." She decided to skip the pineapples and inched her cart down the aisle.

"I bet you're wondering how I know that." The man continued, relentless in his quest to engage her in conversation. This was the first time anyone had attempted to pick her up in a grocery store.

"Not really."

"I used to work on a pineapple farm in the Hawaiian rainforest."

"No kidding." Increasing her speed, she skirted around the end of the aisle, passed the bananas, and charged across the produce department toward the mushrooms. Her pursuer caught up with her as she approached a display of lettuces.

"It was hard work, I'll tell you. Not as glamorous as it sounds. You're new around here, aren't you?"

"Look, I'm trying to shop and don't really have time to hear your tales of the rain forest." She snatched the first head of lettuce she could reach and charged away from the fruits and vegetables. If he followed her into the cereal aisle, she would call for help.

Kate gave the heavy wooden door a swift shove with her hip and rushed toward the kitchen, lugging six plastic bags of groceries, praying her arms wouldn't break. Annie was leaning over the counter on her tip-toes, staring out the window into the backyard.

"Unbelievable! They didn't have any portabella mushrooms or pancetta. How can people cook around here?" Kate dumped the pile of groceries on the scratched wooden table and continued her protest. "I'm not sure how your mushroom risotto is going to turn out. I had to get white mushrooms and regular bacon instead. Surprisingly, they had Arborio rice—weird." None too gingerly, she unloaded cans and boxes into the pantry, shoving older items aside to make room. "And get this, while I was in the produce section, I got hit on by some guy with dreads hanging to his waist. How do I attract these kinds of people?" She gathered up the plastic bags and then turned to look at Annie, still craning her neck over the window sill. "Have you been listening to anything I've said?"

"Of course, dreadlocks and Arborio got it."

"So far I've encountered the oddest people in this town. Remember the chatterbox at the post office telling me I should get a Vera Bradley tote bag to carry Gram's mail? Do I look like the quilted bag type? The sooner I get out of here and back to work, the better." Kate pulled her cell phone out of her purse but found no new messages from the office.

"How was your grandmother this morning?"

Before stopping at the market, Kate had gone to the hospital to check on her. The morning after they arrived, Kate and Annie had gone to the hospital, only to find Gram groggy on pain killers. "She was much better this morning, more lucid. She's got a good attitude and is ready to get out of the hospital, but she has to go to a rehab facility." She sat on a kitchen chair and dropped her head in her hands. "She wants me to stick around and keep an eye on her house while she's in rehab. They told me this morning it might be six weeks."

"Six weeks? What did you tell her?"

"What could I tell her? She's my grandmother. I'm all she's got. Plus, I can't even name all the times she's been there for me. Of course I told her I would, but what am I going to do? I told Patrick I'd be here for a week or two. We have a trial coming up next month." She leaned across the table and lifted the cover of her laptop. "No internet. I've got work to do. I wonder if there's a Starbucks in town."

"Hmm. Maybe." Annie turned from the window and smiled at her friend. "Listen, I know it's not what you planned, but I think it's nice. You should stay and help your grandma until she's back home."

"I know, but…" With a heavy sigh, Kate slumped against her seat and snapped the laptop shut. "What about my career? The promotion? Grant Goldman all but promised me I'd get it. I *have* to win this."

"I understand losing this promotion is not an option for you—losing never is—but, they can't fault you for a family emergency. Surely, they'll understand if you can't keep up."

"Oh, I'll keep up. Don't worry about that."

"That's my Kate. To be the best you must work the hardest no matter what."

"You know me well."

"I do, but in the meantime, you might as well try to enjoy yourself." Annie waved Kate toward the window. "And I know one way to do that. Come here. Look at this."

She crossed the room and looked through the window at the tidy backyard with its large spreading oak tree, red wooden shed, and white picket fence. There used to be a tire swing hanging on a branch where her grandfather would push her to the sky. She and her dad helped Grandpa paint the fence when she was young, each man patiently teaching her the proper way to stroke along the wood's grain. But her warm musings over the familiar yard turned cold when she saw a tall, shaggy-haired man, sporting a little more than the typical five o'clock shadow, disassembling the wood pile that normally lined the fence. He was tossing the logs into a heap in the yard. "Who's that and what's he doing?"

"I don't know. He got here about ten minutes ago. Check out his arms—so well defined, but not too bulky. Wait until he turns around... that guy is *built*."

"Seriously? You want me to check out some unknown, hairy...*interloper*? He doesn't look like he's bathed in a month."

"Kate, are you kidding me? He's obviously been working hard, tossing logs or whatever he's doing. You should go talk to him. From what I can tell, under those stained ripped jeans and dirty t-shirt is one hunk of a mountain man."

"Now he's going in Gram's shed. Not only is he making a mess of the yard, but he's breaking and entering, trespassing, destroying property—"

"Okay, okay, settle down. Why don't you go find out what he's up to before you slap a restraining order on him. And," Annie shouted to Kate as she stormed out the back door, "try to be nice!"

Kate marched down the back steps through a thick carpet of leaves that snapped and crackled under her feet. She heard a heavy bass beat thrumming through the mountain man's ear buds and she poked a pointy fingernail into his shoulder while he was bending over in the shed.

"Excuse me," she shouted, continuing to poke.

The mountain man stood up and turned, pulling the small speakers out of his ears. He looked at her through squinted lids. His dark, almost black eyes drilled into hers, then looked down at her finger still levitating in mid-air.

"Excuse me, but what are you doing? You have no right to trespass on my grandmother's property." She paused, the stranger's penetrating gaze making her squirm. But after a moment she drew herself up to her full height and met his stare full-on. "Your attempts to steal tools out of her shed have been thwarted. If you don't put down that hammer and leave immediately, I'll have to take matters into my own hands."

With a shake of his head, he turned, ignoring her warnings, and walked deeper into the shed, only to reemerge a few short moments later with a handful of nails.

Kate assumed the stance she'd learned in *tae kwon do:* locking her legs in place, one in front of the other, and raising her arms, bending at the elbow. "What are you planning to do with that? How did you gain access into the shed? What about these logs? Why are you taking my grandmother's wood pile apart? Start talking."

"You must be Katherine." He looked down at her hands, flattened palm up, and walked past her toward the back porch.

"How did you—"

"There's a loose gutter over the back door," he said as he glanced at her over his shoulder. His voice was deep, its volume low; his mild-mannered response felt out of sync with the intensity she felt in his gaze. She could practically feel his eyes blazing a path over her body as he took in the sight of her, somewhat deflated but still determined in her pursuit.

"Oh." Kate looked up at the rain gutter hanging askew over the back porch. "Well, you didn't answer my questions about the wood pile. What are you doing with it? It looks to me like you're just making a mess. Who asked you to do this? I expect this to be cleaned up."

He walked toward the porch once more, gave his head a quick shake, but stayed quiet.

"Wait, stop. Don't you go in there."

He raised the hammer and said, "The gutter?" He was tall enough that he didn't need a ladder. Instead, he lifted the aluminum tube and slammed the hammer three times against the existing nail before drilling another one in beside it. He walked past Kate and replaced the hammer in the shed, snapping the padlock shut on the door.

"You had a key?" She followed him around the side of the house, where a 1980s-era Ford pickup sat loaded down with fresh-cut wood. "Were you planning to leave that here? I didn't order this wood and won't pay for it."

She watched him lift a gray wooden pallet with one hand off the top of the woodpile, and couldn't help noticing the strain of his bicep against the hem of his t-shirt sleeve. The air was frigid and her teeth started to chatter. She had rushed outside so quickly, she hadn't bothered to put on her coat, but here he was working in short sleeves.

"Who are you anyway?"

He didn't answer—just walked into the backyard and placed the pallet flat on the ground against the fence.

"Did you hear me? I didn't order this wood and want you to take it away. There was plenty of wood in the pile that you've now demolished." Kate was close to blowing up, doing all she could to restrain herself from landing a punch between his shoulder blades. She drew in a deep breath and slowly let the air ease from her lungs. "Stop and answer me."

He lifted the bill of his dirty ball cap, shook out his over-grown, sandy-colored hair, and replaced the hat before turning around and giving her that soul-deep stare.

"I will when you take a breath," he said.

"Fine." She uncrossed her arms and held them tight against her sides.

"I'm Brody Fisk." He removed his tan leather glove and extended his hand to her. She shook it, feeling the firm pressure in his grip and a strange warmth in her chest. "Somebody been kicking your cat?"

"What? I don't have a cat." Kate pulled her hand back and cleared her throat as Brody walked toward his truck, loaded several logs in the crook of his arm, and arranged them on the pallet. She was presented with his wide-shouldered, contoured back as he bent over and placed the logs tightly in a row. She couldn't hold back another moment and stomped her foot, frustrated at his cool, unaffected response to her questions.

"How do you know who I am? How do you know my grandmother?" She reached up and tugged on the thin earbud cord. "Are you going to answer me or not?"

He dropped the last log in place and leaned against the trunk of the oak tree. His sandy hair peeked below his hat, nearly touching his shoulders. He rested his foot against the tree trunk and Kate looked down at his scuffed leather boots.

She huffed out a sigh, took a step back, and said, "I asked how you know my grandmother and how you knew my name. And for the last time, why are you bringing this wood?"

"I brought your grandmother wood last year and figured she'd need more. You don't have to pay me and neither does she." He scratched his chin, making a sandpaper-on-wood sound, then continued. "You'll probably want to keep the fireplace going because her house isn't very well insulated."

"How do you know?"

"I've been inside."

"You have?"

He blew out a sigh and readjusted his cap. "Have you ever heard your grandmother mention her friend Imogene?" He leaned over and picked up a crisp, brown oak leaf, twirling it between his fingers.

"Yes, I remember Imogene. I met her years ago."

"She was my grandmother. And I knew who you were because your grandmother talks about you all the time. As soon as you came storming out of the house, I knew it was you."

"What's that supposed to mean?"

"Let's just say your grandmother described you well." The leaf fluttered to the ground as he pushed off from the tree, a slight grin tugging at his lips.

"What? But Gram—she would never say anything negative about me."

"Who says she said anything negative?" Brody turned, replaced his ear buds, and strolled to his pickup, where he loaded more wood in his arms.

Kate stalked back to the house, letting the back door slam on her way in. Annie was waiting for her, still stationed at the window.

"Well, how'd it go? What's he like? Is he as hot as he looks from here?"

"Aren't you practically engaged or something? What would Kip say if he heard you talking like that?" She made a hasty retreat to the living room, where she adjusted the thermostat for the third time that day. Annie followed right behind.

"I'm not blind and Kip has nothing to worry about, so spill it. What did he say?"

"Apparently our grandmothers were best friends and he always brings Gram wood in the winter. He says her house is cold and I'll need to keep a fire going. I don't know how to build a fire." She walked over to the brick fireplace with its white-painted mantel. She rested her hands on her hips and shook her head as if she'd never seen such a structure.

"Perfect. Ask him to come in and show you how," Annie said.

"No way. I'll freeze to death first."

"Why? What's he like?"

"Rude. Obstinate. That long hair and dirty hat—ugh." Kate forced an exaggerated shudder, but remembered his dark mocha eyes and sinewy arms. The warmth she'd felt in her chest crept up into a blush on her cheeks.

"Really? Not a sweet, southern gentleman? Didn't take your breath away?"

"Hardly. I'm convinced this town is full of nothing but weirdos and creeps."

"I thought you loved Highland Springs."

"I love visiting my grandmother and yes, the town is nice, but some of the people—" Kate tipped her head toward the backyard and then bent down to study the fireplace. "Well, suffice it to say, I'm not asking for his help."

"Hmm, I don't know. I think with those muscles he could've swept you off your feet and carried you to his mountain cabin, where he would make sweet love to you in front of a roaring fire."

"What are you talking about, Annie? You think this is some bodice-ripping romance novel? Are you insane?" She picked up the heavy metal poker and tapped it against the grate.

"I just thought since you might be here for a while, it would be fun for you to have a little fling."

"With who? Or is it whom?" She glanced over her shoulder as Annie stretched across the sofa. "Anyway, I'm here to take care of my grandmother, not have a fling. And I have work to do. Besides, I seriously doubt there's anyone interesting with *whom* to have a fling. I don't plan to be here long. Drop it, would you?"

Kate reached inside the fireplace and pushed the flue handle, causing a torrent of black crumbs and an old bird's nest to fall onto the log grate.

"First thing tomorrow morning, I'll call to have Wi-Fi installed so I can search how to build a fire. I'm sure there's a video on YouTube."

"Shame. There's a perfectly healthy, warm-blooded expert in your backyard who could show you how."

"Like I said…I'll freeze to death first."

The door bell rang out a brief Mozart composition and Annie scurried to the door. A thin, blonde woman stood there holding an oblong casserole dish in her oven-mitted hands.

"Hi. Kate?"

"No, sorry, I'm her friend Annie."

Kate came to the door, wiping the soot from her hands onto her jeans. "I'm Kate, can I help you?"

"Oh, hi, I'm Riley from next door. I was the one who called about your grandma."

"Yes, of course. Thank you," she said, not making a move to let her in. Annie returned from the kitchen wearing thick, rooster-adorned oven mitts and took the casserole from Riley's hands.

"Come on in. This smells delicious," Annie said.

Kate's eyes bulged out at Annie and she shook her head, but Annie smiled sweetly back at her.

Riley twisted her fingers and timidly stepped into the foyer. "So, um, how's your grandma today?"

"She's doing better than expected. She broke her femur, you know, and has to go to the rehab center for a few weeks," Kate said.

"Oh, wow, I'm sorry to hear that. But she'll get back home, right?"

"I'm sure she will. No reason she shouldn't. How long have you lived next door?"

"Let's see," Riley rolled her eyes in her head as if to consult a calendar lodged in her brain. She took a not-so-subtle step toward the door. "It's been…eight months. I moved here in February."

"What brought you to Highland Springs?"

"Um, well…" Riley side-stepped toward the exit again, this time making no effort to hide her intentions, and reached for the doorknob. "Just needed a change of scenery." She rushed onto the porch, saying over her shoulder, "I hope you like the casserole. Call if you need anything." Before Kate could reply, she was gone.

"She seems nice," Annie said.

Kate shook her head. "Didn't you find her strange, like everyone else around here?"

"How so?"

"She couldn't get out the door fast enough."

"Maybe she's shy. Or, more likely, you made her nervous. Spending some time in this little town might be good for you."

"Oh, Annie, I wish I had your optimism." She flicked the door knob to the locked position and walked toward the kitchen.

"It's not hard to achieve, you know. For instance, right now I'm wondering how that sexy mountain man is doing with the wood pile." Annie scurried over to the window.

"I hope he dropped a load on his foot." Kate stood with her hands on her hips and took in the familiar surroundings. The house was small with only a kitchen, dining room, bathroom, and living room on the first floor, and two bedrooms and a bathroom on the second floor. It was an adorable Craftsman-style home set on a quiet residential block in downtown Highland Springs, within walking distance of Main Street. As a child, she had loved coming here, spending a month in the summer alone with her grandparents, getting spoiled with their affection and Gram's mouth-watering cooking. It was a great place to visit, but she couldn't imagine living here.

It was hard to believe this tiny house was the only one her grandparents had ever owned, and was where they had raised her dad until he married her mom. Her parents were high school sweethearts...and Kate was living proof of their young love. Her mother was expecting before graduation. Passing up their dreams of college, her dad joined the navy and her mom started her life as a military wife. Because they'd missed their chance, Kate vowed to never let anything get in the way of her goals and dreams—a vow she'd made to her dad the day he died.

"Nope, he's not limping," Annie said as she peered out the window. "It looks like he's just about finished. All the new wood is stacked and he's putting the old wood back on the pile."

"Good. I told him he needed to clean up the mess he was making."

Annie shook her head and turned to face Kate. "Did you ever think to simply say 'thank you'?"

"He was destroying her yard and I didn't know who he was."

"Well, now you do, so why don't you go out there and show some gratitude?"

"Fine." Obviously, Annie wouldn't let it go, so Kate went outside to make her happy. Brody was picking up the last three logs from the pile in the yard when she said, "Thanks for bringing the wood. I'll be sure to let Gram know you were here."

"Appreciate that." He tipped his hat and walked toward his truck.

"Okay." She returned to the kitchen, letting the door shut behind her.

"Well?" Annie said with a twinkle in her eye. "How'd it go?"

"Annie," she sighed. "Give up on your dream of me and the mountain man. He's not my type, I'm not interested, and neither is he. And besides, I'm going to be busy while I'm here—too busy for a fling. Remember?"

"Whatever you say."

FOUR

Kate gripped the steering wheel and pressed the gas pedal to the floor, willing the car to keep moving forward, but all she got in response was sputtering and jerking and a dead stop. Since Annie had left to return to DC, she had driven Gram's car several times without any problem.

"Damn it." She dropped her forehead to the steering wheel and let out a frustrated growl. Her grandmother's 1995 Buick just might have seen its last trip, dying with her inside along a country road outside Highland Springs.

She dug her cell phone out of her purse and attempted to search for a towing company. *No service—no surprise.* She climbed out of the car and spun three hundred sixty degrees while holding her cell phone in the air, hoping to find a connection somewhere, but there was nothing. With her back against the door, she squeezed her temples between her outstretched fingers and tried to think of what to do. The rehabilitation facility was another three miles north and it looked like walking was going to be the only way to get there. The wind was whipping across the grassy field and she knew it would be a long, cold trek in her leather jacket and high heeled boots.

Just as she reached inside to get the bag of clothes she was bringing to Gram, she heard a vehicle in the distance and hoped it would be a nice person who could go for help. She shut the door and raised her hand as the pickup truck grew nearer.

She let a string of unsavory words escape her lips, even as she plastered them into the semblance of a smile. Murphy's Law just might have a sense of humor.

"Having trouble?" Brody reached across the bench seat and rolled down the passenger-side window. His long hair was tucked under the same ball cap he had on the other day, but this time his thick arms were covered by a navy twill jacket.

"Um, yeah. Gram's car just gave out. I don't know what's wrong with it."

"Where were you headed?"

"The rehab center to visit Gram." As much as she didn't want to accept his help, she was praying Brody would give her a ride. She was shivering from the cold and wasn't looking forward to the three-mile hike.

"Hop in. I'll take you." He pushed open the door then eased back behind the wheel. "I'll give Travis a call. He'll tow it to his shop and see what's wrong."

"How do you plan to do that? I couldn't get a single bar out here."

"Yeah, cell service is spotty. I'll call when we get to the center."

He shifted into first and rolled slowly down the unlined road. She looked behind her, through the back window at the mound of logs in the back, and then over at Brody, whose left arm was draped over the steering wheel while his right hand rested on the gearshift. He was looking straight ahead with steely concentration. She rubbed her bare hands across the tops of her thighs, letting the friction thaw her already-frigid fingers.

"Where were you headed, if you don't mind my asking?" she said, breaking the tomb-like silence.

"I don't mind." He gave her a brief glance and then went back to studying the road ahead. "Taking some wood to a lady I know."

"Do you only have female customers?"

"I don't have customers. Just people I help out." He lifted his cap and repositioned it on his head.

"But how do you make any money if you don't sell the wood? You don't sound like much of a businessman."

"Who said I was a businessman?"

She sighed and turned toward him, laying her bent knee on the seat between them. "Okay, 'lumberjack' then. How do you live? How do you pay the bills? How do you put food on the table?"

"Got a lot of questions, don't you?" He made a left turn onto a wide gravel lane that trailed through a thick stand of trees. A panicked tingle crept up her spine as she looked frantically through the passenger side window. There was nothing around—no houses, no stores, nothing but trees.

"Wait, where are you going? The rehab center was on that road—the one we were on." The gravel lane dipped down a steep hill to nowhere. "Where are you taking me?" She looked over at Brody as a white-hot warning traveled up her back. She could feel her eyes bulging as she saw him shake his head with a small grin on his face.

"Listen, Mr. Fisk—"

"Brody."

"I should warn you that whatever you're planning...you won't get away with it. I know *tae kwon do*."

"Is that right?"

"I'm more than capable of protecting my—" She gripped the dashboard and braced herself against the back of the seat. As though she were descending the steep drop of a roller coaster, she locked her arms as the truck's brakes strained and the engine roared with each downshift. "Oh my god, are your brakes going to hold out?"

"Hopefully."

"What hellish pit are we driving into?" Surging with fear, her body couldn't decide which was scarier: dropping to her death or being trapped out here with the mountain man.

"We'll be there soon." His lips pressed into a strained grin as he shoved the gearshift forward.

"Look, if we don't die from this drop, let me tell you my grandmother will call the police if I'm not there in a few minutes. She was expecting me by ten-thirty." The truck had slowed to no more than five miles an hour and she considered jumping out, but reconsidered when she saw how close they were driving to the edge of a steep hill on her right. "I'm an attorney. You'll be prosecuted to the fullest extent of the law." Her voice squeaked and she squeezed her eyes shut when the truck rumbled over a pothole, sending her bouncing off the seat. They finally leveled off and she opened her eyes to an old iron bridge crossing a wide creek. The opposite hillside was dotted with a dozen tiny cabins and single-wide trailers. "What is this place?"

"Cash's Holler."

"And...why are we here?" Kate released the dashboard from her white-knuckled grip and rubbed her damp palms on her jeans. She'd always had a fear of heights or maybe a fear of falling. Whichever it was, the last few minutes had left her terrified.

"See that wood back there?" Brody brought the truck to a stop in front of the one-lane bridge and let another pickup cross. He turned toward her, resting his right elbow on the back of the seat and lifting up the bill of his cap. "Like I said, I'm delivering it to a nice old lady who needs it. Now, I'm not sure what you thought I was going to do or what was going to happen," His dark eyes bored into hers as her heart thumped in her chest. "But you can rest assured I won't be committing any crimes today."

He dropped the truck into first and eased it across the bridge. With her cheeks surely burning red, Kate turned toward the window and took in the scene before her: unpainted, one-room shacks lining the creek, broken down cars resting on cinder blocks, mongrel dogs tied to tree stumps and rusted-out machinery rounded out the scene. It was like she had stepped into a movie—one in which something horrible was about to happen. Brody followed a narrow, semi-graveled path and pulled into the muddy yard in front of one of the cabins.

"I'll just be a few minutes. As soon as I unload the wood I'll take you to see your grandmother. Just wait here."

"Maybe I should help you." Kate looked through the windshield at the rundown cabin.

"It's okay. I got this." He smiled and she watched his eyes trail from her jacket down to her jeans. "Wouldn't want you to get dirty."

As soon as he climbed out, she began to fume. What did he mean by that? Was he implying she was some weak woman who couldn't stack a few logs?

She climbed out of the truck and immediately stumbled on the uneven ground, dotted with rocks and gullies. "I *will* help you. The sooner we unload, the sooner we can get out of here."

"Get back in the truck. I'll be done in no time."

She held on to the back of the truck with one hand and fisted her other on her hip, giving him a stern look. "If you're implying I can't *handle* this task, you're sorely mistaken." She reached over the truck bed and picked up a log, lodging it in the crook of her arm the way she'd seen him do. After her fourth log, she decided that was all she could handle and walked on her unsteady heels toward the neat pile lining the side of the cabin. As she placed the logs on the stack, she noticed the deep silence of the holler; only her labored breathing and Brody's boot steps disrupted the soft sound of wind blowing through the trees. They worked in silence, passing each other on the way from the truck to the woodpile, his loads more than doubling hers.

"So, who lives here?" she asked as she reached into the truck bed.

"Clara Cloud."

"I'm surprised she hasn't come out to say hi or thank you."

"She's nearly deaf. Probably doesn't know we're here."

Kate placed her last load on the pile and took a moment to look around before climbing back in the truck. A heavy mist rested like a blanket over the tree tops, blocking out any chance of sunshine. The eerie quiet unnerved her and the steep hills surrounding the holler made her claustrophobic. She wrenched open the door and climbed onto the bench seat, feeling somewhat safer in the cocoon of the truck cab. Brody climbed onto the porch, two steps at a time, and rapped on the door. A tiny woman in a threadbare gingham dress stepped onto the porch, spoke a few words to him, and gave him a warm hug. No money changed hands.

They drove out of the holler a few minutes later, climbing slowly up the steep incline, without a word between them. Out the corner of her eye, she saw him look at her, then redirect his focus on the gravel lane ahead. He'd barely spoken a word to her on the trip and her curiosity was getting the best of her.

"So, is this your full-time job? Lumberjack?"

"Not full time." He repositioned his ball cap.

"I noticed she didn't pay. How can you make money?"

"You're kind of fixated on that, aren't you?" He reached for the radio knob and soon the cab filled with a sports report. Obviously he wasn't interested in answering any of her questions. She let out a hearty sigh and turned her attention to the forest passing by.

After another silent five minutes, they pulled into the parking lot of the rehab center. Brody walked around to Kate's door to help her out. She ignored his outstretched hand and climbed out herself, brushing past him toward the entrance. Once outside her grandmother's room, she turned around to face him.

"Thank you for the ride. I'll find a way home."

"I'll wait for you."

"No," she sighed and ran her fingers through her long hair. "I'll probably be here a while. I'll call a cab or something."

"There are no cabs out here."

"Is that you, Brody?" Kate's grandmother came out of the room, using her good foot to propel the wheelchair forward.

"Yes, ma'am. How are you, Virginia?" He leaned down and landed a peck on her cheek while Gram wrapped her arms around his shoulders and gave him a warm hug.

"You been out delivering wood?"

"Yes, ma'am."

"How's that project coming anyway?"

He grabbed the handles of Gram's wheelchair and guided her back into the room while talking about a deck he was building behind his house. Kate followed and sat in the corner on a folding chair while her grandmother kept up an animated discussion about what she'd done in physical therapy that morning. Kate tapped on her phone, happy to find cell service, and scrolled through the numerous emails she'd received from the office within the past hour.

"I'll call Travis and have him tow the car to his place. You two enjoy your visit." Brody walked toward the door and turned. "I'll check back in a little while to see if you're ready to leave."

Kate waited until he was gone before she moved her chair closer to her grandmother.

"How you feeling, honey? You look awful pale." Gram rested her soft, bony hand on Kate's cheek. "Everything okay?"

"Yeah, I'm fine. It's just been a crazy morning, that's all." Restless, she went over to the bed where she'd laid the bag of clothes and took the garments out, refolding them before she placed them in the dresser.

"I'm sorry about my car. Travis has been after me to have it looked at," Gram said.

"It's probably time for a new one."

"Pff, it's only got sixty thousand miles."

"But it's almost twenty years old. They might not even make parts for it anymore." She hung the last shirt in the closet and returned to her seat.

"It must have been kismet, Brody coming along to help you like that." Gram flashed a mischievous grin at Kate and wiggled her eyebrows.

"Kismet?"

"Fate, a God-incidence, destiny."

"Oh, no, don't even." Kate groaned and slumped lower on the seat, stretching out her long, thin legs.

"What do you mean?"

"Don't play innocent with me. I know that look."

"I'm not sure to which look you are referring." Gram pursed her lips and wiggled her eyebrows again, making Kate laugh. "I'm just saying…"

"Well, don't say." Kate popped out of the chair, as if she'd just been burned, and began pacing around the room. There was nothing her grandmother loved more than probing into her love life—or lack thereof.

"I'm just saying Brody is a wonderful man. He's a real catch."

She stopped her pacing and threw her head back. "Ha! You can't be serious? He's a lumberjack, for god's sake."

"Well, now, honey, that's not all—"

"And what about that shaggy hair and scruffy beard? He's not my type. Besides, I'm going back to DC as soon as I can."

"You shouldn't judge a book by its cover."

"Okay, Gram," Kate chuckled and sat beside her grandmother, giving her a few pats on the knee. "I hear you."

"Seriously. Take you for example. On the outside you look angry, stressed, tired—"

"I *am* stressed and tired. You would be too if you worked the kind of hours I do." She leaned back in her chair and rolled her head from shoulder to shoulder.

"Why do you work so hard? You're young, pretty; you should be having fun."

"Gram, seriously. We've talked about this so many times." She leaned forward, propping her elbows on her thighs. "I'm this close to getting an early promotion, to proving I'm the best associate at the firm." She pinched her thumb and finger in the air releasing a heavy sigh. "And I promised Dad."

"Your daddy didn't expect you to kill yourself just to get ahead."

"But he did expect me to be the best…he said it often enough."

"I don't think that's what he meant."

"Let's change the subject." She slumped back in the chair and tapped her toe on the tile floor.

"Fine." Several silent moments passed before Gram said, "I did have something to talk with you about." She scooted her wheelchair closer and picked up Kate's hand, holding it between her warm, soft ones. "I won't be able to get to any of my meetings this month and I was hoping you'd sit in for me."

"What meetings?"

"Well, the main one—the only one I really shouldn't miss—is the community center board. I'm supposed to be chairing the fall fundraiser and need someone to oversee all the plans for me."

"What does that entail?" Kate sat up straighter and thought this could interfere with her work. She needed to dedicate every extra moment to getting that promotion.

"As I told you, we're just about ready to purchase that old school out on Dry Fork Road and turn it into the community center. Right now our programs are scattered hither and yon—sports at the high school gym, the food bank at the Methodist church—it's a logistical nightmare. It's too bad you aren't staying. You could teach martial arts to the kids."

"Martial arts? What's that? It's been so long, I'm not sure I remember the forms."

"Well, maybe someday you can get back into it. Anyway, this fundraiser will help raise money for the renovations and we'll have everything under one roof. The bank is going to match any money we raise."

"Okay, so what kind of fundraiser are you planning?"

"It's called 'Bag a Bachelor or Bachelorette'." Gram flashed a sparkling smile at her. "Cute name, huh? I thought it up."

"Um, Gram, what exactly goes on at this fundraiser?" Kate laid her hand over her grandmother's in a tight clutch.

"There'll be a silent auction to bid on a date with some of the more eligible singles in the area. Instead of paying for a ticket, each person who attends brings a bag of groceries for the community center food bank—that's where the 'bag' part comes in. We'll be selling pepperoni rolls, country ham sandwiches, sweet tea, all sorts of good food, and we're raffling off some nice items donated by area businesses."

She fought to control the laugh threatening to explode from her gut. "Gram, are you sure about the name? It implies...well...something more than what your singles are probably offering. You might want to reconsider."

"Too late. The posters have been printed. We like the name. It's catchy."

There was no arguing the point, apparently. And if no one involved in the planning so far had realized the blunder, maybe no one would notice at the fundraiser itself. "Sure, I'll attend the meeting in your place. I'll be glad to help." *Hopefully, it won't take up too much time.*

"Oh, honey." Gram gasped and then clapped her hands together once. "You know how you can *really* help?"

She had a sinking feeling. "No, Gram."

"You would be a wonderful bachelorette. I bet as pretty as you are, you'd bring in the most money. The men would be fighting over you."

"Um, again, no." She leapt to her feet and paced a path across the room. "I have no intention of sucking up to a bunch of country boys in hopes of getting a date to god knows where. I'm not that desperate. There are better ways to spend my time."

"Katherine Marie McNamara, that's a hateful thing to say. There are some wonderful young men in this town—smart, successful. Brody for example." Gram's indignation and pointed glare made ice water run through Kate's veins. "You're no better than they are—remember that."

Thoroughly chastised, she dropped back into the chair and picked up Gram's hand. "I apologize."

"It's for a good cause. This money will go toward furniture or art supplies or sports equipment. The children in our community need this."

"I'm sure."

"Plus, I've already mentioned to the committee you might do it."

"What? When did you have time to do that? You've been in the hospital."

"I might have made a couple of phone calls from my hospital bed." Gram winked and gave her that irresistible smile again.

"Ugh. What happens once someone wins the bid?"

"He'll take you on a nice date somewhere. It won't cost you a thing. You'll have a good time."

Kate walked to the room's wide window and sucked in a deep breath. As much as she loved her grandmother, sometimes she could drive her crazy. The last thing she wanted to do was go on a date with some townie and spend the evening listening to his tales of deer hunting or the latest NASCAR news. But how could she say no? She let out the breath she'd been holding and rotated back to Gram.

"Okay, I'll do it. You never know when the ins and outs of gutting a deer will come in handy."

FIVE

It wasn't like Kate had never been in a bar. She'd been in plenty of them, including places with wood floors and country music blaring through the speakers. Her beloved Olde Towne Tavern back in Georgetown, where she played Thursday night trivia with Annie and Derek, attempted to mimic the vibe The Brass Rail had oozing from its dark wood paneling—but succeeded with far more sophistication. Swimming in a sea of flannel and Old Spice, she stood inside the entrance and surveyed the landscape of tobacco chewing, back slapping, and hearty laughter while pool balls clattered under low-hanging lights.

"There are two seats at the bar. Why don't we sit there?" Riley gave her arm a gentle tug.

She shook off her uneasy feeling by straightening her spine and following her neighbor toward the tall, wooden stools in the center of the action.

"Hey, Riley. You guys came."

"Hey, Liza," Riley said, climbing on her stool. Kate smiled at Liza, the tiny bartender she'd met earlier in the week when she had stopped by the florist shop where Riley worked. While picking up a bouquet for Gram, Liza had come into the shop carrying a wooden tray of her watercolor cards. Her pink hair and facial piercings had caught Kate by surprise.

"What can I get you?" Liza asked, tossing cardboard coasters on the bar in front of them.

"What do you have on tap?"

"We've got your usuals: Bud, Miller, Coors—"

"Hmm. Anything more interesting?" Kate said.

"You bet." Liza smacked the top of the bar with a hearty laugh. "I knew when I met you we'd get along great."

When they had met in the florist shop, Kate's wary impression of Liza quickly melted when the lively, unpretentious woman engaged her in conversation. Somehow, she had convinced Kate and Riley to come to "the best bar in town" where they'd meet "all kinds of interesting people." At the time, Liza's enthusiasm had given Kate hope there just might be an interesting nightlife in Highland Springs, a welcome break from her long days of poring over legal documents. But an evening with a bunch of country folk wasn't her idea of a good time.

"How about a milk stout from a local micro-brew? Do you like dark beers?" Liza asked, bringing Kate out of her worrisome trance.

"Yeah, as a matter of fact, I do. I'll have that."

While Liza expertly filled the pint glasses, tilting them at just the right angle and scraping away the excess foam, Kate swiveled on her stool to look more closely at the people in the bar. Directly behind her was a group of men all sporting the same gas company hat. One of the workers shot her a wink and a lascivious smile. She spun around to face the bar at record speed.

"This probably isn't the crowd you're used to back in Washington, is it?" Riley leaned close to her ear, looking over her shoulder.

"Not exactly. Sure more plaid than I've ever seen in one place." She shot a quick glance behind her, but turned back around when Liza delivered their beers. She lifted the heavy glass and took a hesitant sip.

"So, what do you think? Great, huh?" Liza was watching her closely.

"Yeah." She swiped her tongue along her upper lip. "Really good. What do you think, Riley?"

"Love it. I always order Misty Mountain."

"I really wasn't expecting it to be this good. Thanks for the recommendation," Kate said.

"My brother and his friend Tucker own it. Actually, my brother is more like a silent partner with Tucker doing the brewing. Be right back."

"Is she always so energetic?" Kate watched Liza whirl away, her pink, braided ponytail swinging as she walked to the other end of the bar.

"Always. She runs this whole bar by herself and you never have to wait long for a drink."

"What's with the pink hair? She's beautiful. Why would she do that to herself?"

"I guess it's the artist in her. Did you look at her cards? She's talented."

"Yeah, they were nice. Beautiful technique."

"In fact, she's from a talented family. The brewery isn't her brother's only claim to fame. He's an award-winning songwriter. They say he has an amazing voice, but I've never heard him sing. Maybe he's here." Riley rested her elbows on the wood and leaned forward, looking down the length of the bar. "I don't see him. He's not around much."

"Does he live here?" Kate picked up the cardboard coaster and spun it between her fingers, letting it tap on the bar after each rotation.

"He does now. He used to live in Nashville and New York, but something happened. I've heard everything: he lost all his money, he went insane, he's wanted for killing someone." Riley chuckled and took another long sip. "There's never a shortage of gossip in this town."

"I can only imagine." She took another drink and then turned her chair in Riley's direction. Since their first awkward meeting, they had spoken several times across the neighboring fence, striking up a budding friendship. "So, what about you? You're not married, I presume. I haven't seen anyone but you next door."

"Nope. Single."

"Anyone special in your life?"

"Nope. Hey, want to play pool? I know that guy at the table playing by himself." Riley hopped off the barstool and headed toward the back of the bar. Not wanting to be left alone with the gas company crowd, Kate followed. She drew up short when she noticed the man Riley was talking to at the pool table. It was Travis, the dreadlocked guy from the supermarket, who also happened to be the mechanic who had fixed her grandmother's car. She looked back over her shoulder, weighing her options: sit with the matching ball cap boys currently taking shots in unison or play pool with the pineapple-picking mechanic. Not much of a choice.

***

Why hadn't Brody learned to ignore his sister when she insisted he do something? She'd been after him for weeks to come down to the Brass Rail and he'd always come up with a believable excuse…until tonight. He had convinced himself that she was right—he needed to get out more. Now here he was sitting in a dark corner of the bar, watching Katherine McNamara play pool with Travis and Riley, wishing he'd followed his first instincts and just said no.

"Why don't go over there? Join them," Liza said. She placed a freshly poured beer in front of him.

"Rather not." He took a sip and leaned his elbows on the bar. "Pink this time, huh?"

"Don't change the subject to my hair. You're just going to sit here like a lump and not talk to anyone?"

"I believe you were the one who suggested I sit in the corner of the bar and only talk to you. That's what I'm doing." He looked up at the football game on the overhead TV, trying to ignore the pinched look on Liza's face.

"I didn't mean that literally. I was just trying to ease you back into society. I thought after a few minutes, you'd break out of your reclusive little shell and talk to people."

"I'm not reclusive."

"Okay, sure, whatever." She did an about-face and walked to the sink, where she furiously scrubbed glasses and then dipped them in the next two sinks to rinse.

He was having a hard time keeping his eyes off the pool game. Beads of sweat were forming on his forehead as he watched Miss High and Mighty lean over to line up her shot. Katherine was the last person he wanted to see tonight. He could think of a million other things he'd rather be doing than sitting alone in a bar, staring at the woman who had accused him of breaking and entering, and abduction. Regardless of her ball-busting rudeness, he had to admit she intrigued him. If he went over there to join in the game, it would be hard for him to avoid looking into those emerald green eyes of hers and listening to her deep, sexy voice. His encounter with her in her grandmother's backyard had left him confused and frustrated, and his trip to the rehab center hadn't helped.

"Why don't you go over and talk to her?" Liza was back, standing in front of him with her hands on the bar and an accusing look on her face.

"Who?"

"Virginia's granddaughter. Or are you staring that lustfully at Travis?"

"I'm watching the game."

"Oh, yeah, who's playing?"

Brody picked up his glass and drained half of it. He didn't need this hassle from his sister. Talking to Katherine would be a mistake. She was brash, bossy, hot as hell, but trouble. He felt it in the way his chest tightened the day she rushed across the yard accusing him of stealing tools from the shed, and he felt it now.

"What's wrong, big brother? Lost your swag?"

He snapped his attention back to Liza, whose lips curled in a smirk.

"You're a pain in the ass." Brody grabbed his beer and walked toward the pool table, where once more he was entertained by Katherine's perfect form over the edge of the table. If she copped an attitude with him this time, he was leaving. His sister's voice in his head chimed uninvited: *"Whatever you say, Brody."*

***

"Eight ball, corner pocket." Kate pointed with her pool cue at the left corner across from her and leaned over, sighting the ball that would give her and Riley the victory. They were playing two against one and she felt only slightly guilty for beating Travis so soundly. As it turned out, he was a funny guy, not the threatening freak she had thought he was in the grocery store.

"Watch out—it's Minnesota Fats for the win," Travis said. He threw up his hands in surrender. "Oops, Minnesota Skinny I should have said."

"Shut up, Travis. I'm about to sink this one." With a flick of her wrist, she tapped the white cue ball, sending it careening into the black eight ball, but sinking both in the pocket.

"Yes!" Travis did a double fist pump. "There is a god. Watch out, girls, you're about to experience the agony of defeat."

"I wouldn't listen to his bullshit if I were you."

She snapped around at the sound of that smooth, familiar voice. Her arms went limp and her cue stick slid between her fingers to rest on the floor. Brody was behind her and a nervous heat coursed through her veins.

"Hey, stranger, where the hell you been?" Travis rounded the table to shake Brody's hand. "These beauties are trying to beat me at my own game. I could've used your help earlier."

"I was watching you from over there and figured it was time I gave you a hand." Kate kept her back to him while she rubbed chalk over her pool cue, but watched them covertly out the corner of her eye.

"What've you been up to? Haven't seen you in a while," Brody said.

"Been busy, man. Had a lot of requests for new locks lately," Travis said.

"Yeah, I heard there've been some break-ins. Any idea who's doing it?"

"Maybe." Travis tilted his head and Kate followed its path, her eyes landing on the table of gas workers still hammering back the shots. "We never had a crime problem around here before those guys started fracking out on Camptown Road."

Kate lightly nudged Riley. "What are they talking about?"

"There have been several break-ins in town and Travis thinks it's one of the frackers."

"Oh, really?" She stared at the dartboard in front of her on the wall, thinking about her grandmother living alone. Fully confident she could protect herself, she worried about her grandmother once she returned home and Kate went back to DC.

"Hi, Riley," Brody said.

Kate's spine went stiff when she heard his voice. She kept her back to him, but felt a warm blush in her cheeks.

"Hello, Katherine."

The flush grew warmer as she plastered on a pleasant expression and turned around as if surprised to find him there.

"Hi, Brody. Any destruction of property or kidnapping charges filed against you this week?"

He glared at her, then shook his head while taking a drink of his beer. The corners of his eyes crinkled as he watched her over the brim. "Actually, I think you were the only one who had a warrant out for my arrest." He kept his dark eyes locked on hers as he took another sip. "Cops never did show up at my place. You must've dropped the charges."

"Since you fixed Gram's gutter and rescued me from the side of the road, the least I could do was let it all slide." With a wry grin, she tipped her beer mug toward him.

"Loretta and I appreciate that. We wouldn't have been too happy if the police showed up, guns blazing."

"Loretta?" An unexpected weight settled on Kate's shoulders and she had trouble holding back the shock on her face.

"She doesn't much care for unannounced guests at our place."

So, the mountain man has a wife. She'd have to report this important piece of evidence to Annie, even though she knew it would ruin the fairytale ending her friend had concocted. She couldn't help but notice his scruffy whiskers were growing into a thicker, smoother beard. He looked so different from the afternoon she'd first met him. His hair was brushed back from his face and he was wearing a light blue shirt and dark jeans. She never thought she would be attracted to a country boy, but she had to admit, he looked pretty good standing there with one hand stuffed in his front pocket and a beer mug in the other. It was a good thing he was off limits.

"Why don't we call it even and start a new game?" Riley said.

"Good idea. Brody and me against you girls." Travis threw out his arms and then tapped them on his chest. "Unless one of you wants to play with this pool shark."

"I'll be on your team, Travis," Riley said. "I think that would make us more evenly matched, don't you?"

"Sounds like a plan."

Kate looked over at Brody, who didn't seem too happy about this decision—his brows were furrowed and he was staring at the table. When he glanced over at her, she cocked an eyebrow and shrugged her shoulders.

"I guess we're a team," Brody said.

"What kind of skills have you got? I don't need somebody holding me back. I like to win."

"Don't worry. I'll cover you." He picked up the chalk and slowly rubbed it over the tip of his cue.

"Oh, think you've got what it takes?" She chuckled as she snatched the chalk cube from his hand.

"Only one way to find out."

SIX

Brody and Kate were up two games to one against Riley and Travis and they planned to complete their hat trick with this round. Kate stood directly behind Brody, imagining what was hidden under those jeans as he lined up the shot to start a new game. She tore her eyes away. *He's married. Don't be that girl.* She was starting to like his laid-back, country-boy vibe and quick wit. Who would've thought a lumberjack could be so clever? She drained her beer and teetered over to the table to deposit her empty glass. Brody broke the cluster of balls, sending them scrambling across the green felt, pocketing two solids.

"Not bad." She raised her hand and they slapped a high five.

"Solids again. Let's hope we'll be just as lucky this game," he said.

"It's not luck. We've got skill." This time when she raised her hand, he grabbed hold, wrapped his fingers around hers, and pulled her against him. Her breath quickened as she was propelled forward, but he just bumped his right shoulder against her left, like she'd seen men do a hundred times. Like married guys did.

"Hey, Brody." Slinking up behind him walked a petite, bleach blonde wearing tight faded jeans and a crop top. *A belly ring? Didn't they go out ten years ago?* Kate watched him spin around and straighten up, glancing down at the woman whose hand was now rubbing his arm. "Haven't seen you in like, forever. How ya been?"

"Okay." He looked over his shoulder at Kate and raised his eyebrows.

"Well, you're sure looking good. Want to come sit with me?" she asked.

"Actually, I just…" Brody stepped away from her soothing hand and tipped his pool cue at Kate. "Just started a game."

The blonde rounded on Kate and raked her eyes from head to toe, seeming to drink in every inch of Kate's appearance. "Oh, sorry to interrupt. Hi, I'm Holli-with-an-I."

"Kate-with-a-K." She raised her eyebrows back at Brody and saw him muffling a laugh behind his hand.

"Oh, well, I guess I'll let you get back to it." Holli faced Brody and stepped in, closing the gap between them. Just above a whisper, Kate heard her say, "Call me. We can pick up where we left off all those years ago."

"Old friend of yours?" Kate said once Holli was out of earshot.

"Something like that. We sort of dated in high school."

"Sort of dated?" She gave him a knowing smirk. "Is that what you call it?"

"What do you mean?"

"I know her type. Look at her. I'm sure she was very popular." She air quoted with her fingers and then picked up her pool cue.

"You don't even know her." He loomed over her and she could see she'd hit a nerve. Could it be their past was more involved than he let on?

"I just mean I don't think Loretta would be too happy seeing you with her."

"Loretta? Why would she care?"

"Seriously? How can you ask that? Unless you have a very open marriage, I don't think most wives would appreciate their husbands spending time with someone like Holli."

"Are you two going to play or are you going to stand there jawing all night?" Travis sidled between them and tapped Brody's pool stick with his own.

"Sure. We're playing." Brody studied the pool table's landscape, rubbing his chin in deep concentration. He off-handedly said, "We were just talking about my wife Loretta."

"Your wife?" Travis scratched his head. "What the—"

WHATEVER YOU SAY | **49**

"She's the best wife a guy could ask for. Right, Travis?"

"Huh? Oh yeah." Travis chuckled and turned to face Kate. "If you ask me, she's a real bitch."

"I can't believe you just said that." She was shocked Brody would stand by and let his friend speak so disparagingly about his wife. She glared at him, willing him to defend his wife's honor.

"What Travis is trying to say is that Loretta is, um, unique."

"Unique?" She felt her eyes bulging, still confused at his lack of support.

"Right." Travis scratched the back of his head and winked at Brody. "Loretta is a different breed. Her interests aren't like other females."

"What do you mean?"

"Well, um, you tell her Brody. Describe Loretta's interests," Travis said.

"Let's see. For one thing, she likes to hunt." Brody took a drink of his beer, keeping his eyes on Travis.

"Hunt? What does she hunt?" Kate asked.

"Rabbits mostly," Brody said.

"She does a good bit of tracking, too, doesn't she Brody?" Travis said.

"There's nothing she loves more than walking in the woods and following a scent." Brody took a quick sip of his beer and pointed his finger at Travis. "And she loves riding in the bed of my pickup. Isn't that right, Travis?"

Who is he married to, Elly May Clampett? Just when Kate had started to like the guy, he turned out to be an even bigger hillbilly than she first thought.

"You look surprised," Brody said.

"A little. I'm surprised she likes to hunt rabbits. Does she skin them herself and then cook them? I can't even imagine." Kate knew she was staring at him, but she was trying to size up what kind of man he actually was and couldn't tear her eyes away. "I don't mean to be rude, but does she like doing that? Is that something you expect her to do? She sounds like a very...old-fashioned wife."

He sat his beer on a neighboring table and leaned on his pool stick. "Listen." With his eyes cast downward, he rubbed his forehead and said, "Loretta's not m—"

"I mean I didn't know women like that even existed anymore. Maybe it's an Appalachian cultural thing. Is that it?" She looked toward the opposite side of the pool table and then quickly surveyed the bar. "Where's Riley? Maybe she can explain it to me."

"I think she's in the bathroom," Travis said, chuckling as he lined up his next shot. "Riley's probably fond of rabbit, too."

"Hey, guys, anyone want another beer?" Liza walked over, tucking an empty drink tray under her arm, but stopped suddenly. "Sorry, did I interrupt something?"

"Not at all. We were just talking about Loretta," Brody said.

"Sweet Loretta. She's the best dog."

"Dog?" Kate fairly shouted. Brody and Travis burst out laughing, patting each other on the back like champions. She didn't appreciate being the brunt of a stupid joke. "All this time you were talking about your dog?"

"Of course I was talking about my dog. You heard Travis call her a bitch, didn't you?" He was wiping the tears from his eyes, his shoulders still shaking with laughter.

"I thought you were just an ass who wouldn't defend his wife."

"Come on. It was a joke."

"An idiotic joke." She gathered her wallet and keys from the table, and slipped into her jacket, refusing to look at Brody or Travis. "Very juvenile."

"Now look who doesn't have a sense of humor." Brody bent over and whispered in her ear. "Be careful or Travis might call *you* a bitch."

She drew in a sharp breath and stood on tiptoe, straining toward eye-level with him. "We wouldn't want that now, would we?" She shoved her pool stick into his hand. "Finish the game without me." Fuming, she circled around the table and walked out of the bar.

Kate pulled the white Buick into the church parking lot and cut the engine. It replied with a few chugs and a muffled bang. Maybe Travis needed to take another look at this car before she drove it much more. Then again, that would mean actually talking to Travis, a prospect she wasn't looking forward to after the scene at the pool table.

As she grabbed the handle to open her door, determined to find another mechanic even if it meant going to the next town over, a shiny black SUV pulled into the spot behind her. She looked through the rearview mirror at the driver, whose aviator sunglasses and crisp white shirt were the only things she could see through the sun-glinted windshield. Rather than get out, she stayed in the car watching a tall, lean man climb out of the SUV wearing a navy blazer. He turned slightly and Kate drew in a quick breath. Brody. She took her time getting out of the car.

"Good morning." Brody waited at the church door, holding it open for her.

"Oh, um, good morning," she mumbled as she brushed past him into the dimly lit hallway.

"I didn't expect to see you here."

"Gram wanted me to attend on her behalf."

"Okay, well…welcome." He pointed down the hallway and led her into a small room with a conference table and ten chairs.

It had been three days since they'd played pool at the Brass Rail and she had hoped she wouldn't run into Brody anytime soon. She had continuously replayed his stupid joke in her mind and felt silly for over-reacting. They were just having a little fun at her expense and she blew up. She was just embarrassed for being so uncharacteristically gullible.

"Good morning, everybody. Let's get started. We have a lot to go over." The chairman of the board, Sam Smiley, was also the local funeral director. "I want to introduce Kate McNamara, Virginia's granddaughter, to our meeting. She'll be sitting in for Virginia while she's in rehab."

The meeting began with the customary reading of the minutes and roll call, and she couldn't help glancing at Brody sitting directly across from her. He'd had his hair cut since Friday night and his beard was trimmed. He didn't look anything like the mountain man she'd seen in her grandmother's backyard. Come to think of it, he hadn't really looked like such a hick that night at the bar, but today he looked downright professional. She caught him staring at her, lightly tapping his pen on the table, his lips pursed in concentration. When she arched her eyebrows at him, he didn't flinch, seeming to be in a trance.

"So, Kate, your grandmother tells me you're going to be one of our bachelorettes."

She noticed Brody sit up straighter and shift his stare to Mr. Smiley.

"Yes, unfortunately she talked me into it."

"No, no, that's very *fortunate* for us," Sam said. "You'll be a huge asset to our event."

When another member asked about the number of country ham sandwiches needed, she looked over at Brody again and saw him scribbling words on a Post-It notepad. He appeared to write a few words, flip to the next page, and write a few more. While the meeting droned on around her, she continued watching Brody, whose concentration was solely on the words he was writing on the yellow paper. She looked away when he stopped and settled his gaze on her.

"It looks as though we'll be able to take possession of the building next week." A pencil-thin gentleman with white hair was reading from his notes. "We can move most of our activities to the new building even though there's still a lot more work to be done. We've already identified which rooms need renovated and that work should begin shortly after closing. Our first payment on the million-dollar insurance policy is due on the twelfth."

"Excuse me," Kate interrupted the man's report with a tip of her hand. "I'm sorry, I don't know your name, but did you say one million dollars of coverage?"

"My name is Arthur Hansrote and yes, ma'am, I did say one million."

"Is that just on the building itself?" she asked.

"No, it covers liability as well."

"You can't be serious." Kate looked around at the blank faces around the table. "Who gave you such a ridiculously low quote? Let me just look—" She started a search for recommended coverage on her phone's browser.

"Why now, we feel confident this will be plenty of coverage in the event of an emergency," Arthur said. She sensed his hackles rising. "Our program has never had a claim in the five years we've been in existence and we don't anticipate having any in the future."

"Right, only the first time someone slips and falls on the icy sidewalk, you're going to have a lawsuit on your hands." She buried her nose in her research, lightning-fast fingers tapping the cell phone screen.

A plump, rosy-cheeked woman sitting at the end of the table cleared her throat. "Well, now, Kate—oh, I'm Darla by the way. I'm not sure how things are done where you're from, but here in Highland Springs, people aren't quick to sue, especially a place like the community center, which is such a blessing to the children in our area."

"I appreciate the fact that the center is blessed, Darla," Kate said as she continued to scroll through her phone. "But the truth is even with all the love and support of your community, accidents will happen and people will want to be compensated." She leaned her elbows on the table and pointedly looked at each person around the table—all except Brody, whose eyes she could feel searing into her. "I guarantee when one of the children falls on the slick basketball court, cracks his head on the floor or breaks his leg, his family will sue for compensatory damages, medical bills, pain and suffering, and pecuniary loss, past and future. It won't be cheap."

"That's if they don't have insurance, right?" Sam asked.

"It won't matter if they have insurance or not. The massive payout will be the same."

"I can't believe this." Arthur slapped his hand on the table and his scarlet cheeks seemed to swell.

"Believe it, Arthur. There are cases like what I'm describing all the time. Look here," she said, gesturing to her phone. "Here's an example of what a lawsuit can do to a place like this. 'Final arguments were presented today in the case of *Tyler v Charles County Parks and Recreation*, in which a twelve-year-old boy fell twenty-five feet from a rock climbing wall resulting in paralysis from the neck down. His family is suing the center for ten million dollars.'" Holding out the phone, she rotated it around the table to prove her point. "Let me see if I can find a follow-up report with the decision."

She went back to scrolling, but stopped when she noticed the heavy silence in the room. A chill ran down her spine; their dead stares and slack jaws were centered on her. Surely, they understood when something bad happens to a child, it was only natural to want to assign blame. It was just the way of the world.

Kate looked around the table, hoping to see someone who connected with her example, who understood her reasoning. But each person dropped their gaze when she tried to meet it—everyone but Brody. His lips were pressed to a thin line and his stare was dark. Their eyes locked for a moment, but Kate tore hers away when the chairman cleared his throat.

At last, Sam broke the silence. "Well, I'm not sure what to say. I guess we should look into this a bit further."

"That's ridiculous. Our budget is tight. The insurance premiums are going to kill us as is," Arthur said.

"Look, I don't mean to frighten you, but I've seen it before, worked on similar cases," Kate said.

"I don't think we're frightened, young lady, just surprised you think we'd be so neglectful," Arthur said.

"Let's focus on the positive," Darla said. "I mean, we shouldn't let modern technology keep us from caring about one another." Her eyes focused on Kate's phone.

"All I'm saying is you need to seriously reconsider your coverage and find a way to pay for additional insurance."

"Young lady—"

"How much do you charge for your activities?" Kate scooted to the edge of her seat, interrupting Arthur's next tongue-lashing.

"Um, well, we don't charge much. We want the community center to be available to everyone, regardless of income," Sam said.

"Maybe it's time to review your fee schedule. There is money out there. Have you looked into grants? Have you established an endowment fund? Do you have regularly scheduled donations? Do you have governmental support?"

"We've been very blessed with generous donations. I personally think God will provide all we need." Darla's tiny voice could barely be heard over the rustle of papers and nervous coughs.

"You better pray he keeps on providing enough to cover your insurance premiums at the very least." Kate was losing patience with their naiveté. She let out a heavy sigh and sat back in her chair, crossing her arms over her chest.

"That's downright disrespectful, young lady," Arthur said, once again slapping his palm down on the table. Angry voices erupted, all talking at once.

Brody stood up and buttoned his jacket before raising his hand. "Excuse me, folks, but I think she's right." He waited until the chatter stopped. "Times have changed and we can't ignore our potential liability. How about I ask my attorney what he'd recommend and then get some more insurance estimates?"

I'm an attorney, Kate fumed. *What's wrong with asking me?*

"Brody, that's so sweet of you." Darla beamed.

"We wouldn't want to put you out now, Brody," Sam said.

"It's not a problem. I'll be glad to look into it and report back at our next meeting."

"Tremendous. Finally the voice of reason." Arthur reached across the table and shook Brody's hand before stabbing a hostile glare at Kate.

So now Brody was going to be a hero and calm all the board members' fears by talking to his attorney. Why would a lumberjack who lived out in the sticks with his dog need an attorney? She looked closer at him, taking in the well-tailored jacket and leather portfolio lying on the table in front of him. Who was Brody Fisk?

SEVEN

As soon as the meeting was over, Brody watched Kate gather the stack of fundraiser posters and hurry out of the room, not stopping to say goodbye. He caught up to her in the parking lot as she tossed the posters into her grandmother's car.

"Katherine." She leaned into the car and came back out with a heavy leather bag in her hand. He skipped out of the way to avoid getting hit by the swinging satchel. "You rushed out of there pretty fast."

"Didn't seem like anyone wanted to swap recipes with me, did it?" Her anger blazed in the deep crease between her brows and flush of her cheeks. She slammed the door and marched toward the sidewalk. He rushed to catch up with her.

"They just don't understand. In their minds, Highland Springs is still a small town. Hasn't changed since—"

"They better wake up and realize this isn't Mayberry anymore. They have chain restaurants and the internet. This town has been dragged into the twenty-first century, whether it likes it or not." Kate stepped into the intersection, ignoring the Don't Walk sign, dodging between oncoming traffic.

"You didn't exactly make it easy on yourself," he said as he caught up with her outside the coffee shop.

"What? Oh, because I didn't sugarcoat the truth for them?" She whirled around and pinned him with a dark stare.

"I'm just saying a little patience and understanding go a long way."

She opened the door to Sit and Sip, the local version of a Starbucks, not bothering to hold it for him. "Wait," he said.

"What?"

"I, um…" He took a step back. Damn, she was intimidating. That wrinkle in her forehead and fire in her eyes made his pulse quicken. The other night in the bar, before everything went to hell, he'd started to enjoy her company, had suddenly and completely realized how beautiful she was. Damned if she wasn't even more beautiful angry—and a little terrifying to boot. Why the hell didn't he pay attention to the warning bells and back off? "I wanted to talk about the other night."

"I'd rather not."

"I wanted to apolo—"

"A venti caramel macchiato, skim milk, no whip." Kate barked out her order, ignoring his apology, as she thumbed across her cell phone. He noticed the blank look on the cashier's face and was just about to translate when Kate spoke up.

"Do I need to repeat myself?" She glared at the cashier, who was beginning to wither under the intense heat.

"I don't know what a macchiato is."

She leaned across the counter and lifted the largest paper cup from a stack beside the cashier. "Take a large cup." She handed the cup to the cashier. "Fill it with foamy milk, add two shots of espresso, top it off with caramel and no whipped cream. Does this sound familiar?"

"Yes, but I think we're out of caramel," the cashier squeaked. Brody could have been mistaken, but it looked like the cup shook briefly in her hand.

"How can a coffee shop be out of caramel?" With each pronouncement, her voice grew louder and more patrons turned to gawk. He stepped in front of Kate and smiled at the cashier.

"Brittany, just give Ms. McNamara a large vanilla latte with no whipped cream, please. That'll be fine."

"Excuse me." Kate nudged in front of Brody and turned on him. "I can handle this, thank you very much."

"I don't think you're handling it at all." He brushed her aside and ordered a small coffee with cream for himself, as he reached for his wallet.

"I can buy my own coffee," she said.

"You're obviously having a bad day. Let me get it for you."

"How do you know I'm having a bad day?"

"Well, I hope to god you're not like this just because." He handed the cashier a ten and mumbled under his breath. "Although it's starting to seem that way."

With an audible huff, Kate stormed across the coffee shop and sat at a corner table, seemingly oblivious to the stares cast her way. Brody rested his back against the counter while he waited for the coffees. Kate pulled her laptop from her bag, slammed it on the table, and then drew out a stack of file folders. Her high stress level was apparent to everyone in the café, but he doubted she'd get any sympathy

"Here." He handed over her coffee, though she didn't bother looking up to acknowledge him. He waited while she rapidly tapped the keys of her laptop. He waited a full minute, counting the seconds off in his head, before pushing the laptop closed. Her attention snapped to him like a lightning bolt. "Let me give you a piece of advice," he said, leaning in over the computer until he was just inches from her face. "This behavior may work in DC, but not here. People don't give a shit if you're stressed or overworked or unhappy if you're rude to them. Show a little kindness and respect, and they'll be your best friend."

"Is that so?" He could see the fluttering pulse in the soft divot at the base of her throat.

"Yeah. Try to be more pleasant. Your time in Highland Springs will go a lot easier."

"I'll try to remember that. Now," Kate lifted the screen and looked pointedly at him. "I have work to do."

Brody released a loud sigh and scratched his forehead as he looked into her emerald green eyes. She was the most impetuous, haughty, tough-as-nails woman he'd ever met and if he knew what was good for him, he'd run for the hills. Still, for some reason, he was drawn to her. What he felt was equal parts dislike and desire—a lethal combination. Ever since their pool game Friday night, he'd been replaying how snarky, funny, and gorgeous she was without really trying. He felt guilty about carrying the joke too far; he'd obviously crossed a line, but he wasn't sure which one. She was invading his every waking moment, and if he knew what was good for him, he'd avoid her at all costs.

***

"Kate, you work on the jury instructions; Jason, start formulating the first set of witness questions, and we'll meet again on Friday. How does that sound?" Patrick Stone efficiently doled out assignments before closing the file in front of him.

"You got it," Kate smiled at the laptop camera while typing a few notes. Regular trial prep meetings were held in Patrick's office, but today it was taking place in a conference room so that she could participate via video conferencing.

Patrick pulled off his reading glasses and leaned toward the camera, his face filling her screen. "How's it going out there in west-by-god?"

"Going well, thank you. My grandmother is improving."

"Any idea when you'll be back?"

"Well, um, the thing is…she, um, needs me." How could she tell him that when it came to her grandmother, she was a total pushover? Two days after the Sit and Sip fiasco, she had tried to tell her grandmother she needed to get back to DC. Somehow she'd ended up agreeing instead to stay at least until her grandmother was back at home and feeling confident on her own. The woman had a power over her that no one else ever had. Somewhere in the back of her mind, she heard the echo of a line from a movie about love making people do crazy things—like jeopardize promotions, for example. "It's complicated."

"I understand. Although not ideal, we're moving along with trial prep on schedule. Just keep me posted as soon as you have a date. I want you in court," Patrick said.

"Absolutely. Wouldn't want to miss it." She held her breath and her smile until he finally disconnected. How could she keep putting Patrick off? He had been more than patient with her, but soon she feared he wouldn't even consider giving her the promotion. She'd met all her deadlines, kept up with her billable hours, but still, the fact that she wasn't in the office working alongside the staff gave her reason to believe she'd get passed over.

A loud crash echoed through the house. She snapped the laptop closed and ran to the front door. When she swung the door open, she found an enormous stack of lumber piled in the yard.

"What in the world?"

"Good morning."

Jumping at the sound of his voice, she stepped onto the porch to find Brody walking toward her, his arms full with several planks of lumber. He dropped them on the existing pile and pulled off his leather gloves.

"What are you doing?"

"Didn't your grandmother tell you? I'm building a ramp, you know, to make it easier for her to get in."

"No, she didn't tell me."

"That's funny. She told me yesterday when I was there she'd let you know during your evening visit." He lifted his ball cap, ran his hand through his hair, and repositioned it on his head.

"I didn't make it over there last night."

"Oh?"

"I had work to do. We're preparing for an important trial." She didn't like the look he was giving her, silent and expressionless but still somehow... *accusing.* "Don't give me that look."

"I'm not giving you a look."

"Yes, you are. I can tell you're disappointed or shocked or something." With her fingers twisting in knots, she drew up taller and gave him her most confident glare. "I have important work to do. I can't be expected to visit her every single day."

"I didn't say you did, but—"

"I'm up for a promotion and her accident couldn't have come at a worse time."

"Accidents aren't usually scheduled." Brody slapped his leather gloves, one against the other. He turned away from her, but not before she saw sadness wash over his face. "It'd be nice if they were."

"Oh?" She cleared her throat, all her bravado gone as she realized she'd struck a nerve. "Did you know someone in a serious accident?"

"Yeah." He tilted his face to the cloud-covered sky and squeezed his eyes shut. He released a heavy sigh and slapped his gloves together once more. "Good friend of mine. Wish I could have visited him in rehab."

"Did he die?"

"Yes." Still looking anywhere but at her, Brody slipped the leather over his hands. "Better get back to it. I don't want to keep you."

She knew exactly how he felt, having lost her father suddenly to an accident. Strange that she'd not considered her grandmother's fall could have been much worse. "You're not bothering me."

"What, no work to do?"

Self-conscious of her daily mantra, she chuckled. "Always." She stepped back to the door, turning to him before she went inside. "I'll be sure to visit Gram this afternoon."

"She'll appreciate it." He turned back toward the truck and picked up some more planks.

Kate entered the house, slowly shutting the door behind her. She lifted the sheer curtain just an inch and peeked outside at him still unloading lumber. There was so much she didn't know about him, and it seemed each time they spoke she discovered something new. She was so ready to feel defensive, to write off the guilt she thought he was trying to make her feel...but then he mentioned his friend, and all those feelings just sort of melted away. She knew what it was like to lose someone without warning.

She took another glance out the window and drew in a quick breath when Brody pulled off his jacket. Just like the first day she'd seen him in the backyard, his muscles strained against his thin t-shirt, but this time she wasn't put off by his shaggy hair, beard, and boots. This time warmth ooze in places it hadn't in a while. She watched his long-legged stride back and forth to the truck, his strong thighs shifting beneath the faded denim. As he leaned over the bed of the truck, his shirt tail rose and she got a quick glimpse of his flat stomach. She had the urge to swallow. No way could she work with him outside. She gathered her jacket, purse, and keys, and decided now would be a good time to visit her grandmother.

She gave a quick wave to him as she backed out of the drive and yawned deeply. She realized she'd been up since six, plugging away at the brief she'd promised to have to Patrick by the end of the week. Cravings for another vanilla latte from Sit and Sip nagged at her taste buds, but she wasn't sure she'd have the nerve to go in there again. Brody had made it perfectly clear her behavior was unacceptable to the Highland Springs coffee crowd. She wasn't exactly sure why she'd gone off on the meek little cashier. Even for Kate, she'd been too brash. The only thing she could blame her behavior on was the small-minded committee.

Her stomach let out a roaring growl and she did a U-turn in the intersection. It was one o'clock and she hadn't eaten all day. She wanted a sandwich and a latte from Sit and Sip. If she had to live in this town for the next few weeks, she'd have to play their game.

As soon as Kate entered Sit and Sip, the comforting aroma of brewed coffee and freshly baked bread buoyed her resolve. She glanced around the café, noticing nearly every table filled, except for the corner table she'd occupied yesterday. With a little luck, it would still be open after she placed her order. As she approached the counter, the same cashier—Brittany, wasn't it?—stood behind the register, but instead of fear or anger, Kate received a hearty welcome.

"Hello again. We have caramel back in stock. Want a macchiato?"

"That would be great. Thank you. And a turkey on ciabatta. Please." Kate gave the cashier a sheepish smile while she dropped a five in the tip jar. Brody's advice might carry her further than she suspected after all.

EIGHT

Images flickered across the TV screen: a woman cooking pasta, fourth down in a football game, a commercial for motor oil, a man and woman locked in a romantic kiss. Kate hit the off button and threw the remote on the sofa. There wasn't one thing worth watching on TV and she was going to go stir crazy if she didn't find something to do. She grabbed her phone off the sofa and scrolled through her emails and text messages. There was a legal memo due tomorrow and Patrick was expecting jury instructions by the end of the week, but she just couldn't concentrate.

It was Thursday night—the night she usually spent drinking beer and playing trivia with her friends back in DC. She'd had a good visit with Gram that afternoon and since coming home from the rehab center, she'd done a half load of laundry, vacuumed the living room, and cleaned out the refrigerator—anything but work. She was turning into Annie. She tossed her cell phone on the coffee table and puffed out a loud sigh.

The mantel was flanked by bookcases brimming with paperbacks on the upper shelves and photo albums stored along the bottom. She had been tempted many times to pull out an album and take a look. Although she should be working, she couldn't resist any longer. She gathered three albums into her arms and dropped back onto the couch, spreading the first book open across her knees. A black and white photo of a handsome boy going for a lay-up covered the first page—her dad at maybe age sixteen, probably before he met her mom. Flipping through his high school album, she learned her dad was on the winning state baseball team his junior year, and was awarded Athlete of the Year when he was a senior. Page after page of Johnny McNamara's accomplishments filled the book. On the last three pages were pictures of him fishing with a buddy on the river, standing in front of an ice cream shop downtown, and sitting in his old Chevelle with his arm around her mom, beaming proudly. Kate wished she could have known her parents back then. The one thing she knew for sure after looking through the albums is how happy he looked.

She tossed the albums aside and raked her fingers painfully through her hair. More than likely, her dad's success hadn't come naturally, but had been nurtured through practice and hard work—a model she always tried to follow. She flipped open her laptop, determined to finish that brief, but instead stared blankly at the screen. An image of Brody materialized and she wondered what he'd been like as a teen. Once again, he invaded her thoughts.

"I need some air," she muttered, and once more shoved her laptop aside.

She stepped onto the front porch and took in a deep lungful of cold autumn air, only giving a quick glance to the lumber stacked in the yard. She looked up at the bare trees, noticing every last leaf had fallen. Before long there would be a foot of snow. She glanced next door to Riley's and could see her standing at the kitchen window, probably washing dishes. Kate scurried back inside, threw on a jacket, and grabbed a bottle of white wine out of the refrigerator on her way out the back door. Riley answered after the first steady knock.

"Hey, Kate." Riley stood back and let Kate enter the small kitchen, similar in appearance to Gram's: white painted cabinets, blue vinyl flooring, white appliances.

"I'm bored and hoped you might want to join me for a glass of wine."

"Sure. Sounds great." Throwing open the cabinet over the sink, Riley reached up on her tiptoes and brought down two stemmed glasses. "I better rinse these off. I haven't used them in a while."

"I hope you don't mind my barging in on you. I saw you in the window."

"No, not a problem. I got home from work about an hour ago and would love a glass of wine. It was crazy busy today. Lots of funerals for some reason."

"When it rains it pours?"

"I don't think that applies to dying, does it? I hope not." Riley dried the glasses with a thin towel and retrieved a bottle opener from the drawer. "Let's go in the living room."

Kate took in the sparse furnishings in Riley's house, so unlike her grandmother's, which was cluttered with pictures and mementos on every table. Riley's house looked like she had just moved in and wasn't planning on staying. They sat on one of only three pieces of furniture in the room—a tan sofa—and propped their feet on a wide ottoman. The room was illuminated by a lonely lamp on a single end table.

"Ahh, I'm beat." Riley crossed her feet at the ankles and rested her head against the back of the couch.

They sat in silence for several minutes, sipping wine and relaxing in the soft lamplight. Kate had tried all afternoon to get Brody out of her head, but for some odd reason, she couldn't. She kept picturing his tight t-shirt from this morning, his thick muscles as he lifted the lumber, and she'd feel warm all over. Thinking about him made her head spin, but then again, everything about him made her head spin.

"How well do you know Brody Fisk?" Kate asked before taking a long sip of wine.

"Not very well. I met him a few months ago at the Memorial Day picnic. Liza introduced us." Riley sat her half-empty glass on the end table and turned toward Kate, propping her knee on the sofa between them. "And I talked to him for a while when Liza had an art show up in Morgantown. Other than that night at the Brass Rail, I hardly ever see him around. Why?"

"I don't know. He's such an enigma. He comes off as a quiet, unassuming country boy, but then he—" Kate leaped to her feet and paced a circle around the sofa and ottoman, reciting her thoughts as if she were rehearsing opening arguments. "What does the guy even do? I know he's a lumberjack, bringing free wood to old ladies. He drives that crappy truck but then he shows up at the meeting this week driving a Cadillac or a Lincoln or something, dressed in a tailored jacket and really nice jeans and looking nothing like the scruffy guy I first met. How can he afford that on a lumberjack's salary? Maybe he makes enough with his building business. He's putting up a ramp on Gram's house, you know." She stopped her trek long enough to refill her glass. With a nod of encouragement from Riley, she continued. "At the Brass Rail he was cleaned up, looking like, well, nothing like himself, and was actually fun until he tricked me into thinking he was married. I didn't think it was funny at all. Then on Monday after the meeting, he got all self-righteous in the coffee shop."

"What do you mean?"

She came out of her hypnotic rant and looked at Riley, sitting on the edge of the sofa. "He pointed out I should be kinder to the locals."

"It *is* a small town." Riley stood up, shook the empty wine bottle, and padded toward the kitchen, where she dropped the bottle in the trash and retrieved another one from the refrigerator. The cork popped with a loud *thwonk* and she returned to the living room to fill up Kate's empty glass.

"Is he seeing anyone?" Kate didn't want Riley to get the wrong idea, but she was curious.

"No, I don't think so. Why?"

"Just wondering."

"I think if he were in a relationship, Liza would have told me."

"Oh, the town busybody, is she?"

"No, she's his sister."

"Liza is Brody's sister?" Kate felt shockwaves from head to toe. That cute little pink-haired pixie was the lumberjack's sister? They looked nothing alike. Liza was short, thin, a bundle of energy. Brody was tall and laid-back, with soft, sandy hair; bulging biceps; thick, broad shoulders...

"Kate." Riley shook Kate out of her reverie. "I thought you knew that. Liza is Brody's younger sister. She lives in a little house on their farm. He's in business with Tucker. They own Misty Mountain Brewery. I think she would have told me if he was dating anyone."

"So, he's a lumberjack, carpenter, and brewmaster?"

"And a songwriter. That's his real career."

"What?" The wineglass nearly slipped out of her hand and she felt lightheaded. The surprises just kept coming. "He's a songwriter?"

"I told you at the bar. Liza's brother had a big songwriting career in Nashville and New York."

She downed the last of her wine, wiped her damp palms on her jeans, and dropped onto the sofa, feeling the effects of too much wine too quickly. The mystery known as Brody Fisk just kept getting more interesting. Time to go home. If she wasn't going to use her finely-honed research skills to use for the law firm, at the very least she could dig up some answers about Highland Springs' most enigmatic bachelor.

The next day, Kate jumped at the sound of Brody's voice and caught her toe on the leg of her grandmother's walker, sending it clattering to the tile floor. She reached down to pick it up, her face feeling flushed with embarrassment, and righted the contraption along with her composure.

"Brody, what are you doing here?"

"I was just—" He reached over and aligned the walker directly in front of Virginia. "Coming back from Clarksburg and thought I'd stop in. I hope it's okay."

"Absolutely, honey. Pull up a chair." Virginia waved her hand toward the folded chair in the corner. Kate watched him open it and sit back, resting his ankle on his knee. Last night she'd done some research and discovered Brody was quite an accomplished artist, even earning a few awards. The numerous images of him at concerts, awards shows, and interviews portrayed a much different man from the one sitting in front of her now. Sure, he'd always worn his hair a little longer, but he looked more youthful in the photos, more vibrant. She couldn't put her finger on it, but if she had to guess, there was a story behind the lines and shadows on his face. Her mind spun with possibilities as Brody and Gram carried on a lengthy conversation.

"You should go with him, honey." Gram's quick tap on her shoulder drew her back into the conversation.

"Where?"

"I'm stopping at the community center building on the way back, to check on the renovations."

Gram's eyes lit up. "Katherine, why don't you go? He can show you around."

"I'm not sure she'd want to—"

"Sure she would. She went to the board meeting, so she should see what the center is all about. Right, honey?" Virginia leaned over to pat Kate's knee then winced in pain.

"Gram, are you okay?"

"My leg is aching me, that's all. They really worked me hard in rehab today. Had me trussed up in a leather belt with a leash on the back. I think she thought she was taking a dog out for a walk." Though she let out a hearty laugh, Kate could still see the pain in her eyes.

"I'll go find the nurse. You need some pain meds."

"Now, honey, don't bother them. They'll be around with my medicine in a little while."

"No Gram." Kate planted her hands on the arms of her grandmother's wheelchair and gave her a paralyzing look. "You're in pain and I'm going to get something for it. No arguments."

***

Kate marched out of the room, shoulders squared and determination in her eyes. *I'm glad I'm not a nurse around here*, Brody thought to himself. He glanced at Gram and caught a mischievous look on her face.

"Don't worry, she's all bark and no bite," Virginia said.

"You sure about that?" He chuckled and dropped back into the chair in front of Virginia. There was one thing for sure: Kate McNamara didn't waste any time getting what she wanted. It had been a long time since he had felt that sense of urgency.

"I'm sure. Under that prickly exterior is a heart of gold."

"Hmm, maybe when it comes to you."

"Mark my words, in time you'll see there's more to my Katherine than just a pretty face and a wicked tongue."

No sooner had Gram uttered the words than Kate returned with a pill-toting nurse who efficiently administered Virginia's medication. As soon as she was gone, Kate picked up her coat where it had been strewn across the bed.

"Okay, then. I guess I'll go with Brody to the community center. There was a discussion about liability at the meeting." She cocked a wry grin at him before turning back to her grandmother. "Maybe if I see the building for myself I'll be able to make some recommendations."

"Oh, that's a lovely idea." Gram clasped her hands to her chest and beamed joyfully. "Take some pictures, will you?"

"Sure."

"You all together…working on this project. It's just wonderful."

"We're just checking out the building, Gram. Nothing more."

Gram winked at Brody and gave Kate's elbow a quick squeeze. "Whatever you say, honey."

NINE

Ten minutes after they left the rehabilitation facility, Kate pulled the Buick beside Brody's SUV in the old elementary school parking lot and they met one another on the sidewalk.

"So, this is the future community center, huh? This was an elementary school?" She walked into the yard to look in a window and her spiked heels sank into the damp soil. "Damn it."

"You might want to invest in a pair of sensible shoes."

"Sensible?" She tiptoed back to the sidewalk. "Like what Gram wears?"

He chuckled and extended his arm, urging her toward the entry door. "I'm just saying, you'll need something with a flat sole, preferably waterproof, something good in snow and rain."

"I don't plan on being here once the snow starts."

"That could be any day. Come on, let me show you around." He pulled out a ring loaded down with dozens of keys of varying shapes and colors, and shuffled through the pile until he found the key he thought would open the front door. When that one didn't work, he searched again, and finally found the right fit.

As they stepped inside, he smelled the dank mustiness of the aging, closed-up building. The first warm day, they needed to open all the windows and give it a good airing out.

"Right down the hall here is the gym." He opened one of the double doors and led Kate inside. "You can see the floor is in good shape, but needs refinished, and there's a set of working bleachers along that wall." He took a deep breath, drawing in the familiar gym smell of his childhood. He had played recreational league basketball here from the time he was in second grade until he left middle school, moving on to the high school team. "We'll have all our sports activities in here."

He took her from room to room, guiding her around lumber and paint cans, explaining some of the programs they planned to hold in each space once renovations were complete. She said very little, only occasionally asked a question, but seemed interested. The last room they entered was the old cafeteria.

"We were thinking about offering cooking classes since the kitchen is still fully equipped, but as you can see the tile floor needs replaced."

"What about renting it out for parties? They would have access to the kitchen for storing and preparing food, and have this big room for their event."

"That's a great idea. Good way to bring in more revenue."

"I can see a lot of potential for this building beyond just the current programs."

"You want to put some ideas together for the board to review?"

"Do you think they'd be open to any of them?"

"They're not that narrow-minded, believe me. Plus, anything that brings in money will be welcome." He guided her toward the kitchen. "We're most excited about the kitchen because we can hold the annual Thanksgiving dinner here. We've held it at different churches each year and now it will be held in one place."

"You have a community Thanksgiving dinner?"

"Yeah, it's open to anyone who doesn't have plans with family and friends, or who can't afford to put on a Thanksgiving meal of their own. Most of the ingredients are donated, so we don't charge anything, but we do have a donations basket sitting by the door. It's been going on for longer than I can remember."

"Great idea. Who does the cooking?"

"Usually the board members and any volunteers we can round up. Your grandmother is usually in charge of the mashed potatoes. You think you could handle it for her this year?"

"Me?" Kate spun around and looked at him as if he'd just asked her to bungee jump off the Empire State Building. "Make mashed potatoes? I can't cook." He noticed the flush in her cheeks. Was she embarrassed about not cooking? "Don't look so surprised. I hate to break it to you, buddy, but not every woman can cook."

"Okay, okay," he said, holding up his hands in surrender. "I shouldn't have presumed."

He took a step back, allowing some space between them. He was glad she'd mistaken his smile for disbelief. That fiery spirit of hers just did something to him.

"It's not a crime that I can't cook." She leaned against one of the stainless steel prep tables and looked down at the floor.

"I get it. Liza can't cook to save her life, but she survives. Although she does end up at my house once a week for dinner like a stray dog hoping to be fed."

"Very benevolent of you."

"I could have you over one night for dinner." Where did that come from? He lifted his ball cap and gave himself a mental shake. Now that it was out of his mouth, he sort of liked the idea.

"I'm not a stray dog."

"Didn't say you were." He tucked his hands in his pockets and turned toward the double ovens behind him as if they needed inspection. He just couldn't seem to say anything right. "But, um, seriously, why don't you help out on Thanksgiving? You don't have to make the potatoes, but how hard can it be? Just peel, boil, and mash."

"Why don't you do it?"

"I would, but I'm in charge of sweet potatoes." He turned back around to find her sauntering toward the washroom area.

"I'll tell you what," She looked at the deep triple sink and empty shelves. "I'll help in some way, but I'd suggest you keep me out of the kitchen. I can set the tables, serve drinks, clean up, whatever. Just don't let me near a stove." She spun around and gave him a heart-stopping look, eyebrows arched and lips pursed. "I could be dangerous."

"I can only imagine."

Brody ushered Katherine out of the cafeteria and down the main hallway, trying to think of something to delay the end of the tour. "So, what do you think? Good space, huh? And, the upgrades should be finished in another week or two." The past hour walking with her through the center, listening to her ideas, made him want to hear more. All his warning bells were telling him not to bother, but he wanted to be with her.

"Yeah, it seems like the perfect set up for what you want to offer."

As they approached what had been the school's main office, he realized he hadn't shown her through that area. That would give him at least another five minutes with her.

"I haven't shown you this. Come in here." Finding the door locked, Brody shuffled through the keys until he found the right one, then held open the door for her to enter. "This was the main office and I think we're going to use it for administrative space." They peered in each of three small offices and then came to a solid wood door at the end of the corridor.

"What's in here?" she asked.

Once again he searched through the keys and unlocked the heavy door, then flipped the light switch. The fluorescent strip flickered a few times and then illuminated a large storage room lined on three sides with gray metal shelving. A small cloudy window sat high on the wall across from the entryway.

"This is a really big closet. Will you need all this storage?" She walked to the far side of the room with him following close behind.

"I was thinking we could use it as—" His response came to an abrupt halt as the closet door slammed shut with a deafening bang. They both startled and burst out laughing, Kate's hand pressed against her heart.

"My god that was loud. Nearly gave me a heart attack," she said.

"Maybe I can prop it open with something." He attempted to turn the door knob, but got no movement. He jiggled it again and shoved his shoulder into the door. "I think we're locked in."

"What?" She rushed over, nudging him out of the way, and tried the handle herself. "That can't be. Get the key."

"We can't use a key from the inside. See?" He pointed to the perfectly smooth chrome door knob. "It must lock automatically from the outside."

"Well, we can't stay in here." She rummaged through her purse and pulled out her cell phone, rushing toward the window. "I've got things to do. A brief to finish." She held up the cell phone, frantic to get service. "One bar. Who should I call?"

"I'll call Travis. He's a locksmith."

"The mechanic and pineapple farmer is also a locksmith?"

"Yeah," he chuckled and tapped a few buttons on his phone. "Among other things." He kept his eye on Kate as she paced like a caged panther back and forth under the window, her long, dark ponytail whipping around each time she turned. She held on to her cell phone like a lifeline and continued to scroll her thumb across the screen even though he had this under control. After several rings, Brody hung up and sent a text instead.

Need help. Trapped in closet at new comm ctr. He tapped the send button and then had a brilliant thought. He composed another short message.

Take your time.

TEN

"How long has it been since you called Travis? Maybe you should call again." Kate had kept up her pacing and scrolling, keeping her cell phone in a death grip. "Maybe we should call Riley or Liza."

"Nah, I'm sure they're both working. Besides, they wouldn't be able to get in." Brody was sitting on the dusty floor with his back against the wall, one knee bent, enjoying the view of her long legs as they passed by him for the hundredth time. She'd tire out eventually. "Why don't you have a seat?" He patted the space beside him but only got a sneer in return.

"We can't stay in here all day. I have a pile of work waiting for me. There has to be someone who could get us out."

"Nope, Travis is the only one."

"What about one of the other board members?"

"I have the only keys." He shook the bundle of keys at her and was once again rewarded with an angry scoff. The tinkling of piano keys alerted him to an incoming text and she stopped her pacing, her eyes fixated on his phone.

Got my head up the ass of a crappy compact. Be there when I can.

"What did he say?"

"He'll be here soon. Why don't you sit down and relax until he gets here? Tell me your life story."

"I can't relax, and there's nothing to tell." She only stopped her pacing long enough to check her phone and glance at her watch, then resumed her path. "Besides, hasn't Gram filled you in? You said she talks about me all the time."

"She does, but she hasn't told me anything interesting."

"I'm not interesting?" She planted her feet in front of him and looked down at him with furrowed brows. A hot quiver coursed down his spine—an involuntary reaction to her angry beauty.

"I didn't say that."

She at last plopped down near him, crossed her legs, tucked her feet under her thighs and actually put her cell phone away in her pocket. She gathered her hair in her hands and swept the bundle over her shoulder.

"Well, what do you want to know?"

"Okay, let me see." Brody rubbed his forehead, choosing his words carefully. He decided to start with safe questions. "Where do you live in DC? Who do you live with?"

She told him about her life in Washington, her friends, her neighborhood, her weekly routine. He couldn't tear his eyes away from her, mesmerized by the way her eyes sparkled when she told a funny story or how her lips pursed when she was thinking. The urge to lean over and kiss those lips was making him crazy.

"Are you listening?" He snapped to attention and replied with a nod. "Because it seems like you weren't listening."

"No, I was listening. I'd like to meet your friends sometime."

"Maybe you will."

"That's cool." Brody stretched out his legs and noticed she'd finally seemed to relax. It was the first normal conversation they'd had since they met. "I was wondering, what's keeping you so busy? I know you're working, but it seems like you're under a lot of stress."

"Yeah, I'm a little stressed." With a forced laugh, she eased against the wall and stretched her legs in front of her. "I'm up for a big promotion—I think I told you that—and I can't let up just because I'm here. It should have been mine from the start, but now I have to show them I deserve it by working even harder. My competition would like nothing better than to get the job over me."

"Your grandmother is at the rehab place for another few weeks, right? Couldn't you go back until she's home? Most people would just leave her care to the professionals."

"I'm not most people." Kate rubbed her palms across her outstretched thighs, keeping her eyes cast down.

"I just mean that her friends could look in on her until she's home."

"She asked me to stay, to take care of her house. My grandmother stepped in when my dad died, helped take care of me when my mother went back to school. I spent many summers here with her. She and Grandpa even paid for my college tuition with the money they'd saved for my dad." She leaned her head against the concrete wall and stared up at the tiled ceiling. "I feel like I owe her this. Besides—" Her head snapped around and her arresting eyes locked on his. "I can handle this. That promotion is mine. If I have to go without sleep, that's what I'll do. Nothing's going to stop me."

Brody scooted across the dusty floor, bringing himself closer to her, brushing his shoulder against hers. "I know what it's like to feel the competition breathing down your neck, to have a goal so big you can't think of anything else. You'd do anything to be number one."

"Yeah?" she said, nudging his shoulder with her own. "How do you know that?"

"I don't just cut wood and build ramps. I—"

"You're a songwriter."

"I was."

"Not anymore?"

"Let's just say I'm taking a sabbatical," he said, flicking away an imaginary spot from his jeans.

"Do I know any of your songs?"

"I doubt it."

"I'm sure I do. You're a successful songwriter."

"Was."

"Fine, was. I know you wrote country music. I bet I know some of your songs."

"Yeah, I bet." He stood up and brushed the dust from the back of his pants. He leaned against the wall as Kate climbed to her feet. She walked over to the shelf where she had left her purse, pulled out a tube of lipstick, and swiped it across her lips. Something about her cool, city girl vibe made him doubt she'd ever heard a country song—Taylor Swift, maybe, but not a real country song.

"I do. They play country at the Olde Town Tavern where we play trivia."

"Okay then, what's your favorite country song?"

"Um, well." She laughed and tossed the lipstick back in her purse as she did a slow rotation away from the shelves.

"Uh-huh. Thought so," he said.

"Now wait, I just don't know *titles*." She turned her back to Brody and ran her hand across one of the dusty shelves. She hummed a few bars before singing softly. "And it's all so trivial, yeah trivial." She spun around and bopped her head back and forth as she sang a few more lines of the chorus.

"*Trivial.* That's the title," he said.

"Yeah, I love that song. The guy who runs game night plays it each week before we start—kind of like a theme song."

"But the song's not about trivia."

"I know." She took a few steps toward him, clapping the dirt from her hands. "It's about not letting little things get in the way."

"Yeah, but more about focusing on the things that truly matter."

"You've really given it a lot of thought, huh?" She stopped a few feet in front of him and tilted her head, studying Brody as if seeing him for the first time.

"That's because I wrote it."

"No way!" She gripped his arms in both hands and tugged him forward, giving him a full body shake. Her touch sent a warm surge through his chest.

"Yep, sure did. With my partner."

"What else did you write? I bet I know more of your stuff." She dropped her grip, but stayed so close he could smell the allure of her perfume. Her eyes had softened and a small smile tugged at her lips.

"'Wasting Words'?" He watched recognition cross her face. "'Time Ain't My Enemy'. How about 'Fast Women in Fast Cars'?"

She threw back her head and let out a sharp laugh. "That song—please don't tell me you wrote that. It is so objectifying."

"Don't you like it?"

"Well." She laughed again and then looked on either side of her as if someone might be listening. "I hate to admit this, but when it comes on the radio, I crank up the volume and sing along really loud."

"I'd like to hear that." He inched a little closer.

"No, you really wouldn't. I don't have much of a singing voice."

"You sounded okay a minute ago."

"Yeah, sure. How about you sing? I've heard you have a great voice."

The last time Brody had sung for anyone other than Loretta was in a nightclub in New York. He and Kyle had done an acoustic set of some of their hit songs. It was during a songwriters' conference and the room was full of their peers, only adding to the nervous tension. When he had urged Kyle to leave Nashville, he thought they'd make it big in New York, but they never felt like they belonged—especially Kyle. Through a record executive, they'd been paired with Second First Chance, the top pop band at the time. What they'd written wasn't their best work, but they made tons of money. It wouldn't have mattered what the band sang—they'd go platinum overnight. Even with all the success, Brody couldn't stand to look at himself in the mirror, remembering how it all came to an end.

"Come on, Brody, sing for me."

How could he refuse those big green eyes? "Okay, what do you want to hear?"

"Anything. A love song. Something you've written." Kate spun around and walked a few feet away as if she sensed he needed performance space.

His mind went blank. She was looking at him like she expected the world and he couldn't come up with a single lyric. Maybe it was because, at that very moment, he realized he'd never written a love song. Sure, he'd written some sweet words, even a few intended to melt hearts, but none of them were written with someone specific in mind. He had the sudden urge to jot down new words that were ricocheting in his mind as he looked at her eager gaze.

"I caught you off guard, didn't I?" she said.

"Yeah." He cleared his throat. "Just a little."

"I just want to see if you live up to the hype." She smiled and challenged him with a toss of her head.

"Fine. I'll sing something you might recognize." He took a few steps to his right and then crossed back, his hands loosely folded. "I wish I had my guitar." He kept his eyes cast down, as he began his own pacing. This was ridiculous; he'd never had trouble singing in front of anyone, but something about singing to Kate was making his vocal chords lock up. He cleared his throat again and began. A nervous drum beat in his chest, tapping out a steady rhythm while her eyes locked on him as he sang.

"Oh, Brody, it's beautiful. I love that song." She grazed his arm with her nails, stopping his momentum. "But what have you been working on lately? Sing something I've never heard."

"I don't have anything new."

"Why? I thought artists were constantly working on new projects. Don't you hear music in your head that needs to be written down?"

"Not lately."

"But why?"

She was getting too close, asking too many questions, ones he wasn't ready to answer. It was time to deflect, get her talking about something else.

"So, this promotion. Why so ambitious?"

"You're changing the subject." She gave his chest a playful poke while her brows arched.

"Maybe." He chuckled as he reached for her hand, catching only thin air.

"You want to hear about my career?" When he dipped his chin she continued. "Fine. I've worked really hard and deserve that promotion.

And my dad always told me to be the best. You know? The least I can do is live up to his expectations."

"Have you always been an over-achiever?"

Her cheeks turned red as she tore her gaze from his. "Ever since I was twelve," she whispered.

"What happened when you were twelve?"

"My dad died."

He drew in a sharp breath, kicking himself for pushing. It had totally slipped his mind she'd lost her father at a young age. He watched her turn from him, once again the panther resuming her cage behavior, loping back and forth across the room.

"I'm sorry," he said.

"It's okay. You didn't know."

"Actually, I forgot. How did your dad die, if you don't mind my asking?"

"No, it's okay. It was a training accident. He was in the Navy, assigned to an aircraft carrier. They were practicing flying runs. Something went wrong that day and he was hit and killed. It happened not far off shore; he wasn't deployed to another part of the world or anything. I was at school when the news came in." Brody could see her hands shaking, her fingers in knots. "I can still remember the principal coming into the classroom and calling my name to come to the office with her. Most of the kids I went to school with had military parents. It had happened to other kids before so I knew it meant bad news. It was awful. And…strange, I guess, because I can see it all as clear as if it happened yesterday. Worst day of my life."

Brody stopped her trek by stepping in her path and capturing her shoulders in his hands. She released a heavy sigh and buried her face in his chest. There were no tears, no heaving sobs, just a limp, wrung-out Kate, collapsed against him. She wrapped her arms around his waist, gave him a quick squeeze, then stepped back and smoothed her hands across her jeans.

"Sorry," she said. "I haven't talked about my dad in a while."

"Maybe it was good to take some time, to remember him." He reached out his hand, but she took a step back. "I didn't mean to upset you."

"It's okay."

She ran her fingers through her dark hair, letting the thick ponytail flop on her shoulders. Feeling like he was watching a transformation, she shook her head and raised her chin. "We've been here for over an hour. When's Travis coming?" And just like that, the tender-hearted Kate who'd only a moment ago rested her head on Brody's chest disappeared.

"Katherine." He reached for her hand.

"Most people call me Kate." She snatched her phone out of her pocket and turned her back on him. "I've got to get out of here. Do you realize how much work I have waiting for me?"

"Okay." For the life of him, he didn't know where he went wrong or what caused the change. "I understand."

"Do you?" The wind sucked out of him as her green eyes turned to dark olive pools. "I don't think so." She raked her fingers through her hair again and looked down at the floor. She let out a heavy sigh. "Look, this promotion is important to me. Ever since high school I've set certain goals for myself with deadlines attached. No surprises, always focused. My goal now is to make senior associate then partner, and I was on track until...well until Gram fell, and well—" She was out of breath and her cheeks were fully flushed.

"I get it..."

"Really?" She gave a stilted laugh and threw her hand out in his direction. "Look at you, all laid back, easygoing, not a care in the world. It doesn't seem like you have a set schedule or, you know...direction. Why are you here and not in Nashville?"

Brody felt a sting but didn't care to acknowledge that her words hurt a little. "I know you don't think I do anything all day but show up when I'm least wanted, but I've been in your shoes. I know what it's like to chase after money and fame, but eventually I realized I was only chasing my own tail."

"I'm not chasing money and fame."

"Okay, maybe not. But you're chasing something. You might catch it, too, though it will never satisfy. Remember, when you reach for the brass ring, there's a good chance you'll fall off."

"Thanks, Confucius." Kate wrapped her arms around herself and kicked at an imaginary object on the floor. "Did you read that in a Hallmark card?"

"Listen to me." In two strides he was in front of her, blocking her trek to the other side of the room. "You can make all the jokes you want, but I can see what you need."

"Really, now you're some kind of mind reader too?"

"You should lighten up, don't push so hard. Enjoy the time you have here with your grandmother. Enjoy small town life." His face was so close to hers, if she didn't stop him first, he was going to have to kiss her. He couldn't help himself. "Let me help you."

"I don't need help." Her face was tilted up, her eyes locked on his.

"Are you sure about that?"

"Maybe it's you who needs help." She spoke just above a whisper, her lips mere inches from his.

"Maybe it is." He angled his head and was just lowering his lips to hers when he heard the metal scraping of Travis's tools in the lock. He threw open the door just as Brody and Kate stepped apart.

ELEVEN

Problem at the shop. Be there ASAP.

Kate closed the text message from Riley and shoved her cell phone in her coat pocket as she pressed the buzzer outside the Brass Rail. Ringing a doorbell to enter a bar was just one more thing she found odd about life in West Virginia. It wasn't like they ever refused entry; in fact, they seemed to let anyone in.

"Hey, girl. It's good to see you." Liza slapped a coaster on the bar in front of Kate before she sat down. "I was hoping you'd come back."

"Yeah. It was fun the last time I was here. It's sure busy tonight."

"Sure is. It's pay day and they have cash to burn."

"I'll bet." She leaned around to hang her coat on the back of her chair, fished her phone from her pocket, and caught a glimpse of the same gas company workers sitting at the same table as last time. She received a wink from one of the guys she'd noticed leering at her before. "I'm supposed to meet Riley here, but she's held up at the shop."

"Let me get you a beer. Same as last time or something different?"

"Surprise me."

She couldn't stop herself from surveying the crowd, wondering if Brody was there. She scanned the length of the bar, silently humming along to the Brad Paisley song blaring through the speakers, and felt a prick of disappointment when she didn't see him. After their encounter at the community center last week, she hadn't been able to get him off her mind. He had worked on the ramp a few days which made it that much harder to concentrate. She found respite from her unplanned attraction to him by working in her little corner at the Sit and Sip. Distance from Brody was necessary if she wanted to stay on task and win the promotion.

"Okay, here you go. This is Tucker's latest brew, a pumpkin ale. Very seasonal." Liza placed the amber mug on the bar and watched as Kate breathed in the spicy, caramel aroma before taking a long draw.

"Really good." She took another sip, enjoying the tangy cinnamon flavor. "Where's his brewery?"

"Paula's Creek. It's a little area about ten miles outside town. Only thing there is the brewery, a diner, and the remnants of an old grist mill." Liza talked as she wiped down the bar and cleared empty glasses. "There are a few houses—oh, and a really pretty covered bridge. That's about it."

"I love covered bridges."

"Maybe I could go out there with you, cutie." Warm breath brushing against her cheek and the stale smell of cigarette smoke made her turn toward the raspy voice. The gas company worker who'd winked at her a few minutes ago slid onto the barstool beside her. A quiver of dread surged through her as he raked his eyes over her from head to hips. "What're you drinking?"

"I'm fine. Thanks." She grasped the mug handle while shimmying as far across the stool as she could.

"You can say that again."

She took a long sip of beer and raised her eyebrows at Liza, considering how she'd get rid of him without making a scene.

"I'm Jonas Hinkle. And you are?" He didn't offer his hand, didn't tip his hat, simply leaned in closer, causing her to bump into the man sitting beside her.

"Would you mind scooting your chair over a little? It's rather crowded," she said.

"Oh, sure, anything you say, little lady." At least he obliged by moving his chair away a few inches. Maybe he'd get the hint she wasn't interested in making small talk. She picked up her cell phone and swung her left leg over her right, angling away from his ogling gawk.

"So, I seen you're quite a pool shark."

Kate's cold shoulder and icy glare didn't seem to squelch his interest. Where was Riley? Keeping her eyes on her cell phone, she pretended to be engrossed in an important message.

"Yeah, I seen you here a while back playing pool. You got a good aim," he said.

"Thanks." *Where the hell are you? Being hit on by a fracker.* She tapped the send button, hoping Riley responded with a life-saving *in the parking lot.*

"Thought about cutting in on the game, but you left before I had a chance."

"Sorry."

"You didn't tell me your name."

Damn it, how was she going to get rid of this guy? There was no doubt he would persist until she talked to him. If her cold shoulder and clipped responses didn't give him the hint, what would? She hoped she wouldn't have to resort to stronger measures.

"It's Kate."

"You look like a Kate. A girl as pretty as you should have a pretty name."

"Thanks." Finally, her phone lit up with a reply from Riley. *Sorry. Cooler died. Moving flowers to another one. Might be another hour.*

This evening was quickly becoming a bust. She could either endure the fracker for the next hour or finish this beer and head home. The idea of another lonely night at her grandmother's wasn't appealing, but the alternative wasn't much better. As subtly as possible, she tipped her head in Jonas's direction and signaled Liza with her eyes.

"Another?" Liza asked, nodding to Kate's near-empty glass.

"Let me get that for ya." Jonas raised his hip and reached for his wallet.

"Not necessary," she said and started to rise. "I'm leaving."

"Don't go. We were just getting to know each other," Jonas said.

"Um, yeah…" Kate said as she pulled her coat from the back of the chair. "I don't think so."

"What I think she's trying to say is her boyfriend wouldn't like it if he caught her talking to another guy in a bar. Right, Kate? Wasn't he supposed to meet you here about now?"

"Oh, um, yeah. But, he's been held up." She appreciated Liza trying to help get rid of the guy, but figured he'd see right through her ploy. "I'll just see him later at home."

"Actually, no." Liza glanced at the door. "He just walked in."

Jonas and Kate whipped around, bumping shoulders in their rotation, and saw Brody stroll in. He slowed his progress toward the bar, apparently noticing three sets of eyes watching his entrance.

"See? Now you don't have to leave. Your man is here," Liza said, taking Kate's empty mug with her to the sink.

"Didn't realize you had a boyfriend," Jonas said.

Neither did I.

"Hi, honey." She hopped down from the bar stool and met Brody before he could reach the bar. She wrapped her arms around his neck, and to the unknowing eye, appeared to kiss him on the cheek. In reality, she whispered in his ear, "Please play along. I'll explain later."

Without missing a beat, he enveloped her in a tight hug and whispered back, "What are you up to?"

She froze. His breath against her ear, his strong arm embracing her... this was a bad idea. His tone didn't sound happy and she wasn't sure if he'd play along. She felt sick, felt the blood drain from her face. Oh god, what must he be thinking? Why did she go along with Liza's impromptu plan?

"I'm sorry. It wasn't my idea. Just act like you're my boyfriend...please?" She leaned back and dropped her arms from around his neck, refusing to make eye contact. When she tried to step back, he only increased his hold on her.

"Boyfriend, huh?" He nudged her chin with his hand, forcing her to look at him.

"Who's idea was it?"

"It was—" Releasing the icy tingle of guilt, she thawed into a hot rush of desire. God, he smelled good. Was it a light cologne or his shampoo?

His long, lean body was pressed against hers and his dark eyes were mere inches away, looking deep into her soul—her manipulative soul.

"Trying to ditch that guy over there?"

"Look, I just need you to pretend for a few minutes." Her warm blush was surely turning to a flaming red as her cheeks raged with fire. Even in her high-heeled boots, he was an inch or two taller than her, the perfect height for talking, dancing, kissing. Her eyes fell on his soft pink lips, surrounded by the silky, smooth beard which lay soft against his chin.

"Why not use your *tae kwon do* on him? Thought you could take care of yourself."

The flame blew out and the heat extinguished. "Didn't want to get arrested on an assault charge." With her hands flattened against his chest, she pushed away, but he threw his head back and laughed as she attempted to wiggle free.

"I'll bet."

"Just forget it. Let me go. I don't need your help. I don't need anyone's help. You're right, I can take care of myself." She pushed again, but he only tightened his grip. "If you're not willing to play along, let go, damn it."

"I didn't say I wasn't willing to play."

"Then why are you being so difficult?"

"Just waiting on your cue."

"My what?" She stopped fighting for escape and noticed the humor in his eyes.

"If I'm supposed to be your boyfriend, where's my hello kiss?"

"Oh, I didn't—"

Before she could finish, Brody tilted his head and lowered his face towards hers, stopping a breath away from her lips and said, "Is this what you had in mind?"

***

Intending to plant a chaste kiss on her lips, for appearances of course, Brody couldn't stop himself from pressing for more. Ever since their entrapment at the community center, he'd had a hard time keeping those lips off his mind. He slid his hand along the back of her neck, forking his fingers into her soft, flowing hair and teased her lips open. Damn if she didn't taste better than he'd imagined—warm, tender, dewy, perfect. He finally tore his lips away when he felt Kate dig her nails into his side, aiming a sharp pinch through his shirt.

"Sorry," he said. He wasn't.

"We're in the middle of a crowded bar." She murmured the words against his ear, followed by a melodic laugh that plucked his heartstrings. He reluctantly loosened his embrace but couldn't hold back a self-satisfied grin.

"Okay, let's get rid of that guy." Brody released her and grabbed her hand. His nosy sister was up on her tiptoes, leaning over the bar for a better view. Her eyes were glowing and her smile was stretched from ear to ear.

"Hey, you two. Glad you could make it, Brody." He followed Liza's tilted head and roving eyes to the gas company guy sitting one stool down.

"How you doing?" He acknowledged Jonas, slumped over his beer and wearing a noticeable scowl.

"Not bad," Jonas said as Brody returned his attention to Kate.

"Yeah, I was running a little late. Sorry about that, sweetheart." He pecked a kiss on her cheek and gave her a wink. She wanted him to play boyfriend? He could play boyfriend. Let's see how the little vixen liked that. "What are you drinking, babe?"

"I, um…" Kate cleared her throat and he silently chuckled at the blush in her cheeks. His sweet little nothings were making her nervous. "I was drinking Tucker's pumpkin ale."

"Excellent choice." He patted her heart-shaped butt and slipped three fingers into the pocket of her jeans. "Liza, can you get my girl another?"

He turned to Jonas, gave his shoulder a nudge, and said, "What is it with women and pumpkin? Must be something about the spice, huh?" He chuckled and then tugged Kate closer.

"Let me get a taste of that again." Without giving her a chance to protest he locked her lips under his and slipped his tongue inside for another gut-twisting kiss. If he wasn't careful, this little charade of hers was going to get him in trouble. She didn't hold back and, if he wasn't mistaken, seemed to be enjoying this as much as he was. Then again, she might be pouring it on because of Jonas. When he finally released her, he could have sworn her blush had grown deeper and she was fighting back a smile.

Ninety minutes and two beers later, Brody and Kate walked out of the Brass Rail, keeping up the hoax—for Jonas and his buddies, of course. They walked across the parking lot as tiny snowflakes fell from the midnight blue sky, leaving a frosty coating on vehicles and the ground.

"It's snowing," Kate said.

"Yeah, once the leaves are down, snow usually follows."

When they arrived at his SUV, she kept walking.

"Hey, where're you going?" He reached out and grabbed her hand, spinning her around. Her chest hit his with a thud.

"I'm walking back to Gram's," she said as she tried to squirm out of steely arms.

"No way. I'll take you home."

"Brody." She pressed her palms against his chest while a fine white powder coated his shoulders. "I appreciate what you did for me in there, but you don't need to keep it up. It's only four blocks."

"Exactly. It's only four blocks, so it's no bother. Besides, it's snowing. Get in." As much as he hated to admit it, he had a great time pretending to be her boyfriend and he didn't want the night to end.

"Really. I intended to walk. I don't need you to drive me." She'd leaned back and he studied the determined look in her eye, the steel rod of her posture. Once again, there was that tough turtle shell.

"You have a real hard time accepting help from people, don't you?" he said.

"I accepted your help in there tonight. What do you call that?"

"I'd call that—" *Fun, sexy as hell, dangerously close to falling for you.* "Saving Liza's ass."

"That's the only reason you played along? So your sister didn't look like a liar? And here I thought you were being chivalrous."

"That, too. Plus I thought it would be fun to give them something to talk about in there." Who was he kidding? It was more than that. He'd been fantasizing about kissing her for days. As soon as she draped her arms around his neck, he was done for. Even if it was just a performance for Jonas, Brody enjoyed every minute, maybe a little too much. And that's what worried him.

"That's it, huh?" She dragged her fingers through her snow dampened hair and he finally loosened his hold on her. She stepped back, releasing a cloud of warm breath into the frigid night.

"You've got to admit, we had a good time in there," he said.

"It was fun," she said, with more reluctance than he wanted to hear. "But…"

"But I can't do this. I have—"

"Work to do. I get it. But you need balance in your life. You know what they say, all work and no—"

"It seems like you approach life from the other angle—all play."

"Hey, I work…when I want."

"What about songwriting? You said you haven't written anything lately. Why?"

Brody pressed his back to the driver's side door and looked unfocused over her shoulder. How could he possibly explain how he'd felt since Kyle died? It was all his fault; he'd pushed for more, to the point of exhaustion. It was because of Brody's insistence on getting the demos done to his standards that they'd both stayed at the studio for something like three days, only leaving their work area to meet take-out delivery at the front door. Entire nights passed without them realizing it, mostly because he had flipped out the one time he'd caught Kyle checking the time on his phone. Their success was the only thing Brody could see, and in the end, it was Kyle who paid the price.

"It's hard to explain. I just haven't been able to."

"Look, Brody." She rested her hands on his shoulders and gave him an arresting, green-eyed gaze. "What I know about country music is it's all about storytelling. I get the feeling you have a story to tell. Why don't you write about that? You're too talented not to compose more music."

"Have you been talking to my sister?"

"No, does she say the same thing?"

"Every chance she gets."

"See, then you know I'm right. I'll make a deal with you. If you promise to get back to songwriting, I'll try to relax a little." She pinched her thumb and forefinger together. "Just a little."

"Can we seal the deal with a kiss?" Before he could pull her close, Kate pushed him away, a melodious chuckle escaping her lips.

"I can see you're going to be trouble," she said.

"Funny," he said, his voice as quiet as the fast-falling snow. "I've always thought the same about you."

TWELVE

Only three more things to try on and Kate would have to make a decision about what to wear to the fundraiser. She'd ordered two dresses, two pairs of pants, and four blouses for the big night where she'd be on display for all the available men of Highland Springs. She could kick herself for agreeing to this ridiculous event. Her cell phone rang as she was pulling a silky, form-fitting dress over her head.

"Annie, you caught me at a bad time. Can I call you tomorrow?"

"I just wanted to see if you were ready for your big night."

"You make it sound like I'm being presented at a debutante ball. It's a stupid fundraiser where women parade around like heifers at a county fair." She turned to her left and then her right, analyzing her appearance, then plopped on the bed with a heavy sigh. "I can't believe Gram talked me into this. Do you think it's too late to drop out?"

"Yes, it's too late. Besides, it sounds fun."

"Fun? How would you like being on the auction block for a bunch of slathering backwoods bros? It's insulting."

"You'll probably bring in the most money—you know, new blood and all that."

"Great, I'm the freshest cut of meat at the butcher. That makes me feel a lot better."

"Are you worried you won't get chosen?"

"I've considered it. How embarrassing would that be if no one bid or better yet, I get picked by some reject who couldn't get a date any other way?" She reached back and pulled down the zipper, letting the dress fall to the floor. She stood in just a bra and panties in the middle of the bedroom, looking at the pile of garments she'd ordered. She plopped in the center of them and dropped her head into her hands. "This is ridiculous. Do you have any idea how much money I've spent on clothes for this thing? God, I'm pathetic."

"First of all, you're not pathetic. You're doing your grandmother a favor, plus you're helping a good cause. It wouldn't matter if you showed up in a potato sack—you'll look gorgeous. And you know you won't be left standing on the auction block without a date. Think positive and be your most charming self."

"I see why Kip calls you 'Coach'." She stood up, looked at her half-naked self in the full-length mirror, and flashed a few smiles while doing her best fashion model poses. "You're right. I can do this. Men of Highland Springs better watch out."

Having decided to stick with what's most comfortable—gray pants, white blouse, and a matching gray blazer, Kate tentatively stepped into the banquet hall where the Bag a Bachelor or Bachelorette event was taking place. She had pulled her hair into a tightly wound bun, her only accessory a pair of crystal earrings. She dropped the bag of groceries she'd brought along into the pile with the others. Her hands were already shaking, knowing she'd be on display for the Highland Springs singles scene.

When she first walked in, she didn't recognize anyone. No one seemed to have noticed her…maybe she could just turn around and leave before they did. With an about-face toward the door, she ran directly into her grandmother, who was being wheeled in by Arthur from the board.

"Gram, I didn't know you were coming. I could've picked you up."

"That's okay, honey. I know how busy you've been. Arthur came to get me." Arthur pushed Virginia into the room and parked her at a table away from the drafty doorway.

"But, Gram—"

"Here, honey, give me a hug. I haven't seen you in days."

A guilty, self-disappointed flush warmed her face. "I'm sorry. Work—"

"Work, I know. Katherine, my goodness, you look like you're going to court, not a fun night out."

"I didn't know what to wear."

"That's okay, honey. You still look beautiful. Here, let Arthur pull up a chair for you."

Kate nodded her thanks, feeling ashamed for not picking up her grandmother. It had never occurred to her to ask Gram to come. She should have been the one to bring her—that's what she was in Highland Springs for, to take care of her grandmother. The trial prep work just kept piling on and she wondered what other important things or people she'd forgotten. Tonight she'd be sure to spend plenty of time with Gram and get to know her friends better—starting with Arthur.

"Why don't you sit here, Arthur? You should join us," she said. She gave him a warm smile, hopefully gracious enough to make up for her behavior at the last board meeting. Tonight was all about turning on the charm and if there was anyone she needed to practice her charm on, it was Arthur. "That was so sweet of you to bring Gram tonight. It means a lot to me to have her here."

"It was my pleasure," he said.

"This has to be so fun for you to be out of the rehab place for a few hours, Gram."

"It sure is. I feel like I'm playing hooky."

Kate wrapped her arm around her grandmother and gave her a warm hug, then rested her other hand on Arthur's shoulder. "You've made both our nights really special. Thanks again."

"Anytime, just call me." Arthur's cheeks blushed and he gave her a beaming smile.

"Okay now, first things first," Gram said. "Go over and let Darla know you're here so the bidding war can begin." Her eyes scanned the room as if she were taking inventory of all the potential bidders. "Arthur, you wheel me closer up front. I don't want to miss a minute of the action."

The event had been in full swing for over an hour and Kate was chatting with a pasty pale banker who had an annoying habit of straightening his tie and straining his neck, as if his collar were cutting off his airflow every time he started a sentence. He was in the middle of telling her about his whale watching trip to New England and it was all Kate could do not to yawn. She looked past his shoulder, hoping someone more interesting would interrupt his epic tale. Unfortunately, he was the only man to give her any attention.

"So if I were to win a date with you, I was thinking we could spend the evening in Charleston. Have you ever been?" he said.

"Oh, um, no I haven't."

"There's a really good restaurant on the river I've been to several times for banking functions and afterward maybe we could catch a symphony performance."

"Hmm." It took real talent to keep one eye on the banker, appearing fully engaged, and one eye scanning the room. Thankfully, the inch or two she had on him height-wise gave her a slim advantage. "Um, that sounds nice."

"If it all works out—" Once again he strained his neck and adjusted his tie. "There are several other places we could go, you know, later on, on future dates."

"Oh, that's sweet. But, you know, I was telling you I'm only here temporarily. I'm going back to Washington soon."

"I don't mind driving."

She swallowed the last of her drink and flashed the banker a big smile. "Gee, I just remembered there's something I need to tell my grandmother. It was nice talking with you." Before he could respond, she beelined to Gram, who was sitting at a table with several of her friends.

"There you are, honey. Are you having a good time?"

"It's been, um, interesting."

"Met any nice young men?"

"Some?"

"See, I knew you'd be popular. I'll bet your bid sheet is filling up. I sent Brody over there to check on it for me."

"Brody?" An electric charge shot through Kate and she rose up on her tiptoes, looking toward the table where the bid sheets were set out. "When did he get here? I didn't see him come in." Just hearing his name made her realize that perhaps it was Brody she was searching for while the banker droned on and on. She hadn't seen him for over a week, not since the Brass Rail. Several times a day, she'd look through the sheers, hoping he was working on the ramp, but unfortunately, a week went by without so much as a glimpse.

"He got here a few minutes ago. Came in through the back. He had to pick up bags of ice and it was easier to bring them through the service door."

"Oh." Her view to the opposite side of the room was hampered by the dozens of people milling around the hall. She tipped her head left and then right, but still hadn't caught sight of him. "I think I'll get another drink. Want anything?"

"No thanks, honey. They've got me set up real good."

"I'll be back." Thank goodness they'd decided to hold this event at the American Legion hall, where alcohol could be served, rather than some church basement. Kate didn't think she could get through this night without something to relax her wire-tight nerves. She drew in a sharp breath—Brody was leaning against the bar and had just turned around. His hair was brushed softly away from his face and he was wearing a dress shirt, no tie, and a sports jacket. She was growing fond of his beard—it gave him the look of a rugged outdoorsman mixed with a soft teddy bear. And what a sexy smile he had: beautiful white teeth, full lips, and a hint of a dimple hidden under that soft facial hair. She smoothed her hair into place and took a few steps toward him, but stopped when the crowd parted to reveal Holli, dressed in a skin-tight minidress, looking up at Brody while she twirled a strand of hair around her finger.

Damn. Holli was another one of the bachelorettes up for auction and it looked like she was working hard to snag her winning date. Brody handed her a drink and released another raucous laugh. What could she possibly be saying to make him beam like that? Kate hadn't found her particularly interesting at the Brass Rail.

Just as she was about to turn around, Brody looked up and pegged her with those gorgeous dark eyes of his. He gave her a big smile and held up his finger, asking her to wait a minute. She wasn't going to wait there another second and watch him fall under Holli's spell. She turned away and had only taken three steps when she felt a hand on her shoulder.

"Katherine—Kate, wait. Hi." Brody pulled her around to face him. "You look—"

"Like I'm going to court. I know. Gram already told me."

"I was going to say nice, but you're right. You look a bit too professional for this crowd."

"Sorry to disappoint you."

"No worries. Apparently you haven't disappointed most of the guys. You have a lot of bids. Looks like you'll bring in plenty of money."

"Like a prized heifer."

He threw his head back and laughed. "You look a little better than a heifer."

"I'll take that as a compliment."

"Can I get you a drink?"

"Quite the generous guy, aren't you?"

"What do you mean?"

"You bought Holli a drink, now you're buying me a drink. Why don't you just buy the whole house a drink?"

"Something bothering you?"

"No." She shook her head and pinched the bridge of her nose. She was feeling slightly nauseous, a burning in her stomach that had nothing to do with what she'd eaten that day. As ridiculous as it was, the pang deep in her core was jealousy. It had bothered her more than she cared to admit when she saw him laughing with Holli.

"This whole thing, it's making me uncomfortable. I don't like being on display."

"Yeah, I get that."

"How did you get out of being one of the bachelors?"

"I just said no. I don't participate in stuff like this."

"Very smart of you." She lifted his beer out of his hand and took a long drink. "Mmm, good. Yours?"

"Yeah, we donated a couple kegs. I'll be glad to get you one."

"Maybe later. I'll probably need it when they announce the winners."

He nodded toward a table and placed his hand on her lower back, urging her to sit with him. He pulled out her chair and then gave her the slightest squeeze on her shoulders.

"I can tell you who's got the highest bid on you right now, if you want," he said as he sat down.

"Let me guess, the ghostly little banker?"

"How did you know?"

"He's already got our night planned. Dinner in Charleston along the river and a concert by the symphony orchestra." Kate pressed circles into her temples while shaking her head.

"Sounds…" Brody propped his elbows on the table and leaned toward her, "somnolent."

"Who needs a sleeping pill when you can have a night at the symphony with mister 'my collar is choking me'?"

"It might not be bad. You can discuss the latest interest rates over crème brûlée."

"Thrilling." She released an audible sigh, splayed her hands flat on the table, and shook her head, tipping it towards her lap. Brody looked so good he was making it hard to breathe. What was the matter with her? Only a few weeks ago she couldn't stand the thought of him, but somewhere along the way he'd become a permanent fixture in her mind. Maybe it was Gram always touting his virtues that was clouding her good judgment.

"What kind of a date would you like to go on?"

"With the banker?" She looked at his dark eyes, crinkled at the corners, and his sexy crooked grin. Her heart skipped a beat. It was too bad he didn't participate in these things.

"With whoever wins the bid."

"I don't know."

"Oh, come on," he said. In his best game show announcer voice, he asked, "Kate McNamara, what's your perfect date?"

Her heart rate reached a dangerously high level, threatening to thump right out of her chest. How could she possibly think clearly with his deep brown eyes drilling into hers, his intoxicating smile so close to hers? "Well, I'm not really one for a lot of fanfare. I'm, um—"

"So you like to keep it simple, casual."

"I prefer it."

"Don't need roses and champagne, a chauffeured limo?"

"I never had a desire to ride in a limo, no, but roses are nice." He sat back in his chair, his eyes squinted as if he were trying to read her.

"Are you surprised?" she asked.

"A little, maybe."

"Why?"

"I don't know. I took you as liking the finer things in life."

"I'm not easily impressed with the finer things. It's just not important to me." She pressed her hand against her stomach, trying to calm the wave rolling through it. It was the same nauseous feeling she had when he was laughing with Holli. His eyes lost their amusement and he looked pensive as he turned his cup around in circles.

"Hmm." He laughed unconvincingly and plastered on a wry grin. "Good to know."

"Dinner and drinks and good conversation, and I'm happy." She picked up his cup and drained his beer. "Now, it's time for me to get back out there and drum up another bidder. The banker can't be my final bid."

***

Brody watched Kate's long stride across the room, stopping periodically to speak a few words with several single guys he knew. She'd changed since he first met her. Sure, there were times her snippiness emerged or she'd pull into her protective shell, but more and more he could see the real Kate starting to take over. And he liked it. Having felt nothing but guilt and a certain dull lifelessness inside for almost two years, it was pleasant but frightening to feel that exciting zing whenever she was around. It was too bad she wouldn't be here much longer.

He looked into his empty glass and stood, planning to get another, when his little sister stopped him. "Hey, hold it right there. I have a bone to pick with you."

Looking over his shoulder, he saw Liza charging toward him, her blue hair bobbing with each determined step. He chuckled to himself at his sister's ever-changing appearance.

"What's your bone?"

"Why haven't you bid on anyone? Didn't we have a conversation not long ago about you getting out there and meeting someone?"

"I believe *you* said I should get out there. I agreed to nothing."

"Seriously? Brody, there are a couple of women you should bid on—one in particular."

"Oh, yeah, who's that?" He held his breath as he waited for his little sister to blurt out the name he was expecting.

"Kate."

"I figured you'd say that."

"She's perfect for you. I saw how much fun you were having at the bar that night." Fists planted on her hips, Liza challenged him to refute that he and Kate had a great time faking it. "Don't deny it."

"It was an act, remember?" Brody proceeded to the bar, feeling Liza fast on his heels. He wasn't about to confess to her that it had been more than an act—at least on his part.

"It may have started out as an act, but I saw the chemistry between you." His sister had always been able to read him. Yeah, he knew there was chemistry, at least from his side of things. But Kate had made it quite clear outside the Brass Rail she didn't need him or anyone else. She only agreed to cut back on her work to placate him. He doubted she could do it.

"Chemistry? Didn't you fail that class in college?"

Liza grabbed his arm, spinning him around to face her. "Don't be such a dick. You know what I'm talking about."

"Listen, Kate's a busy woman and she's heading back to DC soon. I know for a fact she's not looking for anything. There's no point. We're just friends. Sort of."

"But maybe you could be more than friends if you put a little effort forth."

"Why? She's leaving. I'm staying. The end."

"She could change her mind, decide to stay. You never know. Come on, Brody, this is what you need. Kate's what you need."

"Let me make a suggestion, little sister. You stay out of my personal life and I'll stay out of yours."

***

A half hour later, all the bachelors and bachelorettes were called to the stage. The winning bids were about to be announced and Kate felt the blood drain from her face as she looked out into the crowd. She spotted the pale-faced banker smiling up at her and the short, stocky physics professor looking at her through his bottle-bottom glasses. Only moments before they had been called to the stage, she noticed a flurry of activity by the bidding tables, but had no idea who might have won. The suspense was killing her. Which insufferable date was she about to go on?

Sam, the chairman of the board for the community center, acted as master of ceremonies and had a flair for the dramatic. He gave a rather lengthy speech about the community center and its benefits. Kate just wanted him to get on with it. Finally, he introduced each bachelor and bachelorette and their winning bidders. He'd gone through all the men and women until only she and Holli were left standing.

"And now for the lovely Holli. I'm happy to announce the winning bidder was—" She sucked in her breath, feeling slightly light-headed. "Phil Krantz." She was weak with relief. The banker had apparently taken a

WHATEVER YOU SAY | 109

shine to Holli. Kate plastered on a pleasant smile and clapped along with the crowd. She never thought she'd be so grateful to Holli-with-an-I.

"Last but not least, the newest member of our community, Kate McNamara. There was quite a battle for this young lady's attention." A quiver of fear surged through her. She couldn't remember who was left of the men she had talked to. She thought they'd all been matched with the other bachelorettes. She grasped her shaking hands together as she scanned the audience, taking a quick inventory of the guys still waiting. Her eyes glassed over and the crowd blurred. *Hurry up, Sam, just announce it already.*

"The winner of a date with Kate—" Sam chuckled and then set his reading glasses back on his nose, "is our own Brody Fisk."

She felt a surging sense of relief and, dare she admit it, excitement at Sam's announcement. She scanned the room, searching for Brody, but when she found him his face was ember red. He flashed an angry scowl at her and stalked out of the room. She stood alone on the stage as the crowd dispersed and winning bidders met up with their prized matches. Confusion worried her mind. Was this a joke or a mistake? Brody said he didn't participate in this kind of stuff and by the look on his face, he didn't mean to. She ambled to the end of the stage feeling deflated. As she descended the stairs, she caught sight of him in the kitchen hovering over Liza. They were in a heated argument. All at once, a light illuminated Kate's dark confusion.

THIRTEEN

"What the hell is the matter with you?" Brody seethed through gritted teeth, doing his best to keep his voice low. There were several volunteers in the kitchen who would love to know what the fight was about.

"Somebody needed to kick your ass into gear," Liza growled right back at him.

"That wasn't your call to make."

"Too bad, I made it. You're so busy wallowing in self-pity, your life is passing you by."

"My life isn't—" He clenched her thin arm in his hand and dragged her into a pantry off the kitchen. "You need to stay the hell out of my personal life. How many times do I have to say it?"

"What personal life? Huh? You sit alone every night in that big old house." She snatched her arm from his grip. "Kate McNamara is the perfect woman for you. She's smart, beautiful, fun, and she won't put up with your bullshit. If you'd crawl out of your hole, you'd see I'm right."

"You don't know what you're talking about. You don't know anything about Kate."

"I know she couldn't take her eyes off you at the bar that night. I saw the smile on her face when they announced your name."

"I can't talk to you." He stormed out of the pantry and hit a brick wall—by the name of Kate McNamara.

***

"Katherine—Kate—" Brody nearly knocked her off her feet. He grabbed her arms with steadying hands and released a heavy sigh. "Are you okay?"

She knew she'd come at a bad time, but had to know what was going on. It was obvious by the angry voices and scowling expressions that he and Liza were at odds.

"I'm fine." She smoothed a few loose strands of hair and gathered her courage. He wasn't happy about the bid and she needed to know why. "Could I talk to you for a minute?"

"Sure." He pressed his hand against the small of her back and guided her outside the kitchen to a secluded corner. "I want to explain."

"It's apparent you were caught off guard tonight. I take it there was some mistake."

"I won the bid, but my sister placed it." He raked his fingers through his hair and glanced toward the bid table. "Hell, I don't even know how much."

"A thousand dollars."

"What?"

"I'm not sure what's going on, but I want you to know I don't expect you to follow through." Her eyes welled up and she silently cursed. Why was this happening? It wasn't like she wanted or even expected a date from Brody. But now that one had seemed inevitable, she felt a searing pain as she watched the angry expression on his face. She looked down at the ground, clearing her throat before she continued. "I'll pay the thousand dollars and let you off the hook." She turned to go.

"Wait. You don't have to do that." Brody propelled her around to face him, but she kept her glassy gaze toward the floor. Damn if she'd let him see her disappointment. "I'm sorry about this. My meddling little sister doesn't know when to stay out of my business. I'll pay the money and take you on a date."

"You don't have to do that. You said you don't participate in this kind of thing and I won't expect you to." After a moment, her impending tears subsided and she shook her head, bringing her gaze back to his. She wasn't so desperate she needed a pity date from anyone. Least of all Brody.

"Really, I'll take you out. I..." Brody rubbed his forehead like he did when he was nervous or uncomfortable—a gesture Kate had come to know too well. "Um, I just didn't plan on bidding. That's all. It's nothing against you; you're fine."

"Thanks, I guess." All of his backpedaling wasn't making her feel any better. There was no way she'd go out with him now. No matter what he said, he'd had no intention of taking her on a date from the beginning. "Let me put you out of your misery. No date. No bid money. We'll forget the whole thing."

"I can't let that happen."

"You don't have any choice. I won't go out with you." She tried to leave once again but was stopped by his large hand on her shoulder.

"You have to. How would it look? Can you imagine the gossip?"

Now her disappointment turned to heat. He was more concerned about his reputation than her feelings.

"Let them talk." She rushed across the room and snatched her coat off the chair. If the townies were going to gossip, now would be a good time to start.

She threw all her weight against the entry door, letting it slam behind her. She walked across the parking lot and caught up to Arthur and Gram as he helped her grandmother into his car. While Arthur put the wheelchair in the trunk, Gram beckoned for Kate to bend closer.

"Honey, I wanted to tell you I'm so happy you're going out with Brody. He's a good man. You two are so cute together."

"Gram, it was a...misunderstanding. Brody didn't place the bid. Liza did." She sighed as she pushed her fingers through her hair, loosening her bun. "Brody had no intention of taking me out."

"I don't believe that. Are you sure?"

"Positive."

"Oh, honey." Gram reached out and pulled Kate's hand against her chest. "I'm so sorry." Her soothing voice beckoned tears back to her eyes.

This was ridiculous. It was just a stupid fundraiser that meant absolutely nothing. Why was it bothering her so?

"I was so sure he'd placed the bid himself," Gram said. "I've noticed the way he looks at you."

"Yeah, with contempt."

"That's what you think?" Gram shook her head, chuckled, and kissed Kate's hand. "Katherine, I'm not blind. That boy is smitten with you."

"Absolutely not."

"Now listen to me, I didn't just fall off the turnip truck. I know what love looks like." She squeezed Kate's hand and pulled her closer. "And if I didn't know better, I'd say you have feelings for him, too."

"Gram, you've got this all wrong." She stood up and held on to the passenger door. "There is nothing between us. I'm going back to DC. You're seeing something that isn't there. And besides, it would never work. We're nothing alike, have nothing in common. I have plans, goals, you know?"

"Who are you talking to? Me or you?"

"What?"

"You sure gave yourself a convincing speech." Gram wrapped her hand around one of Kate's tightly held arms and gave it a gentle squeeze. "Sometimes I think you use work as an excuse not to live. If you keep hiding behind that desk, you'll never be disappointed, but then again you might miss out on something special."

"I'm not hiding. I'm just being realistic."

"Is that right?"

"I know what I'm talking about."

"We'll see about that."

***

When Brody walked into the cold night, Kate was standing in the dimly lit parking lot, watching Arthur's tail lights fade into the night. A cold breeze stirred up the gravel dust and blew a few locks of hair across her face. She brushed the strands aside and turned into the wind, toward the building. He felt more than heard her sharp intake of breath when her eyes met his. His face twisted into a wry smile and he threw his hand up in a wave. He was glad she hadn't gone.

"Hey, can I talk to you before you leave?" He tucked his hands in his front pockets as he approached.

"There's nothing more to say."

"Listen." With determination in his gait, he reached her before she could climb into her car. He stood in front of her with his back to her door, keeping her from escaping, and kicked at some loose gravel with the toe of his shoe. "I handled this all wrong."

"Oh?"

"I'm not mad at you or the situation."

"Really?" Kate crossed her arms over her chest and arched one eyebrow at him. A cold shiver ran down his spine. Her intimidating stare suddenly made him nervous.

"Everything I said in there came out wrong. I was just mad at Liza for meddling in my personal life. She thinks it's her responsibility or something."

"Fine. It doesn't change anything."

"I think we should go out."

"Trying to keep the grapevine under control?"

"I don't care about that." He eased his hands onto her shoulders and tugged her forward. "I don't. I shouldn't have said that." He let his hands slide down her arms until he gathered her hands in his. Their softness felt so good. "I really would like for us to go out—get to know each other better."

"Why?"

"Because I…" He met her searing gaze and thought his heart had skipped a beat when he absorbed her gorgeous green eyes. "We had fun at the Brass Rail and I liked talking to you in the storage closet. You can't leave town without dinner in Charleston and a night at the symphony." He winked at her and a huge weight lifted off his chest when she replied with an arresting smile.

"Please don't do that to me, unless you want me to snore through half the date," she said.

"I wouldn't want that." He pulled her gathered hands against his chest and tilted his forehead against hers. "Am I forgiven?"

"It all depends on where you take me."

"No pressure, right?"

"Right."

Their foreheads were still touching and he had no desire to separate. Her iron-hard shell had melted along with his heart. He couldn't remember the last time he'd felt like this: alive, energized, more like his old self. Having her so near made him take a chance he wouldn't have even a few weeks ago.

He applied just enough pressure to ease her forward and captured her surprised mouth against his. There it was, that perfect kiss, the kiss he'd dreamed about since the night at the Brass Rail. With a single touch, he was on fire. He drew her in closer and spun her around, trapping her against her car, and delved deeper, savoring the luscious feel of her tongue tangling with his.

She wasn't stopping him either. Her arms draped over his shoulders and her fingers crawled up the back of his neck, her long nails combing through his hair. God, it had been so long since he'd felt this—or had he ever felt anything like this? He couldn't let go, couldn't get enough and Kate was telling him with her mouth that she felt the same way.

He needed more. He slid his hand inside her coat, splaying his palm across her silky blouse, wishing it was skin. His fingers inched inside the waistband of her pants and slipped under her blouse to the satin of her lower back.

"Wait." She flattened her hands against his chest. "We can't do this."

"Why?" Reluctantly, he eased back but kept her locked in his arms. Her lips were red, slightly swollen. He ran his finger over her still-wet bottom lip. "Nobody's around. No crowd this time, like at the bar."

"Yeah, but you and I both know it was getting too—" Kate gave him a push and broke their embrace.

"Too what?"

"Heated."

"Is that a problem?" Brody gathered her coat in his hands and tugged her forward. Was she mad because he had his hand inside her blouse? She was twenty-eight or so; he couldn't believe that high school move would've made her apply the brakes. Maybe it was the location. He looked around at the empty parking lot and concluded it wasn't exactly the best make out spot. "I guess it's not exactly a romantic setting."

"No kidding." She wrenched out of his hold and walked a few feet away from him. She stopped and looked up at the lamp post. With her back still toward him, Brody came up behind her and slipped his arms around her waist, nuzzling his mouth against the base of her neck.

"I'm sorry if I got carried away. You're a little hard to resist." He planted a few gentle kisses on her neck before she rotated out of his arms.

"Look, Brody, there's no point in getting anything started. I mean, what do you think could happen between us? Okay, so you're taking me out. What then? I'd start hanging out at your house, maybe watch a movie in front of the fire? I'd stay over sometimes and you'd make me pancakes the next morning." She turned away from him and paced in a circle, staring down at the ground as if the dialogue were written in the gravel. "Maybe we'd start having weekly dinners with Liza and Gram, one big happy family. We'd be seen all over town together. 'Look, there goes that cute couple, Brody and Kate. Like two peas in a pod, always together,'" she said in an uncanny approximation of the local accent. "We'd start finishing each other's sentences and picking out a china pattern. Maybe I'd learn to cook, teach a class at the community center. Get all settled in. For what? For nothing. It won't end well."

Brody leaned against the car, hands tucked in his pockets, and watched Kate argue with her demons.

"You've thought a lot about this, haven't you?"

"Yes—no." She stopped her traipsing and looked at him as if she'd been caught naked in a crowded room. "Why are you smiling? You understand what I'm saying, right?"

"I understand. It sounds like you've got this all wrapped up tight, no room for improvisation."

"I'm getting that promotion and going back to DC. What's the point?"

"The point is…" He reached out a hand and pulled her closer. He cupped her face, looking into those stormy eyes of hers. "We can hang out. You learn to chill and I gain some valuable song material."

"I don't need to chill." She stepped back and her heel landed unsteadily on the gravel. He gathered her safely in his arms before she fell.

"You sure about that?" Brody snaked his hand around her neck and tugged her forward, capturing her lips against his. She stood flag-pole straight, her lips pressed tight, but he wouldn't be deterred. With his persistent kisses and soothing touch, the tension in her back loosened, and she finally leaned into him, heavy and languid.

"Well, maybe I do." She dropped her head against his shoulder, muffling a laugh in his jacket.

"Don't you remember what you promised me in the parking lot? At the Brass Rail?" he whispered against her ear.

"Oh yeah…" She chuckled and leaned back, melting him with a playful grin. "I suggested a deal. If you promise to get back to writing again—"

"You'll try to relax…a little."

"See you just finished my sentence."

"You're right. I did." He slid his hands inside her coat and tugged her tight against him. "But you won't be right about the rest. I promise."

FOURTEEN

"We're running out of glasses, Kate," Darla shouted across the kitchen.

"Coming." Kate was elbow-deep in hot, sudsy water, washing and rinsing dishes as fast as they were dumped into the metal sink. When she got a break, she planned to peek into the dining room to see how many people were eating Thanksgiving dinner in the fellowship hall of the United Methodist Church. It seemed like the entire town of Highland Springs came out for the free meal by the number of plates and silverware that had passed through her hands. Those endless hours of legal writing were starting to look good.

"Hey, Kate." Riley came into the room, tying a floral apron at her waist. "Let me take over for a while. Your back has to be breaking by now."

"Thanks. I appreciate that." It was true, her back was killing her. She had lost track of how long she'd been bent over the deep sink. She reached for a towel and looked around the corner at the busyness in the kitchen as she arched her back. Darla was filling water glasses, Arthur was carving turkey, and Sam was ladling gravy into serving bowls. Several other volunteers were hard at work—folks she'd met that morning, whose names already escaped her. She took a few steps into the cooking area and missed colliding with Brody by an inch.

"Watch out." He held an industrial sized baking dish over his head as he swerved out of her way. "Sweet potatoes coming through." They had been so busy since coming to the church that morning, she'd barely spoken a word to him. As soon as everyone arrived, they kicked into high gear to prepare the annual feast.

"That was close." He swatted her bottom with an oven mitt.

A surging tingle radiated throughout her body and her cheeks grew warm. She smoothed the skirt of her apron and looked down at the floor, doing her best to hide the smile on her face. Brody had worked on the ramp only one day this week, which was a good thing. The trial had started two days ago and she was busy reviewing testimony each day. She didn't need the distraction of his muscles flexing each time he slammed the hammer or picked up a board.

"You're blushing." Liza was at the coffee maker, waiting for the carafe to fill. "Want to tell me?"

"Oh, um." She shook her head and chuckled. "It's nothing."

"You sure about that?" Before she could reply, Liza placed a full decanter in one of her hands and a quart of half-and-half in the other. "Can you walk around and refill coffee? Start at the table by the door. Thanks." With that, Liza was off to the dining room to clear tables and collect dirty dishes.

Kate backed into the swinging door, keeping her eyes riveted on Brody, who was talking to Arthur over a steaming pot of gravy. She felt like a teenager with her first crush. Maybe this deal of theirs could work. She'd learn to relax—well, maybe when she was with him—and he'd start composing again. With a little less sleep she could keep up with her work and still have time left over for him. What was it he said? She would give him some valuable writing material. She looked forward to finding out what that was. She drew back her shoulders and put a little swing in her walk, just in case he might notice.

"Hey, look who's here."

She stopped in her tracks when she heard the familiar, gravelly voice. She turned to her right, finding a table full of guys she recognized from the Brass Rail. It was the group of gas company workers, and Jonas was among them. "It's a small world, ain't it?" he said.

"Hi, everyone." Kate plastered on a smile and began refilling coffee cups. "Hello, Jonas."

"How 'bout that. You remembered my name."

"Yep." She started filling cups on the opposite side of the table from where Jonas sat, going down the row away from him, hoping she'd run out of coffee before she got to his seat. The coffee pot had only one cup left, but before she could empty it and get away from the group, Jonas walked up beside her with his cup extended.

"How about a refill before you run out?"

She obliged by filling his cup and splashed in a shot of cream. She turned to walk away, but he stepped in front of her. "I want to apologize for the other night at the bar. I didn't realize you were meeting your boyfriend there."

"Oh, that's fine. Not a problem." The tiny hairs on the back of her neck stood on end, but she kept a pleasant smile frozen on her face.

"I just didn't want you to think I'm some creeper, stalking you or anything."

"I didn't think that. No worries." Once more she took a step to walk away, but he blocked her exit.

"It's just that, I don't know, maybe I had too much to drink, or I was lonely. Been away from home too long."

"Oh?"

"Yeah, we've been working here and I haven't been home in three months."

With her hackles still up, Kate took a deep breath and remembered where she was. If a guy had been so annoyingly persistent back in DC, she might threaten to take him out. But this was Highland Springs, crime rate near zero, and it was Thanksgiving. In a small town like this, she was expected to show a little more kindness and compassion. When in Rome...

"Where are you from?" she asked, keeping an interested expression on her face.

"I'm from Texas. Been working for this company ten years. Now with fracking, we get sent all over. Kinda makes it hard, you know?"

"I can imagine. When will you be finished here?"

"We've got another month or so, then we're off to God knows where."

"Well, I'm glad all of you could come today. It was good talking to you. Happy Thanksgiving."

***

Brody stood in the kitchen, watching Kate through the service window talking to the gas company guy she ditched at the Brass Rail. He must have been telling her quite a tale because she had that concerned, sympathetic look on her face. Surely she wasn't falling for his line of bull. With a churning in his gut and a need to step in, he gripped the handle of the rolling cart used for clearing tables and backed through the doorway, wheeling it in Kate's direction.

"Hey, sweetheart, want to help me clear the tables?" he said, coming within a half an inch of bumping Jonas with the cart. Her cheeks took on a deep red blush and her eyes a smoky glare. "Hey, man, good to see you again." Brody shook hands with Jonas and gave a quick wave to the rest of the guys at the table. "Glad you all could come. Now, if you'll excuse us, we have some cleaning to do."

He tipped his head at Kate, giving her the signal to follow. She trailed behind him as they crossed the room to a table covered with used plates, cups, and silverware.

"You didn't have to do that," she whispered loudly. "He wasn't bothering me."

"You looked a little worried. Thought maybe you needed me to play boyfriend again." He nudged her with his shoulder and shot her a wink. He liked coming to her rescue, even though he had no right. She chuckled and shook her head as she walked to the other side of the table.

"Okay, I admit it, he gives me the creeps." She glanced over her shoulder toward the gas workers' table. "I feel like he's staring a hole through me."

"Right now he's diving into a piece of pumpkin pie." He looked at the workers, huddled together at the table. Jonas looked up and nodded at

Brody who returned the gesture. Even if it was just a ruse, he'd continue to let Jonas know it wasn't okay to mess with his woman. *His woman*—he liked the sound of that.

The notion gave him a chill. She'd prophesied what might happen if they got involved, but he couldn't help thinking about the possibility. Kate had made it clear she was going back to Washington. They shouldn't get involved. It was pure common sense…but when did he ever listen to common sense? Hopefully, this little deal they'd worked out might lead to more.

"I better unload this cart." He pushed the cart toward the kitchen, resisting the urge to see if she was watching him go.

***

Two hours later, Kate was clearing several tables as the last of the Thanksgiving guests were leaving the church hall. There were a few people lingering over dessert, but for the most part, the dining room was empty. As she piled plates into a precarious tower, she felt a tap on her shoulder. She turned around to find a young woman behind her with an infant on her hip and three children, all appearing to be under the age of five, standing stoically beside her.

"Excuse me. Is the dinner over?" she asked. Kate found herself staring at the frail young woman sporting a purple bruise over one eye and missing front tooth. The children looked as though they hadn't seen a bathtub in weeks.

Finally tearing her eyes away from the filthy kids, she smiled warmly and tried to hide her dismay. "Actually, we stopped serving about fifteen minutes ago."

"Okay. Come on kids." The woman turned to walk out, but two of the children stayed rooted, eyeing the leftovers strewn across the table.

"Wait. I'm sure we have something in the kitchen for you. Take a seat." She pointed toward an empty table nearby. "Sit over there. I'll bring you some turkey."

Besides the trip out to Cash's Holler, this was the first time Kate had come face-to-face with poverty and obvious abuse. It was evident by the children's thin bodies and wan complexions that they weren't getting the nutrition they needed.

"Brody." She rushed into the kitchen, finding him placing the last of the turkey in a plastic container. "Can I have some of that?"

"Taking leftovers to Virginia?"

"No, a family just walked in."

"We're finished for the day. They should have come earlier."

"No, look." She grabbed his wide shoulders and turned him toward the service window. "We have to feed them. Those kids look like they're starving."

He looked around at the kitchen: sparkling clean, all food, pans, and utensils put away.

"Please. We can't turn them away," she said.

He leaned against the stainless steel table and looked down at her. His dark, penetrating eyes bore into her—that soul-deep gaze that always made her wonder what he was thinking.

"Well?"

"Well, okay. Give them something to drink and I'll heat up what we have left."

She found five plastic cups on a shelf and a gallon of milk in the refrigerator, partially full, and hurried out to the dining room. Two of the children were crawling under the table while the third child sat as still as a stone, staring longingly at the milk. As soon as she filled the cups, the whole family drank greedily and she quickly gave them a refill. They slowed down and she went back into the kitchen to check on Brody's progress.

Within fifteen minutes, Brody, Kate, and Darla had heated up four heaping plates of food, including a small plate of mashed potatoes and carrots for the baby. Kate sat down across from the woman, spooning little helpings of vegetables into the baby's mouth while his mother tucked into her own plate.

***

As soon as the young family began to eat, Brody watched Kate talking with the woman and her children. He couldn't hear what she was saying, but noticed one child smiling at her while the other two laughed. What could she possibly be saying to make the dirty waifs laugh like that? Eventually, she reached forward and pulled the baby into her own lap, making an airplane spoon to occupy him and keep him eating. She looked so comfortable, natural, holding the baby, like she'd done it a hundred times. His impression of her as a hard-nosed career woman—definitely not the nurturing type—might not have been entirely fair.

"Looks like Kate's made some new friends." Liza had silently sidled beside Brody, snapping him out of his musings.

"Um, yeah."

"She looks like a real pro."

"Yeah." He cleared his throat and walked back toward the sinks. "Wasn't expecting that."

***

A half hour later, Kate carried the last of the dirty dishes from the dining room and dumped them beside the deep, stainless steel sink. Brody's arms were plunged deep in the water and a mountain of dishes were piled in the rack, ready to dry. She picked up a towel and dug in.

"So, did that family get filled up?" Brody stopped washing to arch the kinks out of his back, but kept his hands dangling in the water.

"I think so. They seemed satisfied." She picked up another plate and continued drying, remembering the desperation in their eyes. "I wish there was more I could do. Did you see her black eye?"

"I did."

"She said she tripped on a rug and hit her eye on the newel post. Somehow I doubt it, don't you?"

"Possible, but not probable."

"Those kids, oh my gosh, I just wanted to take them home with me. Put them in the shower and give them come clean clothes. So sad. I think I'll call the Department of Human Resources tomorrow and see if they can get some assistance. Obviously she's being abused. Is there a women's shelter around here?"

He stopped washing dishes and dried his hands, concern shown on his face. "Is this something you should get involved with?"

"Brody, did you see them? They need help."

"I know, but it could be dangerous."

"What do you mean?"

"What if her husband is an angry, violent drunk? You don't want to mess with someone like that."

"I'm just going to call to see if someone could check on them, maybe offer some services to her." She resumed drying, stacking a plate on the towering pile. If she didn't do something to help, she would never get their sad, hopeless faces out of her mind. "I know I shouldn't get involved. I'm not going to be here much longer, remember? But the least I can do is ask someone who can."

FIFTEEN

The next morning, Kate sat on the stairs and watched Travis test the door knob and lock. His long, thick dreadlocks were pulled back and secured with a leather string. She thought back to the morning in the market when he'd approached her about pineapples and she smiled to herself. If someone had told her that day he'd be inside Gram's house installing a new lock in a little over a month, she would have adamantly denied it. She now considered him a friend.

"Kate, this door knob and lock are fine, so all I need to do is install a deadbolt, and you're good to go." Travis dropped his tools into his canvas bag and stood up, tucking his Allman Brothers t-shirt into his faded jeans. "Let me get a deadbolt out of my truck and I'll be right back."

News of recent and continued break-ins, plus Brody's concerns over her getting involved with the battered woman and her children she'd met yesterday, had made calling Travis a number-one priority this morning. Besides, it would give her peace of mind knowing Gram would be more secure after she went back to Washington.

Her laptop was opened and perched on her knees, and with several taps on the keyboard she found what she was looking for: West Virginia domestic violence laws. She'd barely slept last night, thinking about Ashley, the abused woman she'd met at the Thanksgiving dinner. She'd decided not to contact the authorities just yet for fear of Ashley losing the children. Instead, she planned to arm herself with the facts and pay a visit to the family.

Travis returned and set to work installing the new lock while Kate kept up her research. Once the shrill whirring from his drill died down, she set her laptop aside and took the opportunity to get to know him better.

"How long have you lived here Travis?"

"My family moved here when I was thirteen." He kept his back to her, pulling open the lock's cardboard packaging. "My parents were school teachers, like Brody's, and my dad came here to become a baseball coach at the high school."

"And you must have liked it."

"Yeah, I did, but due to some unplanned circumstances, I left town for a few years."

"Sounds mysterious."

"Not really. I got my girlfriend pregnant and joined the Air Force to support them."

"Must be something in the water." She chuckled as she stepped down off the staircase. "That's how I came to be, too."

"No kidding? Well, it happens."

"I didn't know you had a child. Boy or girl?" She moved behind him and watched as he slid the deadbolt into the door.

"A girl, Carly. She lives with her mom over on Hillcrest."

"Oh, she lives here. Do you see her often?"

"All the time. Carly's almost thirteen and comes over a lot. I officially have her every other weekend."

"And you and her mother? Get along well?"

"Yeah, we're friends. We were young and careless. No one was to blame."

"So you came back here after the service because of Carly?" She strolled over to the mantel and picked up a photo of her dad, mom, and herself as a toddler.

"Yes and no. After the Air Force, I lived in Dallas and then Chicago. Worked as an airline mechanic. Thought I wanted the big city life. Then I spent time in Hawaii, but you already know that. There's just something about Highland Springs. It's home. Even if I didn't have Carly, I would've come back."

"No regrets?" She set the picture back in its place, turning back to watch Travis at work.

"None. I like the slower pace, the way folks care about one another. I have good friends here, and family. Nothing more important than that." Kate dropped into the blue plaid armchair, a lifelong fixture in Gram's living room, and thought about what Travis said. She'd always loved living in Washington with Annie, but her circumstances had changed. Annie would surely move to Maryland with Kip, and there was no guarantee Derek would remain in DC; his job with the FBI could take him anywhere. That only left her fellow employees, but she couldn't exactly call them friends—they spent too much time working to develop a deeper relationship. In the short time she'd been here, Liza, Riley, Travis, and most especially Brody had become important to her. Already close with her grandmother, they'd grown even closer over the last few weeks.

"Have you ever considered sticking around?" Travis interrupted her thoughts. "You know, Marvin Perkins is retiring next year."

"Who's Marvin Perkins?" She sauntered over to the door and watched as he tested the new key.

"He's an attorney here in town. Has a successful practice. Most of his work is for the local college, but he does just about everything else a lawyer does."

"What's going to happen to his practice?"

"Well, when I was working on his Mercedes the other day, he told me he wants to sell it to a young, ambitious attorney, but not someone only looking to make a buck."

"Oh?"

"Someone who cares about the people around here." He stood up, tugging his waistband up over his thin frame, and tested the lock with a flip of the handle. "That'll do 'er." He picked up his tool bag and smiled at Kate. "You should talk to Marvin. Might be a good thing for you."

"Me? Oh, no. I'm going back to DC as soon as Gram is settled back home. I'm not cut out for small town life."

"Huh, could've fooled me. Well, I better get going." He handed the keys to her and reached for the door knob.

"Wait. What about my bill?"

"It'll be seventy-five dollars. Pay me when you can." Before she could reach for her purse, he was out the door and walking briskly toward his truck. She watched him drive away and wondered how many people owed him money, and if he even cared.

The following Monday, the Buick's engine sputtered to a stop outside Liza's small, white clapboard house. The white gingerbread trim along the roof's eaves and cozy front porch brought to mind a child's doll house. Kate had been on her way to Brody's to drop off a packet of information she'd gathered for the community center, but decided to pop in, uninvited, to see Liza. If this had been DC, she would have called ahead.

She rapped on the wooden screen door and took in the surroundings while she waited. Across the gravel lane that led to Brody's house was a fenced field, a perfect place for horses or cows to graze. Surrounding the back of Liza's house was a thick, hardwood forest where woodland animals surely found a pleasant home.

After a few minutes of silence, she gave up, accepting that Liza wasn't home. She glanced off in the direction of Brody's, finding an inviting farmhouse at the end of the lane. It was such a beautiful evening, with the sun starting to dip below the horizon, she decided to walk.

She found her way up the stony drive and noticed a full moon rising low in the sky. She gathered the manila envelope against her chest and wondered what Brody's reaction would be when he read through it. She'd spent Friday dealing with the battered woman and her children, and the rest of the weekend on the contents of this packet. File after file of courtroom testimony was waiting for her when she got back to Gram's.

She'd rushed through a bit of it this afternoon, but planned to make time tomorrow to properly review the material.

Coming up over a knoll, she stopped to take in the beauty of Brody's home. It was a two-story farmhouse with a wrap-around porch, set atop a hill with a sweeping field in front and rolling hills in the distance. The same thick forest dotted a steep rise behind his house. As Kate drew nearer, she came to a stop. Through a window, she caught a glimpse of Brody walking into the room, shirtless, hair damp as if he'd just stepped from the shower. She looked around and dove behind a large evergreen sitting a few feet to her left. From there, she was able to ease her head around the tree to get a second look.

To her delight, Brody was wearing only lounge pants and she felt her heart hammer as she took in his lean, defined chest. He dropped into a desk chair at his computer and sipped from a mug. When she stood on tiptoe, she could just catch a mouthwatering view of his broad shoulders.

She surveyed the room as best she could, noticing several guitars hanging on the wall in front of him and a large whiteboard alongside. The board was covered with Post-It Notes like the ones she'd seen him writing on at the meeting. If only she had a ladder to get a better view. She stepped from behind the tree and walked to the adjacent sidewalk, which led to the porch. Hoping her five-foot-eight height would serve her well, she stood just outside the window on tiptoe to get a closer look.

No sooner had she risen on her toes than a brown face with dark brown eyes appeared in the window, letting out a glass-shattering bark. Her arms flailed like a windmill as she stumbled backward, catching her heel on a heavy object in the yard. She fell to the ground with a breath-halting thud.

***

Girl you've got a weapon, I know you're packing heat...

Brody tapped out the lyrics on his computer and tipped back his chair, picking up the steaming mug of coffee beside him. He stared at the words that had been circling his brain all day. In fact, for the past few days, words, lines, thoughts kept popping into his mind, creating stanzas for potential songs if only he had the music to go along. He'd get to that soon enough. Setting the mug aside, he leaned over the keyboard once more. A tingling rush of adrenaline surged to his fingertips as he typed. *Your sexy walk, your sharp-tongued talk, just hiding what's down deep.* Weird. This wasn't how it usually worked. He'd been the primary music composer in his partnership, hearing notes and chords, even full accompaniments. Kyle usually handled the lyrics, which had always been a struggle for Brody. Suddenly it was the other way around. He was hearing the lyrics first, but knew the notes would come.

He got out of the chair and sauntered to the whiteboard hanging on the wall. Until recently it had been empty, but it was now covered in little yellow squares with words and sentences he jotted down as they came to him.

Spinning out of control.

Two steps forward, one step back.

Green eyes, sad rhymes.

He pulled a few scraps off the board, wadded them up, and tossed them in the trash can. Others he lined up one below the other, hoping to form complete stanzas. He took another sip of his coffee and startled when Loretta split the silence with an ear-piercing bark.

***

Kate was still laying on the ground, trying to catch her breath when she heard "Go check it out, girl." Brody's voice boomed from inside the house.

"Oh, my—" Kate tried to sit up, but a stabbing pain shot through her back. She laid her head against the cold grass and sucked in a sharp breath when she heard a low, rumbling growl. Loretta charged toward her and hovered above her with her upper lip drawn back, snarling, showing a row of bright white teeth. Kate froze in place.

"Anything out there, girl?" His shout came from the porch, echoing off the trees and out buildings as Loretta took another step closer, teeth still bared.

"Good girl," she whispered, "Nice doggy, nice Loretta."

Loretta inched closer, her long, slender snout stretched toward Kate. The dog sniffed her fingers thoroughly, traveling up toward her shoulder. When she reached Kate's face she licked her cheek with her wet, slimy tongue. Her tail wagged fiercely, causing her whole body to shake.

"Good girl, good girl," she whispered, reaching up to scratch Loretta behind the ears and pat her spotted back, praying Brody wouldn't find her like this.

***

As soon as Brody let Loretta outside, he pulled on a jacket, and then spun the combination on the gun safe. He reached inside the heavy door for a twelve-gauge shotgun and pulled a couple of shells out of the box, quickly snapping them into the chamber. If the local bandit who'd been breaking into houses for the past couple months had decided it was time to victimize Brody Fisk, then Brody Fisk was about to make him awfully sorry.

When he rounded the corner of his porch, he could just make out the silhouette of Loretta poised in typical pointer style—snout extended and tail poker-straight. He walked down the porch steps, pumped the action, released the safety, and pointed the gun at the lifeless form on the grass.

"Don't move," he growled as he stepped slowly toward Loretta's catch.

"Don't shoot." A female voice squeaked out the request and he lowered his gun. He inched closer and realized it was Kate lying prone in his yard, her legs draped over a concrete wall.

"What the hell?" The barrel was still pointing directly at her as he knelt down to get a closer look. "Kate? What are you doing here?"

"Get the gun out of my face and I'll tell you."

He engaged the safety and laid the shotgun on the ground beside her. He shoved Loretta away and extended his hand to help Kate up. She swatted away his offer and rolled into a sitting position.

"What did I fall over?" She placed a hand on her back and twisted, wincing in pain. "My back." He slipped his arm around her waist, lifting her to a standing position while ignoring her attempts to resist his assistance. "Do you have your yard booby trapped or something?"

"Not intentionally, but apparently it helps ward off intruders."

"I'm not intruding." She bent back and forth, and then left and right, seeming to test out her injuries.

"Then what are you doing outside my house in the dark? Where's your car?"

"It's not dark. Well, it wasn't when I got here." She swiped her hands over her pants and ran her fingers through her hair, trying to put her ponytail back into some semblance of order.

Brody crossed his arms over his chest, enjoying her attempts to pull herself together. She righted her jacket, brushing the dried grass from the sleeves, and cleared her throat. He thought she was the cutest damn thing as she regained her professional, put-together self. Finding her sprawled across his lawn was a pleasant surprise and he couldn't wait to hear her explanation.

"Were you peeking in my windows?" he asked, trying to keep a stern look on his face.

"No. Not exactly."

"Then, what exactly?"

"If you'd give me a minute, I'll explain." He smiled to himself as she drew herself up tall, shoulders squared, determined. "I came to bring you this." She thrust out a manila envelope, smacking it into his chest.

"What's this?"

"It's a list of fundraisers and other revenue generating ideas I came up with for the community center board. There are several grants they could apply for and I've gone ahead and written a few proposals. They just require a signature by Sam. There's also my recommendation regarding liability with some supporting documents to show how I derived the figure."

"You did all this?"

"Yes. Gram wanted me to help with the board and I have. So, do what you want with it."

She started toward the lane, but he stopped her, grabbing her elbow before she could get too far. "Wait. Hey, you want to come in?"

"No, thanks. I've had enough excitement for one night."

"I'm sorry about the gun. We rarely get visitors out here and I just figured, with the way Loretta reacted—" Kate was looking at him with her big green eyes, putting him off balance with her intimidating stare. He never knew which way his emotions would go when he was around her. Sometimes she excited him, sometimes she scared him, sometimes she pissed him off, and sometimes she made his heart melt. Right now he wanted nothing more than to take her in his arms and kiss her. Obviously he'd scared her with the shotgun and she hadn't regained her equilibrium. He reached out and took her hand in his.

"I'm really sorry I scared you. Is your back hurt?"

"A little. What did I trip over?"

"That's where the old cistern used to be. I guess I need to take care of that." He tugged her closer and raised her hand to his mouth. She let him peck a few kisses across her creamy skin before pulling away.

"You do that. It's a serious liability." She did an about face and hiked down the lane with Loretta fast on her heels.

"Damnedest woman I ever met." Brody huffed out a laugh as he enjoyed the sight of her retreating down the lane.

SIXTEEN

A heavy pounding racked through Kate's head, confused as to the source of the noise. She sat up quickly, but sudden movement made the room spin. She dropped her head in her hands and remembered the cause of her dizziness. When she'd gotten home from Brody's last night, she poured herself a glass of wine and attempted to read through endless lines of testimony, but couldn't focus, couldn't get her mind off Brody's naked chest and tousled hair. With a second glass of wine, she buried her nose in the court case once again, but was interrupted by Derek's text.

Coming your way next week. May I crash on Gram's couch?

Rather than answer the text and get back to work, she poured yet another glass of wine and put in a call to Derek. During their lengthy conversation, they had agreed he would stay with her at Gram's while he worked out of the regional FBI office. Knowing she'd have a friend from home visiting soon seemed to be a good reason to celebrate. At least, at the time that was the excuse she used to kill a nearly full bottle of Chardonnay. If she was honest with herself, she needed the wine to douse the flames ignited by Brody's kisses on her hand. That tender, sexy move was unsettling. She couldn't allow herself to fall for him. There was too much at stake with her career.

A loud pounding came from outside, worsening the pounding in her head. She hopped off the bed and saw Brody in the yard, nailing some planks to the ramp's framework. He was squatting down with his back to her and she could just make out a thin line of exposed skin above his waistband. When he stood up, he stripped off his jacket and pulled the long-sleeved t-shirt over his pants. The thin cotton fabric stretched over his broad shoulders. She swallowed hard as a shiver tingled her core, and she rushed to the shower, hoping the steam would calm her headache and other symptoms. Then again, maybe a cold shower was what she really needed…

Feeling a million times better after two cups of coffee, a piece of toast, and a clear head, Kate placed her empty mug in the sink and looked out at the stark backyard. It had been six weeks ago she had arrived at Gram's, the backyard covered in orange, yellow, and brown leaves. Now the leaves were off the trees and the ground was brown, matted grass, awaiting the warmth of spring to bring the green back to life. Gram was due to be released next week and soon after Kate would go back to her old life.

The steady rhythm of Brody's pneumatic nailer stopped and the house became quiet again. On days he worked on the ramp, she found it hard to concentrate. She could get used to the machine gun sound of his power hammer, but not used to the man using it. Most days she went to the Sit and Sip to get away from the distraction.

She startled when she heard a frantic knocking.

She threw open the front door and her eyes followed the trail of blood from Brody's left hand to the puddle on the porch floor.

"My god, what happened?" She reached for his elbow, pulled him in the house, and rushed to the kitchen.

"It was stupid," he said, holding his right hand under the flow of blood. "Sorry about the mess on the porch."

"Don't worry about that." She returned with a bundle of paper towels she quickly wrapped around his hand and led him into the kitchen. "Did you shoot yourself with that nail gun of yours?"

"Nothing as dramatic as that." She pushed him into a kitchen chair and rushed to the bathroom for a first aid kit. When she came back into the kitchen, he was folded at the waist with his head between his knees.

"Are you going to be sick?"

"Maybe," he mumbled.

"How much blood have you lost?"

"It's not how much, just the sight of it."

She burst out laughing as she unwrapped his hand and surveyed the damage. She found a one-inch jagged tear on the side of his hand, not severe enough to require stitches, but still producing plenty of blood.

"It's not funny," he murmured, keeping is head below his heart.

"I'm sorry. Your reaction to a little blood doesn't go along with the gun-wielding bad-ass I encountered last night."

"It's not a little blood." He raised his head and looked at her. "And I wouldn't exactly say I was bad-ass last night."

"Yeah, but your dog was." She squirted a dollop of antibiotic ointment on the wide bandage and strapped it to his hand. "She's a great watchdog."

"That's what she was hired for." He turned his hand to examine her first aid work. "Thanks. The damn plastic blister pack caught the side of my hand when I was trying to open more nails. I hate those things."

"I always have trouble with them myself."

"Are these your parents?" Brody had noticed the old photos strewn across the kitchen table. Last night, after she'd given up on working, while drinking her wine, Kate had systematically gone through the albums and planned to make copies of her favorites before leaving town. He tapped on a photo of her mom and dad outside a pharmacy on Main Street, drinking from striped paper cups.

"Yes. I'm not sure where that picture was taken." She took two mugs from the cabinet and placed them beside the coffee pot. "Coffee?"

"Sure." He examined the photo more closely. "That's Beautiful Blooms, where Riley works. It used to be a pharmacy with an old-fashioned soda fountain." He accepted the coffee mug and brought the steaming cup to his lips. "It closed my senior year of high school."

For the next few minutes, he looked through the photo album, pointing out all the places he recognized as well as a few familiar faces. She watched his expression as he gave a history of Highland Springs through the photos in the album. She could see his pride in his hometown and warmed at the thought that she was now frequenting the same places her parents did when they were young.

"Oh, wow, is that a Chevelle?" He pointed to a picture of her dad's old car outside a drive-up ice cream stand. Her father was leaning against the car with his arm around her mom. They looked so young, so innocent, so happy. The picture must have been taken shortly before he left for the Navy because her mother was obviously pregnant.

"Yep, he got a seventy-two Chevelle in high school. I can still remember him working on it on the weekends when I was a little girl."

"Where is it now?"

"My mom sold it, I'm sure. I don't remember seeing it again after he died." She noticed Brody draw closer to the photo as realization dawned on his face. "Yep, that's me in there. The love child of Johnny and Tammy McNamara."

"Nothing wrong with that." He smiled and saluted her with his coffee mug.

"There's a lot of wrong with that. My dad had to join the Navy, couldn't go to college. My mom didn't go back to school until after he died."

"It's not the most ideal way to start adult life, but they got you in the bargain."

"Oh, and what a bargain." They tinged their mugs together and shared a laugh. "Seriously, I have to say my mom and dad are really amazing people, considering."

"Oh, yeah?"

"My dad was an incredible athlete, decorated sailor, and my mom— well, my mom has achieved so much with her career since my dad passed. I really admire her—how hard she works." She picked up a photo from her parents' high school graduation and traced a finger across the image as if she were feeling their presence. "I often wonder what their lives would've been like if it weren't for me."

"Surely, you're not blaming yourself."

"No." She placed the photo on the table and looked up at Brody, blinking away the watery sheen from her eyes. "But, I can't help wondering." She gathered the scattered photos into a neat pile, tapping them into alignment against the table.

"What pictures are in these albums?" He opened a pale pink baby book and for the next hour they walked through Kate's life, beginning with her birth through college graduation. She had just finished telling him about her Valedictorian speech when she received a text from the office. She read through it quickly and jumped to her feet.

"Out!" She fairly lifted him out of his chair and shoved him toward the front door. "I have work to do. My memo is due by four o'clock and you're distracting me."

"Hey, you were the one who offered me a cup of coffee."

"I know, but you've got to go."

He opened the door and but stayed planted inside the foyer.

"Are you going?" She asked as she pressed her hands against his back.

"Let's go to the ice cream stand sometime—the one in the picture."

"Sure, sure. But not today." She gave him another hard push and he finally submitted, stepping onto the porch, avoiding the bloody spot.

"We also have a date to plan, remember?"

"Brody, you're stalling. Gram's paying you by the hour and you've wasted the last hour drinking coffee in her kitchen."

He gripped the doorway and leaned in to within inches of Kate. "I'll be sure to take it off my bill. Thanks for the Band-Aid and coffee." Before she could reply, he dropped a soft kiss on her lips and walked down the porch steps. She silently cursed under her breath. How could she concentrate on work after that?

SEVENTEEN

"You know, Kate, you can't allow yourself to be distracted. You've worked too hard and invested too much of yourself for your career to falter. Imagine what your dad—"

"Dad would want me to be here for Gram."

"I know that and it's very admirable, but you need to get back to DC and get back on track. You deserve that promotion, but you can't ease up now. As soon as Gram's home, you need to get back there."

Kate's mother had called as soon as she'd pulled into her grandmother's driveway after spending the evening at the rehab center. It had been several days since she'd visited, but Gram never complained. Her mother was in the midst of a lecture about getting out of that "Podunk" town when Kate climbed the porch steps, noticing a light stain from Brody's bloody puddle. She smiled at the memory from that day. Somehow, she had been able to finish her memo in time even with memories of Brody's gentle kiss invading her every other thought.

"Mom, I agree with you completely. You know how much I value my career and I promise not to disappoint you, but I've got to go."

She cleared space on the kitchen table for her laptop and opened her email account. There were several emails sent from the office in the two hours she was at the rehab center, and she sighed heavily, knowing it was going to be a long night of work.

Wednesday morning, Kate tucked herself into the corner table at Sit and Sip which she had internally dubbed "her table" and flipped open her laptop. She left the house early to avoid Brody. She didn't want to be distracted by his nail gun or power drill or Brody himself. There was a brief due by Friday and Patrick was expecting her testimony review by the beginning of next week. They'd won the trial, but were now in full appeal preparation mode. When she told Patrick she wouldn't be able to attend the trial, she could hear the disappointment in his voice, even though he said he understood. So far, she was miraculously keeping up with her work and hadn't missed a deadline, but she hadn't offered to go above and beyond like she would have a few weeks ago.

She had lost track of time as she tapped away on her computer keyboard, oblivious to everyone around her, having emptied her paper coffee cup long ago. She considered getting another one when suddenly her laptop snapped shut, nearly crushing her fingers.

"There you are. Been looking all over for you."

She tugged her earphones from her ears and looked up at Brody, smiling broadly under his ball cap, looking quite pleased with himself. If he wasn't so damned handsome and boyishly adorable, she would be mad at him for interrupting her flow.

"Can I help you, Mr. Fisk? I'm working here, if you didn't notice." She smiled back at him, joining in his playful mood.

"Yes, you can. You can come with me." He pulled the plug on her laptop and stuffed it into her leather satchel sitting on the floor. "Let's go." She didn't have a chance to protest. He grasped her arm with one hand and pulled her out of the chair while carrying her bag in the other, and guided her out of the coffee shop.

***

"Where are you taking me?" Brody knew he was practically dragging her down the street, but he was so excited. He wrapped his arm around Kate's waist as she stumbled, trying to keep up. Ever since he'd seen the picture of her dad and mom outside the ice cream stand, leaning against the Chevelle, he'd wanted to recreate that scene for her.

"We're going for ice cream." He stopped in the middle of the sidewalk and pointed to a long convertible parked by the curb. "Hop in."

"Ah." She stopped and drew in a quick breath. "Are you kidding me?" She covered her mouth with her hands and then rushed to the car. "Is this yours?" She turned to him, her eyes filled with wonder, and a beautiful, shining smile. In all the time he'd known her, he couldn't remember her looking this happy.

"It's mine."

"It's beautiful. Oh my gosh."

"You like it?"

"Like it? It's a gorgeous car. It's a Cadillac, um—" She walked toward the back of the car, searching for the model.

"It's a seventy-five El Dorado."

"Yes, that's what I thought."

"You know about classic cars?"

"Of course." She strolled around the car, dragging her hand across the body, admiring the pale blue paint job and chrome. "My dad loved vintage cars. Remember, you saw his seventy-two Chevelle?" She stopped in the front and bent down to study the grill. "I guess because of him I learned a lot about them, which is funny considering I don't even own a car." She stood back up, placed her hands on her hips, and looked at him, her eyes sparkling. "It's in mint condition. I love it. Where'd you get it?"

"It was the first thing I bought after I got the first big check from my publisher. It belonged to a friend of Elvis Presley. He used to—"

"Give cars to his friends and family. I know." Kate walked over to where he was planted on the sidewalk and slipped her arms around his waist. "Take me for a ride." At that moment, he would have done anything she asked.

"Exactly what I had in mind." He cupped her face in his hands. "If you behave, I'll even let you drive."

"Deal." She touched her nose to his. "Let's go," she whispered.

Brody slid his hand through her hair and palmed the back of her head, bringing her in for an overdue kiss. He felt that familiar bass drum beating down in his chest as she snuggled tight against him and spread her hands over his back. He could kiss her all day long and never get tired of it. Beauty, brains, and she liked classic cars…he'd better be careful.

***

Even with the rough pavement and occasional potholes, Kate felt like she was floating on a cloud. The El Dorado drove like a motor boat gliding across a glassy lake and its captain looked incredibly handsome behind the wheel. She couldn't believe she allowed him to steal her away from her work, but damn it, she deserved a little fun. Tonight she'd work until midnight or beyond, whatever it took. Taking this ride with Brody was all part of their deal—she had to help him with song material, after all.

The Cadillac rolled to a smooth stop at an intersection and he put it into park. They were on a two-lane road out in the country and hadn't passed another car for at least a mile. He turned and looked at her, draping his arm across the steering wheel.

"Are you warm enough? I can put up the top if you're cold."

"No, I'm fine." It was a warm day by early winter standards. They were driving with the top down, the windows up, and the heater blasting. The sun was shining down and the sky was crystal clear. She drew in a lungful of fresh air, noticing the only sound was the soft purr of the idling engine. At that moment she felt a pang of nostalgia just thinking about leaving here and returning to traffic noise, city smells, and the ever-ticking clock.

He must have read her mind. He picked up her hand, pressed his lips against her palm, and said, "Nice day huh?"

"Perfect."

They rode on through the countryside with him telling her stories about his childhood, pointing out landmarks along the way. Twenty minutes later, they pulled into an asphalt lot in front of an ice cream stand—the same one in the picture—that looked like it would have been right at home in a 1950s movie. It was probably the era in which it had been built and had never seen an update.

"Here we are." Brody walked around to her side of the car and helped her out, not letting go of her hand as they walked to the window.

"The same place as in the picture."

"And it probably has the same menu."

"We should take a selfie in front of your car."

"Better yet, let's get someone to take our picture. Pose just like your parents did."

She squeezed his hand and smiled up at him while he looked down at her. When had it happened? When did she drop her guard, let him in? Was it in the Brass Rail parking lot the night of their charade for Jonas's benefit? Was it in the storage room? At the auction? Thanksgiving dinner? All at once it felt like she'd known him forever, like they were meant to be together. This moment at the ice cream stand, the same one her parents frequented, had been destined to be. Dropping all her past attempts to keep a wall up between them, to shut off her feelings, she tilted her face towards his, inviting another tender kiss, ignoring the nagging worry in her gut.

***

After stuffing themselves on chili dogs, French fries, and banana splits, they were relaxing in the front seat of his car—the only one in the parking lot. Brody draped his arm over the seat back, laid his hand on Kate's shoulder, and then brushed her cheek with the back of his hand.

"You know, we haven't made plans for our auction date yet."

"Hmm, what did you have in mind?" She scooted across the bench seat and tucked herself under his arm. He wrapped his arms around her and pulled her against him, resting her back against his chest. It felt so good to have her in his arms, completely relaxed, like she belonged there. He could get used to this.

"Of course, I have to give you the perfect date—drinks and dinner. I just haven't decided where."

"I'm easy to please."

He laughed and nuzzled her neck. "I seriously doubt that."

"I am." She sat up in protest and turned to face him. "Really, I told you before. I don't need a lot of fanfare. Keep it simple."

"Nope. I'm hedging my bets you're a champagne and caviar girl who's just trying to come off as a beer and peanuts type. I'm not buying it."

"Fine." She resumed her position, reclined against his chest. "It's your money."

An hour later, they headed back toward Highland Springs, taking the long way home on unlined back roads. Brody had indeed let Kate drive and he was now relaxing in the passenger's seat watching her long, dark hair blow in the cold breeze. They'd avoided talking about her work or his songwriting until she asked.

"What were you doing the night I came over to your house? I've been meaning to ask."

"I was just sitting at my computer."

"Writing music? Is that how you do it?"

How could he explain how he wrote music? It had been so long since he'd written on his own and he was just starting to find his way. He'd finally rediscovered the thrill of a new song and he knew it was all because of her.

"Lately, yeah."

She drew in a quick breath and flashed him a dazzling smile. "So you *have* been writing again. I'm so glad. When do I get to hear something?"

"Settle down, missy. I'm just getting back to it." The car swerved and she snapped her attention back to the task at hand. "Keep your eyes on the road." He laughed and angled across the bench seat, dropping a quick kiss on her cheek.

"But you've been composing, right? You're too talented not to."

"Yeah, and when I have something worth sharing, you'll be the first to hear it." Things had changed with Kate today. She was relaxed, happy, didn't push him away when he held her hand or gave her a kiss. If only he could figure out why? He'd come to rely on her resistance, making it easier for him to keep his hopes under wraps. Now that she seemed to enjoy his touch, even invite it, he was afraid he wouldn't be able to stop himself from falling.

Kate rolled the Caddy into her grandmother's driveway alongside the Buick and cut the engine. She had a lascivious smile on her face as she massaged the steering wheel.

"I love this car," she fairly cooed. Seeing her behind the wheel of his favorite ride, her cheeks pink from the cold afternoon air, looking so gorgeous, he couldn't stop himself. He scooted across the seat and tugged her legs around, flattening her on the bench seat with a hearty pull.

She giggled as he eased his body on top of hers and placed a long, gut-twisting kiss on her irresistible lips. He stifled a moan as she reached inside his jacket and under his sweater, where she warmed her hands up and down his back. She felt so good, so right, in his arms. He kept her lips locked against his as he unbuttoned the front of her coat. He'd reached the last button when a muffled ringtone came from inside the glove compartment.

"That's my phone. I have a text." She spoke against his mouth.

"Ignore it." He slipped his tongue inside and greedily kissed her luscious mouth. She responded in kind, seeming to ignore the text, at least until the phone began to ring.

"Brody." She tore her lips away and pushed against his chest. "I have to answer that. It might be Gram calling."

If she had said "It might be work," he wouldn't have let her up. But since it could be the rehab center calling, he acquiesced and sat up, reaching inside the glove compartment for their phones. When they had been a mile outside town on their way to the ice cream stand, they had agreed to lock the devices away for the afternoon. They'd had four blissful hours of uninterrupted time together. Now the real world had come calling again.

He scrolled through a few texts, not paying attention to Kate as she answered the call. She was apparently talking to someone at the office and blurted out, "What? When was it due?" He looked over and saw a dark shadow come over her face. Just that quickly, the happy, carefree girl he'd spent the afternoon with was gone and the stressed-out professional woman was back.

"I'm sure that wasn't what I was told." Kate climbed out of the car and slammed the door behind her. She reached into the backseat, snatched up her satchel, and marched toward the house.

He climbed out of the car and stepped onto the porch, meeting the front door as it slammed in his face. Not sure if he really wanted to go inside, Brody hesitantly opened the door and stood inside the foyer. She was still on the phone, rifling through a stack of papers on the kitchen table.

"Patrick, Jason did *not* tell me the filing was due this afternoon. I promise you." She yanked her laptop out of her leather bag and plopped it on the table, still combing through documents as if she had an extra set of hands. "Tell me what you want me to do and I'll handle it." She fired up her laptop and then stopped, standing ramrod straight. "Oh, Jason *did* email me. Patrick, I'm so sorry. What can I do?"

This was bad. Brody didn't like the look on her face as she tapped off the call. He crossed the living room into the kitchen as she dropped into a chair.

"Damn it." Her fingers flew across the keyboard, her eyes searing onto the screen. She seemed to have forgotten he was there. He placed his hands on her shoulders and began a slow massage, but she wasn't having it. "Stop." She brushed his hands off her shoulders and ejected from the chair.

"What happened?"

"You've got to go." She charged past him and pulled open the door.

"But what happened?" he asked again, reaching out for her hand. She jerked it away and turned on him.

"What happened?" Her eyes bulged as if they were straining to pop from her head. "*What happened?* I'll tell you what happened. I missed an important filing, that's what happened." She slammed the door, causing the house to rattle. "Thanks to you, I missed an email telling me the filing which I thought was due Friday had been moved up to today. Now

Patrick is furious and thinks I'm incompetent." Kate stalked toward him with a crazed look in her eyes.

"I'm sorry."

"Sorry, that's all you can say? This is my damned career we're talking about. I can kiss the promotion goodbye thanks to you and your *brilliant* idea to go get ice cream on a freezing cold winter day. What the hell were you thinking?"

Brody's chest was so tight he couldn't take a deep breath. His emotions warred between anger and hurt, and he felt like he was right back in her grandmother's backyard six weeks ago when she'd accused him of trespassing—only this time it was worse. He felt really bad that she'd missed the message, but even worse seeing her so upset.

"Look." He captured her hand before she could pull it away. "I'm really sorry you missed this deadline. If there was something I could do, I'd do it. From what you've told me, it seems like you've done everything they've asked. One mistake surely wouldn't affect their decision about the promotion."

"Oh, what do you know? You just ride around dropping off wood, showing up whenever you feel like it to work on my grandmother's ramp, only half attempting to write music. Where's your sense of urgency? Your ambition? Your drive?" She wrenched her hand out of his and stormed toward the kitchen, but he caught her before she could get too far. Damned if she was going to throw this in his face.

"You know, I'm tired of you taking out your frustrations on me."

"What are you talking about?"

"Obviously, you're miserable."

"I'm not miserable."

"Do you like living like this?"

"Like what?"

"Constantly working, constantly trying to prove yourself. For what? For some promotion, some bogus standard that says you're worthy? It's bullshit. You don't need someone else's confirmation."

She took a step back and wrapped her arms around herself. "You don't know anything about me."

"Don't I?" He closed the gap and leveled a searing gaze at her. "I know that ever since you got here you've never stopped working, until today. Can't you ever take a break? You don't have to make partner by the age of thirty to be deemed a success."

"You'll never understand. The law is my career, my vocation, the thing I've worked toward since college—before college even. I don't have the luxury to leave it all behind like you."

"What the hell are you talking about?"

"You, the highly successful, multi-award-winning songwriter. What did you do? Make some quick cash and then give it up?"

"Winning awards isn't everything. At least I'm not strung out on caffeine and biting the heads off of everyone around me. Have you ever thought to take a step back and realize you can be an attorney—a damned good one—without all the stress?"

"I've yet to meet an attorney at my age who isn't working eighty hours a week. That's just the nature of the business." Snapping around, showing him a cold shoulder, Kate stomped into the kitchen. "You'll never get it, I'm wasting my breath." She reached for a glass out of the cabinet and filled it with tap water. Brody stepped directly behind her.

"What about right here in Highland Springs? There are people who could use your help, who wouldn't make you feel two inches tall just because you missed a deadline. How can you let them treat you like that?"

"I guess when you have no agenda, no one to answer to, no real responsibilities—" she spun around and paralyzed him with her dark stare "—you can say things like that. But in the real world, where people actually work for a living, we have others to answer to."

"Okay, sure, as always, do your best to put me down when in reality you're the one who's unhappy."

"I'm happy. I'm working toward something, unlike you. You know, now that you mention it, are *you* happy? Are you satisfied chopping down trees and pounding nails? Obviously, there must be more to your story.

I mean, who gives up a career like yours? I read about you." She stalked toward him, fists clenched, eyes blazing. He stood his ground. "The biggest names in country music were clamoring to work with you. As soon as you and your partner pumped out a song, it was snatched up and made into a mega hit. What happened to that guy? Are you happy with your life now?"

He held her fiery stare as long as he could, before he looked at the floor, rubbed his forehead, and released a heavy sigh. "It was a partnership, remember? And I no longer have a writing partner."

"So what? Why is that stopping you? I know a lot of your earlier hits were written by you alone."

"You seem to know an awful lot about my career." Now it was his turn to lean in. "When did you have time to do all that research? I thought you had *so* much work to do."

"I do have work to do and you're keeping me from it. Why don't you do something more productive than criticizing my career and do something with your life?"

"I've spent the last two years coming to terms with who I am and what I've done." He reached out and latched onto her arm. "Sure, maybe I've avoided writing, and understandably so, but I'm coming to terms with it. You need to get this career of yours under control."

"I don't know what happened with you, but I'll tell you this. You're too talented to be wasting time swinging a hammer and chopping trees. At least I'm using my brain and the degrees I earned."

"Hey, I'm content with who I am." He realized he was clutching her arm too tightly and immediately dropped it, then punched his fist against his thigh. He turned toward the window, contemplating a memory from the backyard, and then snapped around. "You're the one who needs to take a long look in the mirror and ask yourself if this is who you want to be for the rest of your life. I can guarantee that right now, you're not the woman your grandmother always brags about." He lessened the gap and glared down at her, nose-to-nose.

"Maybe you need to take a look in the same mirror. Right now you're not the *catch* Gram told me about either."

Brody ended the stand off and stepped around her. "I'm out of here."

"Fine. Don't bother picking me up on Friday night," Kate said.

"Oh, no, I'll be here." He swung around and pinned her with a dark stare. "I may be a lazy, hick lumberjack, but I follow through on my promises. Be ready at six."

He slammed the door behind him and stomped down the porch steps. As much as he hated the idea right now, he'd honor his obligation and take her on the date his little sister had so connivingly arranged. Kate would get her "dream date," but it wouldn't be the one he originally planned. She'd get the one she deserved.

EIGHTEEN

"Hi, Dad. Sorry I haven't come sooner." Kate bent down and tugged a few blades of grass from the base of the tombstone, tossing them into the rushing wind as her jacket flapped open. She stood up, tugged the wool around her, and stared at the carved granite.

"It doesn't look like I'll get the promotion." She brushed her gloved hand across the top of the tombstone with a heavy sigh. "I'm sorry. I hope you're not disappointed in me. I could say I did my best, but obviously I didn't. I dropped the ball."

There were hundreds of gravestones in varying shades of white and gray dotting the grassy knoll where her father lay next to her grandfather and where her grandmother would be buried someday. While visiting Highland Springs, she always made a point to visit her dad, but this trip it had taken several weeks before she had come.

"I wish you were here to tell me what to do. I'm frustrated. The promotion should've been was mine all along, but now I'm going to be passed up because I missed a deadline." Rummaging deep in her coat pocket, she pulled out a tissue and pressed it to her dripping nose. "I feel like I should be doing something more meaningful, like working with Ashley and her kids. The thought of going back to DC after being here…" She dabbed at tears dropping from her cheeks. "I don't know. Mom is going to be pissed if I don't get the promotion. And, honestly, so will I. I'm so confused." She blew her nose soundly and stuffed the tissues back in her pocket. "Right now, I could use a little sign or message from you."

She released a heavy sigh and placed the colorful bouquet she'd been holding at the base of the tombstone. What a silly idea to think her dad could send her a message. Knowing she was expected at the rehab center soon, she returned to the Buick, scoffing at the notion of communiqués from beyond the grave.

Kate watched the busy bird activity at the feeder outside Gram's room. Sometimes she felt like one of those birds, hurriedly flitting from the feeder to the tree branch, trying to beat the other birds to the best seed. As much as she hated to admit it, Brody was right. This isn't the way she wanted to live: working twelve or more hours a day, stressing over deadlines, fighting for a promotion she should have already received. There had to be a simpler way to live. Spending time at her father's gravestone earlier that morning had given her a sense of calm—something she hadn't felt in years. Even though he hadn't sent her a sign, she knew her next move was the right one.

"I've decided to ask Patrick for a leave of absence until after Christmas. It's probably a big mistake, but I need a break. It's so hard to keep up from here."

"Honey, I think you're making the right choice. You've looked terrible the last few times you've visited." Gram walked to the window, unaided by her walker, and placed a hand on Kate's shoulder.

"Gee, thanks, Gram."

"I just mean you seem tired and the stress is showing on your face. You should be out having some fun, not working non-stop."

She laid her hand over Gram's with a contented sigh. Just the soft touch from her grandmother brought her comfort. "I did have fun yesterday with Brody. But I blew it. Patrick called to say I'd missed a filing deadline and I snapped. I took it out on Brody."

"Oh, honey, I'm sure he understands."

"No, Gram." She turned around and faced her grandmother. "He said some cruel things to me and was furious when he left. But honestly, I deserved it." Tears welled in her eyes and she was on the verge of sobbing as she looked at the sympathy on Gram's face. She had already cried enough last night after Brody left and again this morning at the cemetery; surely she didn't have any tears left to shed. "I said some terrible things to him, too."

"What about your date tomorrow night?"

"Brody says we're still going, but I won't be surprised if he cancels."

"Now, Katherine, if I know Brody, he'll be there tomorrow night to pick you up and will understand once you explain what happened. And a sincere apology on your part won't hurt."

"I hope he gives me the chance. Keep your fingers crossed, Gram."

The Beautiful Blooms van backed out of Gram's driveway just as Kate came down the street. She tapped the horn twice when she saw Riley behind the wheel.

"Great, you're home." Riley shouted through the window as she pulled the van to the curb. "I was just about to call you."

Kate pulled in the drive and then walked toward the florist van, meeting Riley in the middle of the street. She was holding an arrangement of red roses and pink star lilies with a bright smile on her face.

"For you," Riley said, extending the colorful bouquet.

"Who would send me flowers?" She drew the bouquet to her nose, inhaling the spicy scent. "They're beautiful."

"You'll just have to read the card."

She tugged the small, white envelope from the plastic stick and handed the arrangement back to Riley for safe keeping. A floral embossed card was tucked inside and she nearly gasped with joy when she read the words.

Looking forward to tomorrow night. Brody

***

Brody pulled the old pickup into Virginia's driveway and laid on the horn. No way was he walking to the door to get her. After the way she acted the other night, she was lucky he didn't cancel. Kate swung open the front door and stepped onto the porch. A few inches of red fabric peeked below her wool coat, making it difficult for him to keep his eyes off her long, shapely legs.

"Hi." Her velvet voice burned a hole in his chest as she climbed into the truck. He didn't bother to answer. Before she could snap her seat belt into place, he backed out of the drive and pressed the gas pedal, making her lurch forward.

"How've you been?" she asked, but he kept his eyes forward, refusing to get sucked into those gorgeous green eyes. Her creamy white thighs invaded his periphery, only making him angrier. He may have committed to this date, but he didn't have to enjoy it—and neither would she.

"I hope I'm not overdressed. You didn't tell me where we're going."

"Doesn't matter."

"Still not giving anything away, huh? Want to surprise me?"

"Something like that."

He rubbed his palm across his faded jeans and kept his eyes locked on the two-lane road ahead. The spice of her tantalizing perfume tickled his nose and he got mad all over again. She'd made it perfectly clear she thought he was a lazy redneck the other night and now she was trying to torture him. Her harsh words, so on target, had sparked him to spill all the thoughts he'd kept bottled up for so long onto paper, resulting in lyrics he didn't know he could write. For the past forty-eight hours, he'd composed music to those lyrics, keeping his phone off and doors locked, as the notes and words tumbled out. It was the most he'd created in two years, but damned if he'd give her credit for it. They rode on in silence until they reached his destination.

"Brody...about the other night." She bobbed off the seat as he drove the pickup across the gravel parking lot, jerking to a stop outside a tan metal building. He looked through the dust-covered windshield at the windowless warehouse, noticing the new sign on the black double doors that read "Tasting Room." Tucker must have just installed it. Six cars were parked in front of Misty Mountain Brewery and several rows of cars were parked at the opposite end of the lot in front of an old silver diner. A red neon sign flashed "Sue's Place."

Brody opened his door and climbed out, never acknowledging her last few words. He pulled open the Tasting Room door and waited while Kate climbed out of the truck. She tugged down her skirt, flipped her silky hair over her shoulder, and slammed the heavy door shut. He couldn't wait to see the shock on her face once she entered the brewery.

They stepped into the sparse, dimly-lit room where only a few tables and a long, rough-hewn wooden bar filled the space. Behind the bar was a floor-to-ceiling glass wall, behind which shiny copper vats stood in even rows. The ripe smell of freshly brewed beer hung in the air. He glanced at her, expecting to see anger flushing her cheeks, but instead was the one to receive a shock.

"You brought me to Misty Mountain? This is amazing." She squeezed his arm and burned him with her heart-stopping smile. "I've wanted to come here." Feeling off balance, he slowly guided her to a pair of stools at the center of the bar adjacent to a row of taps where a tall, burly man was pouring beer.

"Well, I'll be damned if it isn't my not-so-silent partner." He reached across the bar and shook hands with Brody, pulling him in for a rugged hug. "And you've got to be Katherine."

"Yes, I'm Kate." She beamed at the gentle giant who picked up her hand and kissed it like she was a princess. "And you're Tucker, I presume."

"Nope, Tucker's off this evening. I'm Prince Charming." He thumped his open palm on the bar and let out a raucous laugh. "How the hell you been, man? Haven't seen you in, oh, forty-eight hours."

"I'm okay." He looked past Tucker into the brewing room and shook his head.

"Damn, bro, she's better looking than you described. No wonder you had to pay big bucks to take her out."

"Just get us some beer, would you?" Brody said.

"Sure thing. You like beer, Kate?"

"Love it," she said.

"What's your preference?"

"I want to try them all."

"Well, aren't you just an angel from heaven? If I weren't already spoken for—"

"Who the hell are you dating? Just pour her a flight and shut up," Brody said.

Out the corner of his eye, he watched her lean back on her barstool and look around the tasting room. His elbows were perched on the edge of the bar and he greedily drank from the dark beer Tucker had poured for him. Kate shrugged her wool coat from her shoulders and, as she turned to drape it across the back of the chair, he stole a glance at her cranberry dress, hugging her curves in all the right places. How was he going to get through the night when she didn't play fair?

"How 'bout you show Kate the operation, Brody?"

"How about you?" he mumbled.

"Sure thing. Come with me, little lady." Kate followed Tucker to the end of the bar and disappeared through a door marked "Employees Only." Brody watched them through the glass wall as they took in the towering vats, sharing a laugh. He finally took a good long look at her and he felt a stirring where he didn't want to be stirred. Her long, elegant body was draped in a deep red, clinging dress with just enough cleavage exposed to leave him wanting more. Her thick, dark hair cascaded down her back, making his fingers itch to touch it. He drained the pint glass and walked behind the bar for a refill.

A few minutes later, Kate settled onto her barstool and Tucker returned to his station behind the taps. She looked over her shoulder, surveying the scene.

"So what's the deal? Why does every man in this town have a beard?"

"Well," Tucker said as he looked at Brody, "I have a beard year-round because I have an ugly ass dimple in my chin. What about you, man?"

"Hunting season." Brody took a long draw on his beer.

"Hunting season." Tucker snorted and shook his head. "Man, you don't hunt."

"I hunt. I went out last weekend."

"Shit, you don't hunt. Sitting in your pergola doesn't count as hunting."

"Hey, I have a great view from up there. Saw a ten-point buck." He took another sip. "I hunt. I just don't shoot."

"Pansy. You're supposed to be in a tree stand, not on a damn treated lumber deck." Tucker laughed to himself and carried two pints, brimming over with foam, to a couple sitting at the end of the bar.

"So you're a hunter, huh? That's why you have the beard?" Kate propped her elbows on the bar and picked up another double shot glass of amber ale from the wooden sampler rack.

"That's as good a reason as any," he said.

"Hmm." She set down her glass and spun her barstool around to face him.

"What's this pergola he's talking about?"

"It's a travesty. That's what it is." Tucker had returned, wiping his wet hands on the towel tucked in his belt. "He took a perfectly good cowboy hide-out and turned it into an HGTV reality show."

"I'm confused," she said, looking back and forth between the two men.

"You'll have to go out to his house sometime. He's building a deck on a ledge we used to play on when we were kids," Tucker said.

"Stop. You mean to tell me you've been friends since you were boys?"

"Yep. Met the big jerk in first grade," Tucker said. "Been a thorn in my side ever since."

"This thorn is moving on." Brody picked up his beer and walked to an empty table in the corner of the room. Kate picked up her wooden rack of samples and followed. She sat in the chair beside him, draping her sexy leg across her knee. He rubbed his forehead while resting his elbows on the table. They sat in silence for several minutes while he figured out what to say. This date was a stupid idea and he needed an out.

"Tucker's a hoot. I like him," she said, breaking the silence.

"Yeah, he's funny alright." He took a long drink and leaned back in his chair.

"You get along, right?"

"Like brothers."

She inched her chair closer to his and rested her hand on his arm. "Brody, before we pulled in…" She cleared her throat, concentrating on spinning one of the small glasses of beer. "The flowers were beautiful. Did you get my text?"

"Flowers?"

"The roses and lilies you sent. That was really sweet of you, but I can see you're still upset about the other night."

"But I—" *Liza strikes again.*

"I want to apologize for the hurtful things I said…and the awful way I treated you." She stopped swirling the glass and he noticed her hand shaking as she picked up a glass of beer. After a long swallow, she said, "We'd had a really nice afternoon and I ruined it. I shouldn't have taken out my frustration with my job on you, and I'm sorry. You didn't deserve it. It won't happen again."

A punch in the gut couldn't have hurt more. While he was doing all he could to hold a grudge, Kate magnanimously took the blame for their fight, apologizing for her role. For the first time that night, he looked at his date, their eyes locking in a smoldering gaze. He scooted his chair closer to hers and draped his arm across the back of her chair.

"It was just as much my fault."

"No. The things you said to me were—"

"Hateful and I shouldn't have said them. I'm sorry. I know what kind of pressure you're under."

"Well…not anymore. I took a leave of absence until after the holidays."

"You did?"

"You were right. I've been miserable. And it's been harder and harder to keep up with my work. My focus needs to be on Gram, not my work, and I plan on making her my number one priority until she's settled at home." Once again she rested her hand on his arm. Brody thought there was no better feeling. "Forgive me?"

"There's nothing to forgive," he said. He scooted to the edge of his chair, coming as close to Kate as possible without pulling her onto his lap. He played with the ends of her hair as he gathered his courage. "We might have a little problem."

"What would that be?"

"This date of ours."

"It started off slow, but it's getting better, don't you think?" She nudged his shoulder, only making him feel worse.

"The thing is…I was furious at you and decided to change my original plans."

"Which were?"

"I was going to take you to this great Italian place in Clarksburg, but decided to punish you with a trip to the brewery and Sue's Place, next door, for dinner."

"Who would want Italian when I can have beer and diner food?"

What an ass he'd been. Here she was giving him that sexy smile, totally forgiving, accepting his terrible plans. He slipped his hand behind her head, sinking his fingers into her satiny locks, and pulled her lips close to his. "I'll make it up to you." He captured her soft lips under his and shuddered when she grazed her nails across the back of his neck, pulling him closer and deeper.

"So, now listen, folks. Sorry to interrupt." The spell was broken. Tucker had pulled up a chair and shoved in close to them. "I want to talk to you while I have a break."

"Now?" Brody sighed and sat back in his chair.

"Yeah, now. Kate, Brody tells me you're a lawyer, right?"

"Come on, Tuck, not now."

"It will only take a minute." He held up his hand, silencing Brody with the gesture. "We've had a generous offer from a big beer company." He leaned in close to Kate and whispered. "I can't tell you the name but it rhymes with *thriller*."

"Stop, Tucker," Brody said.

"Anyway, Brody thinks it's a bad offer, but I say an offer like this might not come along again. I was wondering if you'd take a look at it."

"What is it? A proposal? A contract?"

"It's a shit load of papers. Buy-sell agreements, operating agreements, all kinds of stuff I don't know anything about. Brody is skittish about selling, but I think we need another opinion—a professional opinion."

"Of course," she said.

"You don't have to do this." Brody gently took her hand in his and looked deep into her eyes. "We can handle this."

"No, I'd be glad to look at your shit-load of papers. I've got nothing but time on my hands."

"Atta girl." Tucker thumped her on the back with his thick, beefy paw and stood up, pulling up his pants up under his protruding belly. "I'll send over a couple of beers, on the house."

As soon as he walked away, she broke into an uncontrollable laugh. "He's something, isn't he?" She drained her last little glass of ale, still laughing to herself.

"Yeah, he's something alright. Listen, you don't have to do this."

"Really, I want to. It will be stimulating to read something other than depositions and witness accounts."

"You need to be stimulated, huh?" Brody wrapped his arm around her waist and pressed his cheek to hers.

"That wasn't exactly what I meant, but since we're on the subject..." She placed her hand on his knee and turned to face him. Her hand slowly glided higher on his leg. He could feel his face turning red as his body temperature surged. She seemed to love making him squirm. "Am I making you uncomfortable?"

"Sweetheart, you always make me uncomfortable." He leaned in and gently nibbled her bottom lip. She broke the connection with a quick peck and short laugh.

"Good."

NINETEEN

"Watch your step." Brody wrapped an arm around Kate's waist, helping her up into the dark, cavernous covered bridge. The bright beam from the flashlight illuminated their path while casting shadows on the wooden trusses. Their footsteps echoed off the walls, competing with the reverberation of their voices.

"Oh my gosh, this is so cool." She tucked herself under his shoulder, slid her arms around his waist, and pressed against him. "But sort of scary."

"Nothing to be afraid of, except some bugs and maybe a few bats."

"Now you're really trying to scare me."

As they walked into the center of the bridge, he scanned the interior with his flashlight, showing her black bats hanging from the rafters, tucked in tight corners. He told her stories of his teenage years, poaching beer from his dad and drinking it out here with Tucker and Travis. They stopped in the middle of the bridge and he snapped off the light.

"What in the world?" She tightened her hold on him as he guided her to the side of the bridge, trapping her against the wall.

"Ever been kissed inside a covered bridge?"

"I've never been inside a covered bridge."

"Well, then, we need to make it memorable." Earlier at Sue's Place, while they dined on homemade venison stew, corn bread, and ham-flavored green beans, she had requested he show her the covered bridge Liza had told her about. Now, with only the light of the moon sneaking through the narrow cracks in the wood, she was able to see Brody's beautiful smile and dark eyes as he slowly lowered his mouth to hers. He kept her plastered to the wooden wall for several minutes, while she savored his tender lips and teasing tongue. He unfastened the three plastic buttons of her coat and moved the wool aside as he snaked his hands around her waist, drawing her tighter to him. With a tiny moan, she welcomed his kisses, applying pressure to the back of his head, needing more. They continued like this, oblivious to their surroundings, until an owl's screech echoed throughout the bridge.

"What was that?" Once again fearful, she clung to Brody. She liked leaning against his thick, strong chest for protection. He quietly chuckled as his arms smothered her against him. She was usually brave in most situations, but that courage disappeared in the presence of a moonlit night and a few random wildlife sounds.

"Just an owl. No worries."

"Let's go back to the truck." She tugged on his hand and charged back toward the entrance.

***

Once back inside the pickup, she slid across the worn bench seat and placed her hands on either side of his face.

"Thank you for my perfect date."

"You sure you aren't disappointed you didn't get a fancy meal by the river and a symphony concert?"

"Didn't even miss the crème brûlée." She touched her lips to his and said, "In fact, I think I preferred Sue's Place by the creek and country music on the jukebox." He rested his elbow across the back of the seat and gathered a handful of her hair in his hand. Her lips were just touching his when she said, "Besides, there's no way to top making out by a covered bridge."

That's all it took. When Kate slipped her hands inside Brody's jacket and pushed it off his shoulders, he couldn't resist the invitation. He eased her down on the bench seat and pressed his body to hers, taking care not to crush her under his weight. He kissed her deeply, devouring her luscious mouth. Her long legs entangled his and the already staccato beat in his chest picked up speed when her long, slender fingers slid under his shirt. He slowly broke the kiss and set his concentration on pushing aside the clingy garment he'd had his eye on all evening, curious what wonder would be waiting underneath.

She didn't stop him; in fact, she helped him by lifting up so he could tug the zipper along the back of her dress. She slowly unbuttoned his shirt, released it from his shoulders, and tugged the cuffs over his hands. She shrugged out of the top half of her dress, letting it dangle freely between them.

Her nails grazed over his chest as she kept her eyes locked on his. The swell of her breasts pressed against lace and he couldn't resist lowering his face, tasting her creamy skin. She held his head in her hands and pulled him back to her mouth. His hand slipped around back and in one fluid movement unlatched her bra. She wiggled out of it and dropped it on the floorboard.

"Kate," he said as he nibbled up her neck, "we shouldn't do this here."

"I like it when you call me Katherine." She shifted below him, aligning her pelvis against his arousal, and wrapped her legs around his waist. "And why not do it here? Isn't that was this old truck was made for?" She splayed her hands across his butt. He responded with a satisfied moan and smothered her in a deep, wet kiss.

Suddenly, a shaft of light lit up the interior.

"What the hell?" He popped his head up, just enough to peek through the passenger side window. A car was sitting perpendicular to the old Ford, headlights pointed straight at them. He could see by the size and spacing those headlights belonged to a large sedan, possibly even a police cruiser. What terrible timing. Or maybe it was good timing. If the car had shown up a few minutes later, he wasn't sure they'd have been able to stop. With a last, longing look at Kate's gorgeous face, he felt all their earlier passion drain away. She looked frightened, confused, and he was determined to shield her from any embarrassment.

"Wait, don't move," he said as he reached for her bra on the floor.

"Who is it?" The car's bright light cast shadows on her face. "What's going on?" She started to rise, but he pushed her back down on the seat.

"I think there's a cop car out there, shining his headlights on us." Brody draped the top of her dress across her naked breasts. "Don't get up. I'll drive down the road so you can dress." He sat up, easing her legs aside, and started the truck. With a quick wave to whoever was behind those headlights, he pulled onto the road. About a half mile later, he pulled over in front of a deserted gas station and dropped the truck in park. Kate sat up and quickly slipped on her bra, expertly latching it closed. She shimmied into her dress and he helped with the zipper.

"I'm sorry about that," he said.

"It's okay."

With his arm resting on the back of the seat, he moved closer, itching to kiss her again, to be sure she really was okay. The piercing glare of the same headlights illuminated his rear view mirror.

"Damn it. What's with this guy?" He pulled onto the road and headed back to Highland Springs.

***

"Oh my gosh." Kate buried her face in Brody's shoulder, smothering her laughter in his leather jacket. "First of all, I've never made out in a pickup truck and second, I've never been caught. That was crazy."

"I wish you could've seen your face." He was laughing just as hard. With one hand on the steering wheel and one hand across her shoulder, she felt lightweight, not a care in the world. They were cruising along a country road, heading back to Gram's with a full moon lighting the way.

"I would have died if he came up to the window," she said.

"Sorry, officer, I tried to tell her not to undress, but she wouldn't listen."

"Funny." She nudged him hard on the shoulder and then snuggled back in. "How would you have explained your missing shirt?"

"Wouldn't have mattered."

"Oh, yeah, a double standard."

"Cop probably would have high-fived me."

"Hmm. So that's how it is around here, huh?"

The rest of the ride home, she stayed pressed against him, laughing and talking so comfortably, like they'd known each other much longer than the six weeks since they'd met. It was crazy to think a couple of beers at a warehouse and venison stew in a diner would turn out to be the perfect date, but it had.

Brody glided the old truck to the curb in front of Gram's house and killed the engine.

"Here we are," he said. He climbed out and, as Kate followed, she caught her heel in a rut. She stumbled against him, bringing her face close to his. She didn't wait for his lead but instead slid her hand around his neck and pulled him toward her for a kiss.

"Would you like me to come in for a little while?" he whispered against her lips.

"Ah." She sighed and pressed her forehead to his. "That would be great, but…"

"But?"

"Walk me to the door." She stepped back and looked at his confusion. Of course he'd be confused. Only minutes ago, they were near the point of no return and now she wanted him to kiss her goodnight. She intertwined her fingers with his and led him to the porch. Once she'd unlocked the door and stepped inside, he pressed her against the opened door and tempted her with another toe-curling kiss.

"What happened between the covered bridge and here?" he murmured against her skin as he dragged his lips down her neck. She raked her fingers through his hair, savoring his tender kisses.

"Nothing happened. It's just that—" Kate placed her hands on either side of his face and reluctantly pulled his mouth from the base of her neck. "I have something to do." She watched the ardor drain from his face, replaced by furrowed brows and pursed lips..

"You've taken a leave, so you don't have work to do."

"I know."

"And you don't have Tucker's papers yet."

"Right."

"So, what's so important it has to be done tonight?" He glanced at his watch, still keeping her back pressed to the door. "It's ten o'clock."

"It is? I'm sorry, but you have to go." She pressed her hands against his chest and gave him a hearty push.

"Katherine, what's going on?"

"I promised someone I'd help them with something tonight."

"It can't wait?"

"No, it can't, but can you?" She reached out, wrapped her arms around his neck, and pulled his forehead against hers. "I'm free tomorrow, all day."

"Is that so?"

"Mm hm." There was no way she'd let him leave mad, the way he had two days ago. She wanted more than anything to lead him upstairs and keep him there until morning. But she'd made a promise and had to follow through. She ran her fingers up and down his spine, and he shivered in response. "How about I come over to your place tomorrow at, oh, say four?"

"Make it two." He threw all his weight against her and devoured her mouth, as if to remind her of what she could look forward to tomorrow.

Gravel crunched under the Buick's tires as Kate slowly rolled down Brody's driveway the next day. She had slept late and woken to find a sweet text from Brody.

Since you didn't knock at two AM, I realized you meant PM. Come over ASAP.

After receiving the text, she hurried to get here, knowing he was anxiously awaiting her arrival. The last time she'd been here was at twilight, when she couldn't fully appreciate the beautiful landscape. The farm consisted of rolling hills, thick hardwoods, and acres of dormant fields, which she imagined grew lush with vegetation in the summer.

She parked in front of a large garage, cut the engine, and was surprised Loretta hadn't come out to greet her with her tail wagging, barking wildly. She climbed out of the car and looked around, trying to get her bearings while turning full circle. Even in the early winter, his farm was stunning. The house was painted pale gray with white trim and black shutters, exuding a hominess she hadn't recognized during her nocturnal visit. In daylight, the house looked much larger than she remembered.

As she approached the house, a cold shiver of wariness coursed through her body. It was too quiet. The only sound she heard was the winter breeze rustling the branches of the evergreens dotting his yard. Where was he? And why didn't she hear Loretta inside? The garage doors were down, none of his vehicles were in sight, and the place looked deserted. After a quick glance over her shoulder, she stepped onto the porch, walked to the front door, and pressed the doorbell. Expecting a loud bark, even the sound of footsteps approaching the door, all she got was silence. After a minute, she gave up.

He knew she was coming, so where was he? She walked down the opposite side of the porch and into the side yard—the opposite side from where she'd peeked in his windows. She took a deep breath, inhaling the crisp, cold air, but it didn't calm her jagged nerves. Ever since last night, she couldn't shake the feeling someone was following her.

The "friend" she had helped last night was Ashley, the abused woman she'd met at the Thanksgiving dinner. Kate assisted in getting her and her four kids to a safe location, and now she had an ominous feeling. What if someone was watching her right now? Maybe those headlights last night belonged to someone other than the police. Something wasn't right about this and the longer she stood in Brody's yard with no sign of him, the more concerned she became. The infernal silence was scaring her. She dialed his phone number and waited for him to answer. The call immediately went to voicemail.

She walked back around the house toward the driveway, hoping to find his truck coming down the lane. Another cold tingle rushed up her spine, putting her on alert. What if Ashley's husband knew she had been the one to usher his wife and children out of the house and to the safety of a shelter? What if he had hurt Brody? The sooner she was back in her car with the doors locked, the better she'd feel until Brody got home. As she rounded the corner, she heard a sound. Were those footsteps behind her? Just as she was about to turn around, a stranger appeared in her periphery and a hand clamped down on her shoulder.

TWENTY

"What the fuck?" Brody curled into a fetal position, trying to ease the searing pain in his back. "Jesus." He coughed a couple of times and rolled onto his knees. "Why'd you do that?"

"Brody?"

"Who the hell did you think it was? Are you crazy, woman?" Taking a deep breath, he wondered if he would be able to stand up. What the hell was the matter with her? She wasn't kidding when she said she knew *tae kwon do*.

"Oh my god, it *is* you." Kate dropped to the ground beside him and gathered his face in her hands. Her eyes bugged, seeking recognition, then she threw her arms around his neck, toppling him over to his back. "I'm so sorry."

"Ouch. You already threw me to the ground once."

"I'm so sorry." She frantically covered his face with kisses and smoothed back his hair. "I'm sorry. Where's your beard? Your hair's shorter."

"I decided to clean up a little." While he lay flat on his back with his arms stretched out beside him, he took a couple of deep breaths as he assessed the damage. He didn't feel sharp pains in his back, so maybe if he stayed put a few minutes, he'd be able to get up. "Wanted to surprise you."

"I didn't know it was you. You look completely different."

"Remind me to warn you the next time I shave."

"I'm so sorry. Are you okay?"

He was now. Kate stretched out beside him and snuggled up against him, laying her warm hands against his bare face. Maybe he should keep acting injured so she'd keep up the TLC.

"I'll be better once you roll over on top of me." He wiggled his eyebrows at her and got a punch in the arm in return. "Ouch. Are you trying to kill me?"

"You asshole. You scared the stuff out of me. Who sneaks up on someone like that?" She popped up and brushed the backside of her jeans. "Where have you been? It's eerie out here, so quiet. And where's Loretta?" She glared down at him long enough that he started to question who was the victim here. "I thought something happened to you. This is no joke." She kicked the bottom of his boot and stormed away. "Stop laughing."

"I can't help it." He rolled on his side and slowly got to his feet. She was pacing back and forth, her arms crossed over her chest. "Come here. Don't be mad."

"I am mad. This isn't funny. I was worried and scared."

"Come here." He wrapped his arms around her from behind and rested his chin on her shoulder. "I should have told you I was shaving this morning." He lifted her hair and planted a few kisses on her neck. "I just thought you'd like my surprise."

"Not when it involves sneaking up on me."

"Trust me. I'll never sneak up on you again." He pressed his cheek to hers. "I might not survive it the next time."

She dropped her arms and turned to face him, shaking her head while examining his face as if it were the first time she'd seen it. She brushed the back of her hand over each of his cheeks and rubbed her thumb over his lips.

"Amazing." She leaned back and cupped his face in her hands. "I can't get over the difference."

"Good difference or bad difference?"

"Just different. It's like I'm with another person."

"How about I remind you that I'm the same guy?" Before she could respond, he enveloped her in a tight hug and covered her lips with his.

Any anger she may have been holding on to dissolved as she pressed herself against him and matched his kiss with equal fervor. After several minutes, they pulled away but stayed locked in each other's arms.

"We good?" he asked.

"We're good."

"I'll never question your ability to protect yourself again."

"Smart man." She gave him a quick peck on the lips and then stepped back. "So, where were you? Where's Loretta?"

"I was on the phone up on the deck and Loretta went to the dog park in town with Liza."

"Oh, the pergola—or should I call it the 'cowboy hideout?'" She reached out her hand. "Show me."

"First, let's go inside. You'll freeze to death in that thin jacket you're wearing."

Brody led the way through the front door of his house and Kate was immediately hit with a cozy, at-home feeling. She stood in the foyer and looked at the beautiful oak staircase and natural carved woodwork. To the left was a formal dining room with an antique mahogany table covered in an inch of dust. *Not much of an entertainer. Noted.* He led her down the hall into a great room where a large stone fireplace filled most of one wall, flanked by windows on either side. This wasn't the room she saw through the window that night.

"Let me find a warmer coat for you. It's a little windy up on the deck." Brody walked through a doorway that led to the kitchen and she took a moment to get her bearings. She knew the room she'd seen him in was on this side of the house. After turning a half circle, she saw a closed door behind her and knew this must be it. Since he was nowhere in sight, she tiptoed to the door and peeked inside. She found it—the room where she had seen him shirtless at the computer. The wall with the window was covered in thick, acoustic foam panels, as was the wall opposite it. Fascinated, she stepped inside to discover what must be his studio.

"Looking for something?"

She jumped at the sound of his voice and could feel the heat in her cheeks. She'd been caught snooping again.

"I was, um, just looking around. I hope you don't mind."

"Does this room look familiar?"

"As a matter of fact—" He was looking at her with a wry grin. "It does. I confess." She threw up her hands and shrugged her shoulders. "Is this a studio?"

"Yeah. I write in here and record demos."

"So this is where all the magic happens, huh?" She strolled around the room, taking in all the little details she'd missed that night. There was a shelf with several awards and framed photos.

"Not the only room," he said.

She spun around, caught his impish grin, and thrilled at his silky voice and overt innuendo. He might not look like the mountain man she'd come to know on the outside, but he was still the same sexy man she was finding harder and harder to resist. They had all day, no need to rush things. Right now she wanted to know a little more about the songwriting side of the man she was coming to think of as endlessly multifaceted.

"Tell me about these awards." She moved closer to the shelf and drew in a breath. "Brody." She picked up a golden gramophone and read the plaque. "So this is your Grammy for best country song." Beside it was another Grammy dated two years after the first. "And another for best pop song." She had done extensive research on him, but was still dazzled by his success. "And a couple of CMA awards." She turned around and found him at his desk with his back to her. He was leaning over the computer, checking emails. She crossed the room and turned him around to face her.

"You're so…so accomplished."

"It's no big deal." He sat on the edge of the desk and tucked his hands in his front pockets.

"No big deal? It's a huge deal." She latched onto his upper arms and looked into the deep brown eyes.

"Does it change anything?"

"What do you mean?" she asked, her voice soft.

"If I never get another one? Would it make a difference?"

The pain was evident on his face and she wondered where these emotions were coming from. He should be proud of his success, maybe even a little boastful. She couldn't understand why he felt he couldn't achieve the same level of success now.

"Not at all." She came a little closer and rested her hand on his cheek. "I'm impressed. You should be so proud of yourself." She draped her arms around his neck.

"It's just, all those awards were with the help of my partner, Kyle. I doubt I could've done it without him."

"You could have and still can." She stopped, realizing this was the very thing she'd said the night of their big fight. The last thing she wanted was to upset him now that everything was so good between them. "I'm sorry. I shouldn't have said anything. I don't mean to push. The most important thing is that you write again—you're so talented."

"Actually, it's okay. What you said to me that night helped get my lazy ass back to work. I've been writing a lot."

"That's great. How does it feel?"

"Feels great. It's going well."

"Anything you're willing to show me?" She raised up and glanced over his shoulder, noticing a smattering of papers strewn across his desk with handwritten lines.

"Are we still talking about music?" He stopped her trek toward the desk with a crooked grin.

"It all depends." She snatched the first sheet her fingers could reach and quickly skimmed the stanzas.

Let's just keep it simple,
No plans, no promises, that's the deal.
We'll spend some time together,
Without hearts to break or steal.
See, I can make it simple,
Down to the cold bare facts.

Your gorgeous eyes, your pretty smile,
Makes my heart go off track.
The simple truth of the matter is,
She mumbled the words aloud. "Mm, interesting. Did I inspire you on this?"

"Maybe."

"And the simple truth of the matter is…what? Care to complete that sentence?"

"Not at all." He tugged the hem of her jacket and tucked his arms inside. "It's still a work in progress." His arms tightened around her waist and his eyes locked with hers. "If you have no further questions."

"Hmm. I guess music can wait."

Like a bull let out of a stall, he grabbed her and locked her in a kiss before she could even take a breath. It was as if he'd kept that kiss secreted away all day and it needed to get out. She pressed herself tight against him, marveling how in only a day's time, things had changed between them.

Eventually, he loosened his hold and playfully patted her tight jeans. "Let's go." He grabbed a down jacket off the desk chair. "Here. Wear this. You'll be warmer."

"Is it yours?" She slipped her arms inside the thick coat and zipped it closed.

"No, it's Travis's. He left it here when he was working on my hot water heater."

"What? Another business?"

"I told you he had too many to mention." Brody held out his hand and intertwined his fingers with hers. "Ready?"

He led her through the great room, into a modern kitchen with oak cabinets, granite countertops, and a stainless steel commercial oven. *So the mountain man cooks?* Before she could get a good look, he dragged her through the back door onto a screened porch, which she'd somehow missed the night she was here. Cushioned wicker furniture was gathered in a circle and she could just imagine a warm night, having drinks with friends by candlelight while soft music played and crickets chirped. She shook her head, scattering the image away.

"It's up this way."

They crossed a narrow yard and Kate looked up at a steep slope where tall, sturdy wood beams held a wide platform extending out of the hillside. A wooden staircase built into the hill wound up through a thick canvas of trees.

"This is where I got all the firewood. It took me over a year to clear this path and set the framework."

She was speechless. This had to have been a huge project and she couldn't imagine him doing it alone. Her thighs began to ache halfway up the stairs, but Brody climbed effortlessly. Finally, they reached the top and they stepped onto a huge deck, covered partly with the pergola Tucker mentioned. It smelled of new lumber and fresh forest. She let go of Brody's hand and walked toward the front of the deck.

"Be careful. I haven't finished the railings yet," he said.

"It's beautiful." She had thought the view from the front yard was pretty, but it was no comparison to this. "The view is spectacular." Not only could she see the mountains in the distance and the winding river, but she could see downtown Highland Springs as well. "What made you decide to build it?" He came up beside her and draped his arm over her shoulder.

"I needed something to focus on when I came back from New York." She detected sadness in his voice and again, that faraway look in his eyes. He dropped his arm and sat on the edge of the deck, letting his legs dangle over the side. The sun was beaming on his hair, picking up natural golden highlights. She inched toward the edge and had a sudden case of vertigo. He turned and held out his hand, then jumped up to help her.

"Sorry about that. I'm so used to it up here I forget how scary it can be."

"I'm okay now." Kate settled on the lip of the deck and took a deep breath of fresh mountain air. "This is amazing." She looked at Brody, who was wordlessly gazing out across the valley. He turned to her with a serious expression.

"No, you're amazing." He tilted her chin, kissed her softly, and she melted again. She felt a hot, rushing wave and thought she could get used to this. Now that she'd put her career on hold, all she seemed to think about was Brody. In a moment of clarity, she felt her cheeks flush from the fear of where this might lead and she pushed him away. They needed to slow down.

"Are you okay?" He studied her face, his brow furrowed.

"I'm just, um, a little warm." She unzipped the down jacket. "The sun is really strong." When she opened the coat, a red plastic lighter fell out of an inside pocket. "Oh, does Travis smoke?" She reached inside the pocket, thinking she'd find a pack of cigarettes, but instead she pulled out a thick, perfectly rolled joint.

"You could say that," Brody said, chuckling as he reached for the joint. He started to tuck it inside his pocket, but she stopped him.

"What are you doing?"

"I'm putting it in my pocket."

"No, you're not. We're smoking it." She leaned across him and snatched the joint from his hand. "What? Why do you look so shocked?" His mouth gaped open and his eyebrows arched.

"An officer of the court smoking weed? What would the partners back in DC say?"

"Right now, I could care less." With the joint lodged between her lips, she flicked the lighter into a flame and glanced over at him once more. She pinched the joint between her fingers and said, "Are you smoking this with me?"

"Light it up." He laughed and shook his head as he watched her take several quick tokes. "You seem to know what you're doing."

"It's been a long—" She broke into a coughing fit as she handed the joint to him, waving the smoke from her face. "Haven't done this since college. I'm out of practice."

"It's probably been longer for me." He inhaled deeply and held it in, speaking while holding his breath. "Used to smoke with Travis before football games."

She took the reefer from his hand and tried again to smoke without coughing. This time it went much smoother and she felt light-headed.

"You can't be serious. Did it help your performance?"

"Nothing could've helped our performance." He accepted the joint and inhaled again. "We sucked."

"Well, no wonder." Kate felt a light, dizzy feeling and she put her hands on the deck to steady herself. "Oh my gosh, I'm such an amateur. I feel it already."

"Good stuff, huh?"

"Where does Travis get it?" She looked out across the valley and thought the view was even more amazing than before.

"Grows it." He exhaled a large plume of smoke and passed back to Kate. "Just enough for himself and a few friends."

"What?" She grabbed his arm. "No way. Where?"

"In his basement. He's got all kinds of plant lights and an irrigation system rigged up. It's pretty sophisticated. You gonna smoke that or what?" She inhaled deeply as she let that news sink in.

"I'd like to see it." She took another quick toke and handed it back. "Will he show me?"

"Probably."

"Wait. I can't. What if the cops come? I can't get caught around anything illegal. I could lose my license." She tugged his arm again. "Oh, crap, you think the police will come out here? Do they know about Travis? That you two are friends?" She leaned out to look down his lane and Brody pressed his arm against her stomach, stopping her from tumbling over the edge. "Now I remember why I don't like to smoke weed." She slid back from the edge of the deck and lay back, closing her eyes and tilting her face to the sky.

"You finished with this?"

Kate opened one eye and looked at the tiny tip of joint Brody had pinched between his fingers. She waved her arm at him. "I've had enough." He lay down beside her and ran his fingers through her hair. She brushed his hand away. "You've got to get rid of that. Hide the evidence. We don't want Travis to get in trouble. If the police question us, we can't lie," she said.

"What?" He sat up and crossed his legs at the ankles, reclining with his hands flat behind him on the deck. "Travis won't get in trouble."

"How do you know?"

"The chief of police is one of his best customers."

TWENTY-ONE

After thirty minutes, ten of which were spent laughing over Kate's paranoia about getting questioned by the police, Brody stood up. It was only after he explained the police chief got pot from Travis for his wife who suffered from MS that she was able to shake off the fear they would get dragged into police headquarters.

He held out his hands to help her up. She stumbled against him and he wrapped his arm around her waist. She had laughed so hard that mascara streaked down her cheeks, so Brody gently rubbed the black marks with his thumb. Then, he tilted his head down and kissed her, tasting marijuana residue on her tongue. She was so damned beautiful with her long, dark hair blowing in the breeze and the sun shining on her face, bringing out a sprinkling of freckles on her nose. How could he let her go back to DC? The thought gave him a sharp pain, like a spike hammered into his heart.

"Come on, Brody, let's walk down to the river." She grabbed his hand and stepped gingerly off the deck onto the long, narrow staircase. All coordination was back and she appeared to have not a trace of fear as she charged down the steps. When they got to the bottom, she took off running across the yard and down the hill toward the river flowing past the field. He chased her, following a few yards behind, down to the river's edge where they dropped onto a grassy mound.

"You recovered fast," he said.

"I'm not sure I'm fully recovered, but the run helped." She raked her fingers through her hair, letting it fall back in place. "Don't let me smoke that stuff again. I get so paranoid."

"I just get lazy. It was all I could do to keep up with you."

The river meandered over rocks, carrying an occasional twig or leaf to its ultimate destination, and they sat in silence as the water flowed by. He was totally at ease—not the drug-induced sedation brought on by the marijuana, but an emotional, almost spiritual contentment he hadn't felt in years, if ever. Trying his best to not think about tomorrow or next week, but only focus on this moment, was a struggle. He wanted to have a lifetime of moments like this with Kate. He reached out and gathered her hand in his.

"Tell me about New York. Why'd you come back?" The spell was broken. Just the mention of New York sent a surging sadness through him. Why did she have to bring it up now?

"Oh, I don't know."

"I mean…" She turned and sat against her heels, covering their grasp with her other hand. "I saw the Grammy for best pop song. Was that while you lived in New York?"

"It's really not something I like to talk about."

"Why? What happened?"

"It's a long story. Not one I'm proud of."

"You mentioned your writing partner. What happened to him? I mean, I read he had an accident, but I feel like there's more to the story."

Brody tore his gaze from the meandering river and locked his eyes with Kate's. "I killed him."

Kate extracted her hands from his and rose onto her knees; her gorgeous green eyes were staring at him as if she were looking at a stranger. He pulled up a thick blade of grass and studied its long, straight lines. His time in New York, the accident that ended his partnership with Kyle, the mistakes he had made were all subjects he'd tried to forget. Now her questions made it impossible to avoid the time in his life that had brought him to this moment.

"I don't believe you. Tell me exactly what happened."

"I'd hate to face you on the witness stand."

"I'm sorry." She broke her penetrating gaze. "I didn't mean to put you on the spot."

"I bet you always get the answers you're looking for in court."

"Yeah, I hate to brag, but I'm starting to get a reputation as something of a pit bull." She stretched her legs out in front of her. "It's okay. You don't need to tell me." They sat in silence a few minutes more when he decided to tell her. If her opinion of him changed after this story, maybe it would be for the best.

"This might take a while. You want to go inside?" he said.

"No, I like it right here, don't you?"

He took a deep breath and drank in her gorgeous face. Something about her tender smile and sparkling eyes made him relax and accept it would be okay.

"I dropped out of college my sophomore year and took off for Nashville to get a singing career going. It was slow at first, but eventually I had a top twenty hit with 'Spin the Bottle of Jack.' But I really didn't like the travel and had sold a few of my songs to some big-time performers, so I decided to stick to composing." He glanced over to find her eyes locked on him, drinking in every word. "A producer friend of mine introduced me to Kyle, who became my writing partner. We hit it off instantly and wrote a lot of hits for about four years. Once we won a few awards, I got too big for my britches, as my grandpa would've said, and decided we should cross over to pop." Kate stirred beside him, curling her legs under while keeping her view on him alone. "Any questions so far?"

"A million of them. But they can wait." She touched her hand to his cheek. "Keep going."

He cleared his throat and let his eyes drift back over the water.

"Kyle never wanted to leave Nashville, but I pushed him. Told him we needed to stretch our wings, make the big money. You sure you want to hear this?"

"Continue, please."

"Anyway, our manager hooked us up with Second First Chance."

"Oh, wow. They're huge."

"Right. They are. We wrote an entire album for them which went platinum, but that wasn't enough for me." He jerked up a handful of grass out of the ground and threw it into the river. "I wanted more."

"So, what happened?"

It was the first question Kate had asked and it momentarily brought Brody back to the present. He looked at her, concern etched across her face, and he turned to sit facing her with their knees touching. All his earlier trepidation had flowed away with the river, making him comfortable talking directly to her.

"Well, we made plenty of money and more opportunities opened up. That Grammy was for 'Waking Up Monday Morning' which was on the soundtrack for the *Atlantis* movie."

"Oh my gosh, you wrote that? I love that song."

"Yeah, so did twenty million other people." He chuckled and rubbed his forehead.

"You didn't like it?"

"It was okay. The thing is, it wasn't our idea. We were told to use that title and write music and lyrics to fit. So much for creative freedom."

"So what happened?"

"We had a lot of interest from other performers and I wanted us to churn out as much music and as many demos as quick as we could. I kept pushing him to produce more." She crawled closer to him and laid her hands on his knees. "One night, we'd been recording demos for days, and Kyle was complaining because he was tired, wanted to go to a bar and relax. I insisted we keep working until we'd recorded everything to my liking. We argued, he eventually gave in, and we stayed at it until like five in the morning."

He leaped to his feet and faced the river, but instead of seeing water flow over dark rocks, he saw skyscrapers and heard the noise of city life. After several silent moments, his nerves settled and he told the story he'd spent two years trying to forget.

"Kyle left the studio on his own, asleep on his feet, said he was going to the diner on the corner. I stayed to lay down some more guitar tracks. About an hour later I got a call saying he was dead."

"Oh, Brody." Kate came up behind him and wrapped her arms around his waist.

"After leaving the diner, he stumbled in front of a bus. Killed him instantly."

"I'm so sorry. That's tragic," she whispered.

"If I hadn't pushed him, if I'd let him go home when he first complained of being tired, maybe he'd still be alive."

"Brody, it's not your fault. It was just an accident."

"You sure about that?" He turned around, tucked his hands into his front pockets, and kicked a stone on the ground. "It sure feels like my fault."

"He could've left at any time. He was a grown man with his own mind, able to make his own decisions. You can't blame yourself."

"I know you're looking at this logically, but for the past two years, I haven't been able to see it that way. Kyle was my friend, my partner. He never refused anything I asked when it came to the work."

"Would you have refused anything he would have asked?"

"Probably not."

"Then it was an equal partnership, a true friendship. It could just have easily gone the other way."

"Maybe." He wiped a tear from his eyes and looked off in the distance.

"You need to write these feelings down. Turn it into a song, a dedication to Kyle. Let the world know what a great guy he was so he'll never be forgotten. And in the process, get your career back to where it was."

With a heavy sigh, he cupped her face in his hands. "You're so beautiful, you know that?"

"You're trying to change the subject. I'm serious."

"Sweetheart, I know you're serious." He slipped his hands inside her coat and pulled her against him. "And I appreciate it. I'll think about what you said."

"But, Brody—"

"It's taken me all this time to realize my original dream, the one I busted my ass for, died along with Kyle. I was killing myself for an illusion—and him along with it. It's different now—I'm happy here, living for something real."

"I don't understand."

"Maybe someday you will." He gathered her face in his hands and pressed his lips against hers. She melted against him and returned his kiss, tenderly, lovingly. If she wasn't careful, he'd never let her go.

"I love kissing you," she whispered. Then she stepped back and zipped her jacket closed. "But I'm starving. Got anything chocolate in your kitchen?"

***

"Pretzels, yes." Kate grabbed a bag of fat, Bavarian pretzels out of the pantry and handed them to Brody, who was hovering behind her. "Food of the gods." She pushed a few cans aside and picked up a jar of peanut butter. "Now we're talking."

"I thought you wanted chocolate." He set the peanut butter on the counter and walked to the opposite side of the kitchen, where he picked up a plastic cake plate.

"Haven't you heard of sweet and salty? Best combination when you have the munchies." Her fuzzy, drug-induced head was clear, but it was still a good excuse for indulging in forbidden junk food. She closed the pantry door and turned around to find him setting the cake plate on the kitchen table. "What's that?" She carried the pretzels and peanut butter to the table and plopped down in a wooden chair.

"I have just the thing for your chocolate craving." He removed the plastic lid with a flourish and presented her with an expertly frosted dark chocolate cake topped with chocolate curls and finely chopped nuts. Her mouth began to water.

"Where did you get that?"

"I have an admirer at the post office." He crossed the kitchen, pulled two plates out of the cabinet, and retrieved two forks out of a drawer. "At least once a month I'm guaranteed a cake or a pie from the lady who runs the counter."

"The talkative lady? The one who gives out fashion advice?"

"The very same." On his way back to the table, he grabbed a half-gallon of milk out the refrigerator and tucked it under his arm. He pinched two glasses between his thumb and fingers and placed everything on the table. "I thought about giving up my post office box, just get my mail delivered out here, but it's worth the trip."

"So, you've got a not-so-secret admirer."

"Jealous?" He carried two napkins to the table and laid them at each place as he sat in an adjacent chair.

"Terribly." She spread the napkin across her lap. "You're pretty good at that. Ever wait tables?" She ripped open the bag of pretzels and unscrewed the lid on the peanut butter jar.

"Plenty of them. I worked at a barbecue place in Nashville for a couple years during the day and played music at night." He jumped up and crossed the room again. "We need some knives." When he returned, he plunged one knife in the peanut butter and sliced the cake with the other. "As soon as I started making enough money to pay my bills, I gave up the serving job. We've talked about me enough. What about you?"

"The jobs I've had? Other than law?" She took a big bite of cake and dropped her fork on the table as if she'd been stung. "Oh my god," she mumbled through her stuffed mouth. Brody started laughing and sprayed a fine milky mist on the table. Holding a napkin to his mouth, he swallowed and laughed out loud.

"You should've seen your face."

"Whaa—?" she said, her mouth too full and sticky to complete the word. She'd taken too big a bite and was having difficulty swallowing, but at the same time, she was savoring every rich, decadent, chocolaty morsel.

"Do you always roll your eyes like that?" he asked.

"Like what?" She took one last swallow and finally emptied her mouth, able to speak clearly again.

"Like that. Like you're in ecstasy."

"I *was* in ecstasy. This is the best cake I've ever eaten." This time, she made sure to take a smaller bite of the cake, but noticed Brody wasn't eating. He was still watching her with a half smile on his face. "Why aren't you eating?"

"I like watching you." He shoved his plate and glass aside and propped his elbows on the table, easing closer to her. She slowed down, feeling self-conscious. His eyes were hooded, glassy, his expression soft, contemplative.

"You're making me uncomfortable." Using the side of her fork as a knife, she cut off a bite of her cake and extended it to him, feeding it to him without protest.

"Mm." He ate it slowly, sensuously, and she became mesmerized by the movement of his mouth, his chiseled jaw. She took another bite and tried to move her lips in sync with his.

"Delicious, right?"

"Delicious," he said in that silky, seductive tone she had come to know so well—the one that never failed to send her heart pounding. With his eyes locked on hers, he slid the fork inside his mouth, depositing another chocolaty piece. Now it was her turn to watch him eat. His lips were soft, full, kissable. They moved fluidly, pressed together, in a circular motion, sucking her in like a slow-moving whirlpool. Her eyes traveled to his jaw, tightening, releasing, with each bite.

"…better than sex," he murmured.

"What?"

"Were you listening?"

"Um, yeah, I was listening."

"She called it 'better than sex cake.'" He chuckled and raised his eyebrows at her. "What do you think of that?" He swiped his finger across the top of the cake and plunged a dollop of icing in her mouth. She let the gooey confection melt off his finger onto her tongue, savoring the sensuous feelings coursing through her body.

"Hm. I don't know…" Returning the gesture, she offered him a fingertip full of icing and rather than take it in his mouth, he slowly licked it from her finger. Damn, he wasn't playing fair. Kate wasn't sure how much longer she could sit here without touching him, kissing him. "What do you think?"

"I think." This time, he took a swath of chocolate and dotted it on her lips, then proceeded to tenderly lick and kiss it from her mouth. "You need to tell me." He whispered against her lips.

"Well." She cleared her throat, feeling the need to pull off her sweater, she'd grown so warm. Scooting her chair back from the table to put a little distance between them, she tossed her cardigan on the chair beside her. Brody wasn't hiding the fact that he wanted more than just cake and now that the moment had arrived, her heart was pounding and her stomach twisted in knots. She picked up her plate and carried it to the sink. "This cake is incredible. It just might be better than sex."

In only a few long strides, he was across the room and scooping her in his arms, folding her over his shoulder. "You want to bet?"

"Brody." She giggled uncontrollably. "What are you doing?" She uselessly pounded on his back, feigning outrage while her head hung upside-down. "Put me down."

"Nope." He bounded up the staircase as easily as if he'd been empty-handed, and entered his bedroom. "There's only one way to find out." He tapped the door shut with his foot.

TWENTY-TWO

Kate arched back, catching a quick glimpse of Brody's impish grin. He still hadn't put her down. "Okay, so you've got me up here. What now?"

"What now?" He lowered her to the floor, slowly, letting his hands glide over her body on the way down. "You need to ask?" He grabbed the hem of his t-shirt and pulled it over his head, baring his chiseled chest. She drew in a shallow breath and took a half-step back. He matched her step and reeled her into his arms. Why now? Why was she suddenly feeling shy around him? Perhaps it was the dappled afternoon sunlight coming through the blinds, exposing his lightly tanned skin. Or the rumpled sheets of his unmade bed, inviting them to explore one another. Or maybe it was the fact that once they crossed the line to lovers, everything would change.

He lowered his mouth to her fisted hands tucked against his chest and pulled her fingers into his mouth, sucking and nibbling until every fiber of her being was marshmallow. She drew in a deep breath, savoring the smell of him—spicy, outdoorsy, male. His eyes were locked on hers as he pecked his way across the back of her hand, only stopping to change course. Now his lips found the pulse thrumming at the base of her neck and trailed kisses to her earlobe, which he captured between his teeth.

Oh, to hell with sunlight, rumpled sheets, and crossing lines. She couldn't resist him another moment. With a quiet moan, she slipped her arms around his trim waist, tilting her head to give him better access to her neck, as she ran her nails up his spine. He released a moan of his own and cupped her face in his large, calloused hands, kissing her hungrily as he backed her toward the bed. With each step, he kissed her more deeply and she opened to him, welcoming his lips, tongue, essence. She wanted him—couldn't get enough—was putty in his hands. She'd deal with the fall out later…much later.

The backs of her thighs bumped the edge of the bed and Brody drew back, raking his fingers through her hair while keeping his dark, sultry gaze on her. "I want you…so bad," he said as his hands found their way under her tank top. Cool air touched her skin as he tugged her shirt up over her head, letting it fall to the floor. "God, you're so beautiful." She shivered. Whether from the sudden chill or his feather-light touch along the base of her breasts, Kate snuggled up to his warm body, planting tender kisses along his chest. He had just enough golden hair to tickle the tip of her nose, bringing a smile to her lips. While she continued to taste his skin, he unlatched her bra, tugging it forward to drop between them. He placed his hands on her hips and drew her tight against him.

"Tell me you want me, too."

His gaze seared into her, causing a delicious flutter in her chest. Of course she wanted him. There was no doubt about that. She couldn't stop now if she tried. She brushed her fingertips across his soft, shaved cheek and placed a delicate kiss on his lips.

"I do."

"Don't move."

Instead of getting a confirming kiss, Brody dropped his hold and disappeared through a door which she concluded must be the bathroom. She heard the slamming of several drawers and some muttered curses. She turned toward the tall bedpost at the foot of the bed and muffled a laugh. Leaning her head against the walnut post, she silently chuckled at their luck. Last night they'd been interrupted by a pair of headlights and now it seemed he was having difficulty finding his stash of condoms. She was on the pill, so at least birth control wasn't an issue.

"Where were we?" He had silently snuck up behind her and drew her bare back against his chest.

"Did you find what you were looking for?" She giggled as he attacked the sweet spot at the base of her neck.

"It took some searching, but yes." As he continued his tender assault across her shoulder, he cupped a breast in each hand, grazing his thumbs over her hardened nipples. "There's no stopping us now."

He spread his hands over her breasts, sliding them ever so slowly down her stomach, to below her belly button, and slipping them inside her waistband. He flicked open the button of her jeans and pulled the zipper, spreading the fabric open and away, giving him better access. While one hand dipped between her legs, the other palmed her buttocks, causing her to release a tiny squeak of pleasure. Warm air brushed her shoulder as he chuckled at her reaction. He was driving her mad and he knew it.

Kate leaned forward and rubbed her backside against his erection, drawing out a deep moan from him. He was making her crazy. The least she could do was return the favor. She snaked her hands up and behind, grasping the back of Brody's head, bringing his face around to meet hers for a deep kiss. As awkward at their position was, she had no intention of moving. Mid-kiss, he plunged a finger inside her and used the base of his thumb to draw circles, causing her to shudder and moan. He continued his delicious maneuvering until she thought she'd burst.

"Brody." His name escaped on a strangled whisper. If he kept this up much longer… She gripped her jeans and shimmied them to the floor, side-stepping out of them and turning in a flash. He followed her lead and removed the last remaining barrier to their lovemaking. He gathered her in a tight hold, sliding one hand to the back of her thigh, lifting it to rest on his hip while the other gripped her butt, grinding her tight against him.

"Katherine," he murmured between kisses. He dropped his hand to her other thigh and lifted her in his arms, coaxing her legs around his waist. He walked to the head of the bed and placed her gently on the mattress, as if he were handling a precious crystal vase, and climbed on beside her. She gathered his face in her hands as he swiped a condom off the nightstand and eased between her legs. He lowered his head, capturing one breast in his mouth, using his tongue to send ribbons of fire through her veins. She threw her head against the pillows and groaned with pleasure.

Using his knees to nudge hers apart, he slowly, painstakingly entered her, creating a swell of desire she had never known. This was right. They fit flawlessly together. He plunged and ground against her until she cried out.

"Look at me, sweetheart." He held her face in his hands, continuing to rotate his hips, watching as she reached the climax. Her eyes involuntarily rolled back in her head. *Do you always roll your eyes like that?* She released a breathy chuckle. He smothered her laugh with a kiss, moaning into her mouth as he reached his own. He collapsed beside her, tucking his lips against her neck.

"So?" he whispered.

"Nope…" Kate panted and turned to meet his eyes. "That cake *wasn't* better than sex."

***

Breakfast. I promised Kate breakfast. The nagging thought forced Brody's eyes to flutter open then squeeze shut from the morning brightness. He rolled over and threw his arm over nothing, landing on the cool, empty sheets. She wasn't there.

He sat up, looked around the room, and for a second he thought maybe he'd dreamed it. Had she really been here last night? Been under him, legs wrapped around him, moaning, calling out his name? A long, dark strand of hair lay across her pillow, confirming it wasn't all a dream. He climbed out of bed, pulled on his jeans from where they'd been crumpled on the floor, and padded downstairs.

Expecting to find Kate sitting at the table, sipping a cup of coffee, he was taken aback with the silence of the house. Pots and pans from last night's dinner were still stacked on the counter, the overhead light was off, and her jacket was gone. As he headed for the great room to look for her car through the window, he noticed a folded note sitting teepee-style on the counter. He flipped open the yellow lined paper.

Good morning sleepy head,

You were dead asleep when I woke up and I didn't have the heart to interrupt your dreams. (Dreaming of me, I hope.) Yesterday was great, dinner was great, everything else was great, but I think you know that. I'll have to take a rain check on breakfast. Derek texted me. He's at Gram's. Maybe I'll see you later.

Love,

Katherine

Brody leaned against the counter, awash with relief, as he reread her note. In the few seconds he'd found the house empty, his chest had tightened and he'd imagined the worst: she regretted last night. Unable to control a full-on smile, he read the note once more and decided she wouldn't need to take a rain check on breakfast. He'd bring it to her. But first, he needed a shower.

***

As quietly as possible, Kate opened the front door and tiptoed into her grandmother's house. The living room was dark, the blinds drawn, but she saw Derek's car outside and his coat draped over an armchair so she knew he had arrived. She hung her coat in the closet and turned toward the stairs.

"You're home awfully late, young lady." Derek's booming voice split the silence, causing her to jump. He crossed the living room from the kitchen with a coffee mug in his hand and drew her in for a hug.

"What are you doing sneaking up on me?" She wrapped her arms around her old friend, feeling an instant calm to her fright. It seemed much longer than a few weeks since they'd last seen one another. "I'm sorry. I had every intention of coming home sooner. Why are you up so early?"

"I have a meeting before training starts."

"Sounds like you have a busy day. Is there enough coffee for me?" She walked into the kitchen and poured herself a cup of the steamy brew. He sat on a kitchen chair, looking uncharacteristically rumpled in a wrinkled t-shirt and baggy flannel pajama bottoms. His baby blue eyes were locked on hers, waiting to see who would speak first in this game of chicken. Whenever he wanted to get information out of her or Annie, he'd stare them down as if he were practicing an interrogation technique.

"Fine, I'll go first. Did you sleep okay last night?" she said.

"Did you?" He continued to stare, but she could see he was fighting back a smile.

"I slept like the dead. Did you have any problem getting in?"

"None. Thanks for leaving the key." He helped himself to more coffee and then leaned against the counter beside her. "Okay, now you have about ten minutes to tell me everything."

***

Brody pulled his pickup in front of Virginia's house a half hour later, noticing a government-issued SUV in the drive next to the Buick. He grabbed the bag off the seat and walked to the porch. As he approached the door, he heard loud music playing, but low enough he couldn't recognize the song. He pressed the doorbell and stepped back.

The door swung open and a tall, shirtless man flashed him a movie star grin.

"Hey, you must be Brody," he said. Brody couldn't help but notice the six—no eight pack abs rippling across his torso. This tool couldn't be—

"I'm Derek. Come on in."

He shook Derek's outstretched hand and stepped inside. R&B music blared through the speakers, making it hard to hear.

"Kate's in the shower. I'll turn this down and go get her." Derek walked over to the entertainment center and turned the knob on an old radio that Virginia had probably owned since the eighties. When Kate mentioned her friend Derek was coming to visit, he hadn't pictured Ryan Gosling's body double answering the door.

"Hey, what are you doing here?" He looked up and saw Kate standing on the staircase, draped in a white terry cloth bathrobe with her hair wrapped in a towel. Why did he feel like he was interrupting something?

"I better get moving." Derek pulled a shirt off an ironing board set up in the kitchen and passed Brody at the bottom of the stairs. "I hope we can get together later." He patted Brody's shoulder and ran up the stairs. "Better get some clothes on, young lady," he said as he passed Kate.

"So, what brings you here so early?" Kate stopped on the bottom step and rested her arms on Brody's shoulders. She gave him a brief hug and a tender kiss, and he felt stupid for ever doubting her.

"As it turns out—" he held up the bag "—I still owe you breakfast."

"What's in it?" She lifted it from his hands and looked inside. "Aw, you brought your own pancake mix and syrup. Sweet." She brushed a kiss across his lips and took him by the hand, leading him into the kitchen. "So, you met Derek." She filled a mug with coffee and handed it to him. "What do you think?"

"Seems like a nice guy." He tried to hide a smirk behind the brim of the cup, but was unsuccessful. "I just wasn't expecting a Calvin Klein underwear model to open the door."

Kate pulled the towel off her head and let it drop to the floor as she shook out her damp hair. She tugged on his jacket, signaling for him to take it off. "He's a great guy and I think you'll really like him, once you get used to his ridiculous looks."

"Are you trying to make me jealous?" He unlaced the sash on her robe and glided his hands around her bare body. "Because it's working."

"Maybe." She snaked her hands under the tail of his shirt and ran her nails up his back. "I like it when you get all hot and bothered."

"Well, then, you should really be enjoying yourself right now."

"Oh, I am." She giggled and pulled him in tight, opening her lips to his. It had only been, what, eight hours since they'd made love before falling asleep last night, and he wanted her like it had been much, much longer. Slowly, she lifted his shirt higher, touching her skin to his.

"I've got to head out." Kate scrambled to cover herself when Derek strolled into the kitchen. She quickly tied the sash on her robe, and Brody turned away, pulling down his shirt at lightning speed. Derek kept his eyes locked on the coffee pot while he filled his travel mug, pretending as if he hadn't just walked in on some serious foreplay. "I should be back around six."

Kate kept her eyes cast on the floor, a deafening quiet hung in the air, as she tried to hide her obvious embarrassment. If Derek had been a few minutes later, who knows what he would have walked in on.

Derek cleared his throat, breaking the silence. "Brody, it was good to meet you. Maybe I'll see you later." He tapped a kiss on Kate's cheek before heading toward the door.

As soon as he was gone, Brody pulled Kate back into his arms. She opened her robe and snuggled tight against him.

"Are you sure I have nothing to worry about with that guy?"

"He's harmless."

"You know I'm kind of selfish when it comes to my woman."

"Oh, so I'm your woman, huh?"

"Something like that."

"You're staking your claim on me, is that it?"

"That's the idea."

TWENTY-THREE

Kate tucked her feet behind her and rested her elbow on the arm of the sofa, sipping her second cup of coffee while savoring the quiet. It was only nine o'clock and she'd been up since six, having breakfast with Derek and seeing him off. After his morning training session in Clarksburg, he was heading home to DC. She was fending off a mild headache, a remnant of last night's trip to the Brass Rail where she and Derek met up with Liza, Brody, and Riley.

As soon as Derek was out the door she had a call from Riley asking her to help sell poinsettias at tonight's Christmas parade and street fair in town. Then came a call from the rehabilitation center reminding her of the patient release meeting this afternoon. Gram was scheduled to come home Monday morning. When she had first come to Highland Springs, her intentions were to stay until Gram got home and settled, but since she'd taken the leave of absence, she was happy she was staying until Christmas. The grand opening of the community center was the tenth of December and Misty Mountain Brewery was having a holiday open house on the thirteenth. She couldn't leave town before then.

A rumbling came from outside and she recognized immediately the sound of Brody's truck pulling in the drive. She scurried to the front door, and sighed against the jam, drinking in his sexy masculinity. He was dressed in his faded, stained jeans and worn navy coat, with his hair tucked under the dirty ball cap, and she couldn't think of any man more handsome.

"Good morning, sweetheart." He gave her a tender kiss while his large hand palmed her bottom. "How's the headache?" He handed her an insulated cup from Sit and Sip as they backed into the foyer.

"How did you know I had a headache?"

"I saw how much beer you drank. You have a headache."

She dropped her head against his chest and giggled. "You're right."

"I also brought you an energy drink." He pulled a narrow aluminum can out of his pocket. "Didn't know your preferred hangover remedy."

"I think you're my preferred hangover remedy."

He scooped her up, lifting her off the floor, and rewarded her with a lingering kiss. She could get used to this each morning. After a few moments, he placed her gently back on the floor and said, "You're keeping me from my work. I planned to finish the ramp today."

"Sorry. I didn't mean to distract you."

"Believe me, you're my favorite kind of distraction, but—"

"But, you need to finish. I have a meeting at the rehab place today. Gram comes home on Monday." She turned him around to face the door and gave him a hearty swat on his back pocket, propelling him forward. "You're on the clock. Get to it."

"This one's called Jingle Bells. See the pink speckles on the red blooms?" Riley was trying to educate Kate on all the varieties of poinsettias available at the Beautiful Blooms booth, but she'd already forgotten most of what she'd been told. Her mind wasn't on petal colors, but on Brody, the man who was making her reconsider all her plans. Where in the world was he anyway?

"I'll just turn the customers over to you if they have any specific questions, okay?" Kate said as she scanned the thickening crowd.

"That works. I'm going to get some hot chocolate. Want some?"

"No, thanks." Her response came out with a white puff. It was bitter cold out with an occasional burst of snow flurries in the air, but that hadn't stopped the huge crowd from attending the annual winter event.

She tapped out a quick text to Brody to find out his whereabouts. Before she could hit send, two strong hands gripped her shoulders.

"There you are." She snuggled into his arms, instantly warmed by his presence. "I was just about to text you. Where'd you disappear to this afternoon?"

"As soon as I finished the ramp I went home, did some writing." She tilted her chin and rose on her toes, ready to receive a hello kiss. "Miss me?"

"Terribly," she murmured against his kiss.

"Good."

She tucked her cold hands in his back pockets, bringing him tightly against her as he warmed her with his lips. "As soon as Riley gets back, we can walk around a little."

"I've got to help Tucker at the beer truck." He gave her another kiss and draped his arm around her shoulder, guiding her behind the poinsettia table. "But I'll come get you when I'm finished."

As he leaned in for a goodbye kiss, an older gentleman clothed in an oversized ski coat and knit cap approached them at the booth.

"Hello, Brody. How've you been? Haven't seen you in years." The man shook Brody's hand enthusiastically.

"Hi, Mr. Perkins. Good to see you. I hear you're about to retire."

"Sure am. Packing it in by spring and moving to South Carolina to be near my daughter."

"Kate." Brody turned to her, gripped her coat sleeve. "This is Marvin Perkins. He's an attorney here in town."

"So nice to meet you," She shook his hand, surprised at the still-strong grip.

"Oh, I think you're the young lady I've heard about. You're a fellow attorney, right?"

"Yes, I am." It always amazed her that people knew about her, were talking about her, as if her appearance in town was big news.

"Right. I think it was Travis who told me about you." Marvin nudged Brody and pointed his finger at her. "He even suggested I talk to you about buying out my practice."

"Did he?" Another surprise for her.

"There sure will be a void when you close your doors, sir. Don't you do a lot of work for the college?" Brody said.

She listened closely as Marvin and Brody carried on their conversation, discussing the merits of his practice, wondering if she would be happy in a small town practice of her own. Did Brody even want her to stay? They'd grown so close and, at this point, she couldn't image leaving Highland Springs.

"Well, you two, I better get down to the beer truck before it's all gone." Marvin patted Brody on the back and shook his hand. "Kate, it was great to meet you. Stop in sometime and we'll chat."

"I'll do that. Thank you." She watched Marvin hobble down the street, wondering once more if she could do it. Would the cases be interesting enough? Would she feel challenged? She imagined she'd work a lot less than her usual eighty-hour week. "He seemed like a nice man."

"He is."

"I think I'll stop in and talk to him about his practice," she said. When she looked up at Brody he was staring at her, eyes furrowed with a wrinkled brow.

"Really?"

"Yeah, it might be interesting to hear what it's like to practice in this quaint little town. You know, discover a typical day in Marvin Perkins's life."

"That's a great idea; you should." And like that, his brow smoothed, and a smile stretched across his face. "You just might like the idea."

"I just might." She draped her arms around his neck and tingled from his warm, tender kiss.

***

Brody weaved in and out of the crowd, milling around the street blocked to traffic after the parade had gone through. Local artisans and shop owners had set up booths along the two-block stretch and festive chatter was in the air. He could see Kate working at the poinsettia booth looking comfortable, like she belonged. He had relieved Tucker at the beer truck for a few minutes and was now hoping to steal her away.

"Hey, beautiful." He snuck up behind her, making her jump. He shifted her scarf so he could nuzzle the creamy skin at the base of her neck. "Can you get away for a little while?"

"What's in it for me?" She angled her head, giving him free access to her neck and shoulder.

"That's a loaded question. What did you have in mind?"

"Hot chocolate and a pepperoni roll."

He stopped his tender assault and tipped his head around to meet her eye-to-eye. "You'd choose hot chocolate and a pepperoni roll over what I'm offering?"

"Right now? Yes. I'm cold and hungry." She wrapped her arm around him and brushed her icy lips against his ear. "I'll take what you're offering later."

He chuckled and enveloped her in a smothering hug. "Deal." As much as he tried to deny it to himself, he was in love with Kate. Until she officially told him she was going back to DC, he would relish every second with her and hope she might consider staying.

They'd only taken a few steps when a heavyset woman with shockingly red hair stopped Kate in the street.

"You're Kate McNamara. Right?"

"Yes?" Kate tightened her grip on his hand.

"I'm Ashley's sister, Tiffany." All at once, Tiffany grabbed Kate by the shoulders and hoisted her against her ample bosom. "I'll never be able to thank you enough." Tiffany's face quickly dampened with tears as she kept Kate in a crushing embrace. "If it weren't for you, I don't know what would've happened."

Seeing Kate's alarm, Brody used his shoulder to open a gulf between the two women. Kate stepped back and straightened her coat while mouthing *it's okay* to Brody.

"How is Ashley? Has she been in touch?" Kate asked.

206 | LEIGH FLEMING

"No, of course not. You know how it works. But I got word yesterday that she and the kids are safely to their destination." Tiffany gathered Kate's hands in her thick ones, fighting back tears. "They said you filed for divorce for her. No one ever stepped in for Ashley like you have. I just hope someday she'll be able to thank you herself."

"She thanked me that night. I was glad to help."

"Bless you, Kate." Kate was jerked forward in another bear hug, but managed to shrug her shoulders at Brody. Tiffany finally released her and sniffled her goodbyes.

Totally confused, he watched her waddle away and then caught a satisfied grin on Kate's face. "Do you mind telling me what that was all about?"

"Let's keep walking." She slipped her arm through his and led him in the direction of the food truck. "Remember our auction date, when you invited yourself to stay over, but I said I had something to do?"

"The disappointment is seared in my memory."

She gave his shoulder a nudge. "I think I've more than made up for that night, don't you?"

"Hmm. Not quite."

"Anyway…" She chuckled and shook her head. "I helped Ashley and her kids—you know from the Thanksgiving dinner? I helped them escape that night. I drove her to Beckley to meet up with a sponsor with the battered women's network in the area. They run a sort of Underground Railroad, helping women escape to secret host families outside the region."

"Why didn't you tell me?" He guided her under a lamp post away from the throng.

"It had to stay confidential. I know I could trust you, but didn't want to take a chance. Her husband was at work and we couldn't risk him getting word she was leaving. If he had returned while I was there, he probably would have killed her and me."

"You took a big risk."

"After meeting her at the Thanksgiving dinner, I couldn't sleep imagining what she must be going through. I decided not to call Child Protective Services, afraid they'd take her kids away, so I handled it myself."

"And you've filed divorce papers on her behalf? Can you do that?"

"I can and I did. I'm licensed in West Virginia. Her husband was none too happy. Apparently, he got violent, trashed a bunch of equipment at work, and was thrown in jail. Best place for him."

Brody gathered her against his chest, thankful she was alright. This was just the kind of legal help she could provide if she stayed. By the look on her face and the determination in her voice, he could see the pride she felt in helping this woman.

"I'm impressed. Really." He tipped her chin up with his knuckle. "That was very generous of you and I'm sure Ashley will always appreciate it."

"I have to say, helping her start a new life has probably been the most rewarding thing I've ever done."

"Without even trying you've got a small practice of your own started here in Highland Springs." He pecked a kiss on her nose. "You've helped Ashley, you read over Tucker's crap-load of papers." He tipped his forehead towards hers. "And you gave him very wise counsel, I might add. If you should ever consider sticking around, I think maybe we can keep you busy here."

"And I do like staying busy." Their foreheads vibrated with her laughter. Maybe his suggestion was too heavy handed, but damn it, he didn't want her to leave. He never intended it to happen, but he was in love with her. She originally planned to stay until Virginia was settled and he prayed it would be much longer than that. *Stay here with me and you'll stay busy, in more ways than one.*

***

Coffee pot off, dishwasher started, lights out…Kate walked through the kitchen, taking a quick glance at the dining room, which would soon be converted to Gram's temporary sleeping quarters, before grabbing her coat off the back of the blue plaid chair. Brody was on his way over. They were going to the medical supply store in Clarksburg to arrange for a hospital bed for Gram's arrival home on Monday. Her cell phone vibrated in her back pocket.

"Hello?" she answered on the second ring.

"Kate. It's Grant Goldman."

"Oh, um, hello."

"It's been a long time. How's your grandmother?" He boomed into the phone, his voice upbeat, jovial.

"She's, um, better." Her vocal chords tightened from the surprise. She hadn't expected to hear from the managing partner. She cleared her throat and said, "Much better, thank you. In fact, she'll be home from rehab Monday."

"Great news. Glad to hear it." If she didn't know better, she'd think she was talking to her long lost buddy, he was downright jaunty. "So, listen, Kate, we've had some changes around here since you've been gone, moved some people, and I was hoping we could meet to discuss it. When will you be back in the District?"

"Well, as I said, my grandmother will be home Monday, but I told Patrick I planned to stay a little longer to make sure she can live on her own, until after Christmas."

"I'm not sure I want to wait that long. Let me just tell you where we stand."

Her legs suddenly turned to jelly and she plopped down on the sofa; her head pulsated and her heart pounded. Surely Mr. Goldman called because he wanted to let her down easy. She didn't think she'd feel so deflated knowing she didn't get the promotion, but she did.

"It's been brought to my attention, in fact to the attention of several of the partners, that maybe we haven't done enough to recognize your contributions to this firm. You've been unfairly overlooked for a promotion—a very well deserved promotion—and we've put you through an unnecessary trial period for one open senior associate spot."

"Oh?" Like a helium balloon suddenly released, she slumped against the sofa back, her head floating in confusion.

"Like I said that day before you left, your performance on the District Hospital case was outstanding. I dare say we might not have won if it weren't for you and the entire team."

"Thank you." Where was this going? Would he just get to the point?

"In fact, we're now ready to offer you the promotion you so richly deserve, including a bigger office and a fifty-thousand-dollar bonus. And the partners all agree you can be sure to make full partner well ahead of schedule."

"Um." She was speechless, literally speechless. She'd thrown that expression around plenty of times, but at this moment her mind couldn't form the words to send to her mouth to speak. He was handing her the dream she'd had since the first day she entered law school. It was too good to be true.

"Kate, are you still there?"

"Yes, I'm sorry about that. I'm just very surprised."

"You shouldn't be. All the partners acknowledge your hard work and outstanding abilities."

"I appreciate that and appreciate your giving me the senior associate position."

"As far as we're concerned, you were the only person who truly deserved the promotion and I'm happy you were patient with us while we made the decision. You have an amazing future with the firm."

"Mr. Goldman, I don't know what to say. I'm honored." Her goal of making partner had just leapt forward by several years. She couldn't stand still. She had to move. She rushed to the kitchen and back again, turning circles in a frenetic dance, unable to control her excitement.

"We're the ones who should be honored. Even while you've been away, taking care of your grandmother, you've managed to produce more in a day than some associates produce in two. You're a great asset to this firm and deserve this promotion. Call me when you're back in town."

"Thank you so much. I'm thrilled. You've made my day. I'll be in touch soon."

She halted the celebratory shuffle and dropped to the sofa with a satisfactory "Yes!" Finally, she was feeling validated, even appreciated. She squeezed her temples to calm her pounding head, smiling so hard her cheeks hurt. She took a deep breath, noticing a tingle up her spine. She looked behind her and found Brody standing inside the foyer, hands on his hips and a decided scowl on his face.

"Sorry. You didn't answer when I knocked and the door was unlocked."

"It's okay." She rose from the sofa and crossed the wide divide between them—a divide that had nothing to do with the size of the room. "The firm called. I got the promotion. I guess you heard?"

"Yeah, I heard." He stuffed his hands in his pockets with a shrug of his shoulders. "It's what you'd been hoping for. Congratulations."

"Brody, listen." She stretched her hand toward him as he took a small step back. "I'm sorry. You know how much this promotion means to me. It's what I've worked for—for so long."

"I know and I'm glad for you." His sweet smile didn't match the dullness of his gaze. "It's great. Really." He drew her into his arms, but she felt she was hugging a mannequin—no warmth or strength lay in his touch. "I, um, had a call from Tucker on my way over. There's an issue at the brewery." He cleared his throat and tucked his hands in his pockets, keeping his eyes tipped downward. "You think you can take care of getting your grandmother's equipment on your own?"

"Sure. Are we okay?"

"You bet. I'll see you later."

TWENTY-FOUR

"Hi, Dad. I'm back again. Twice in less than a month. That might just be a record for me."

After Brody had gone, Kate couldn't sit still, couldn't focus on anything, so she decided to order Gram's bed over the phone. Instead of driving to Clarksburg, she made a trip out to the cemetery. A woodpecker drilled frantically into a nearby tree with overhanging branches that shaded the plot. Until recently, Kate felt like that bird, pecking way at a heavy workload, with little to show for it. Now, she was offered the promotion, validation for all her hard work, but her earlier exhilaration was waning.

"So, I got the promotion…but you already knew that. I should be happy, right? I was happy earlier. Why am I not happy now?" She dropped to the damp grass and tucked her legs behind her. "The thing is I'm starting to really love it here. I miss Annie and Derek, but I have new friends and I've helped a couple of people with their legal issues. Ashley and her kids are safe and waiting for her divorce to be final. I looked over Tucker and Brody's offer and advised them on the beer company's buy-out, and I think they're happy with their decision to pass." She tugged a handful of frosty grass and let the blades trickle through her fingers. Brody's disappointed expression continuously flashed in her mind.

Across the tombstone-dotted knoll, an older couple was huddled together in front of a grave, appearing to gain warmth and comfort from each other as the winter wind blew. How long had they been married, she wondered, and whose grave were they visiting? She quickly wiped an errant tear dangling on the end of her nose.

"I'm in love. That's the real problem." She threw back her head and sniffed deeply, the leafless limbs blurring above her. "Brody lives here. This is his home. I doubt he would ever leave Highland Springs." Like heavy clouds parting to bright sunshine, for the first time she could clearly see the simple truth: she wanted to stay. "But my career in DC is…I've worked too hard to give it up."

She stood and faced John Tyler McNamara's headstone, hugging herself against the cold and confusion. "Tell me what to do, Dad. I wish you could give me a sign or come to me in my dreams or something—anything to help me make the right decision."

Since Kate hadn't heard a booming voice from the clouds telling her what to do about her career, she decided to confer with Gram instead. Her grandmother had been home two hours and they were contentedly sitting at the kitchen table, drinking tea as the old rooster-shaped clock ticked out the seconds. She hadn't seen Brody since he'd overheard her news, but he'd called and texted, and she felt everything was as good as it could be between them. It still didn't stop the burning worry in her stomach—what was she going to do?

"So, what do you think I should do? I mean, I'd be stupid to pass up this opportunity, right? Who would pass up such an offer?"

"Well, now, honey, if what you tell me is—"

"I mean, Gram, come on, it's Bell, Greenburg, and Goldman, the most prestigious firm in the District. Who would even think of giving that up? I didn't kill myself to be in the top ten percent of my class and fight for that Federal clerkship after graduation for nothing. I had a plan, goals, a path to partnership."

"That's true, Katherine, but—"

"And, it's unfolding exactly like I pictured it—even sooner maybe. I need to accept the promotion, right?"

"Honey, take a breath." The warmth of Gram's hands grasping hers settled Kate's heart and calmed her frenzied thoughts. "Everything you say is true. You've worked hard and deserve that promotion. But you've also told me you love it here, too. It pained me to see how exhausted and stressed you were the first few weeks you were here. You hardly had time for anything in your life but work. Couldn't you work here? Start your own practice or go into practice with one of the firms here or in Clarksburg?"

"I've thought of that—I have. But what keeps holding me back is BGG. Most people coming out of law school would give their left arm for the position I have." She dropped her head in her hands and plunged her fingers through her hair, tugging the strands at the roots. "The other thing is, I keep thinking about Dad and Mom. Mom has encouraged me, has pushed me to be successful in my career, and Dad...well...he wanted me to be the best. I don't want to disappoint him."

"Honey, I've tried to tell you that's not what your father expected. He would just want you to be happy, and from what I've seen you haven't been happy until recently."

"I don't know." She grabbed her half-full mug and trudged to the living room where she plopped on the couch. Strewn across the coffee table were three photo albums—one opened to a page of baby snapshots when Kate was about two. "Gram, why do you have all these photo albums out?"

"Feeling nostalgic I guess." With remarkable speed for a nearly eighty-year-old woman, Gram crossed the room unaided by her walker and sat on the sofa beside Kate, taking one of the books into her lap. "Look how pretty you were in your Easter dress. I made that for you, did you know that?"

"I did. In fact, I'm pretty sure Mom still has that hanging in a closet at home. It's beautiful."

"Oh, and look here. This is your first trip to the zoo." Gram tapped her finger against the clear cover at a picture of Kate reaching toward a giraffe's curious face. "Who's holding you? That doesn't look like your daddy's arm, but it's sure not your momma's."

"Let me see." Kate took the album out of Gram's hands and tilted the page away from the lamp's glare. "It might be Uncle Bill. Remember, he came to visit a lot when we lived near Seattle." Flipping through the pages, she smiled at the happy little girl in the pictures and wondered if she'd ever have children. If she went back to the DC firm, she probably wouldn't have a family for a long time. She slammed the book shut and closed her eyes, shaking her head at the confusion she was feeling.

"Honey, you can take this album home with you if you want or any of the albums. I've got plenty of pictures of you."

It was true. Any open wall space had been filled with portraits and candids of Kate at various times of her life. There was no bigger cheerleader in her life than Gram. She gathered her grandmother in her arms and tucked her chin into Gram's shoulder, drawing in the sweet, powdery scent of her. If only she could be as stalwart and resolute as Gram. Maybe she'd be happier with her decision.

TWENTY-FIVE

Blustering winds rattled the windows, tiny ice pellets pinged on the roof, but nature's sounds were overshadowed by the lusty bellows and heavy breathing behind the bedroom door. Kate collapsed on Brody, propped against the headboard by a mound of pillows, and expelled one long breath against the nape of his neck.

"Remind me to send a thank you note to Darla." He released a hearty chuckle, pressing his warm face against her ear. She leaned up and he captured her mouth, pressing his lips against hers. "Thank god she agreed to stay with Virginia tonight."

"We won't have to wake up before the sun tomorrow." She snuggled against him, splaying her hand across his ribs, with a contented sigh. Just like she'd predicted, ever since Gram had gotten home, he ate dinner with them every night, and after Gram went to bed, he would sneak upstairs with Kate, being sure to leave in the early morning before Gram awoke.

Being with Brody felt so right, so natural, so where-she-needed-to-be. Many times, during those quiet early morning hours—just like now—when they lay skin-to-skin, the words "I love you" teetered on the tip of her tongue, and she had so desperately hoped he felt the same. But after days and days of internal debate and consideration, she had decided to accept the promotion. Tomorrow she was heading back to DC—she just needed to find the courage to tell him.

"What are you thinking about?" He tipped onto his side and brushed his knuckles across her cheek.

"Nothing really." She rolled onto her back and the dark wood beams traversing the ceiling blurred in front of her.

"Nothing?" Brody tucked a strand of hair behind her ear and let his hand glide softly down the side of her neck. "I can hear your gears grinding. Talk to me."

With a heavy sigh, she rolled to her side, facing the handsome "mountain man" she'd come to love more than she ever thought possible. "Do you ever have regrets?"

"Regrets?"

"About coming home. The decision to leave New York and Nashville?"

"No regrets. I'm happy here. It's where I belong."

"But all that you've worked for over the years is in Nashville."

"That's true, but the great thing about songwriting is I can do it anywhere."

"Right, you can do it anywhere." Would he be willing to do it in Washington, DC? Could he be happy there?

"Kind of like law—you can do it anywhere." He twisted his finger in her hair, wrapping her dark locks around his knuckle, and hummed a few notes.

"Something you've been working on?" She brushed a few wayward strands off his forehead and touched her lips to his.

"Yeah, while I was driving to the brewery these chords came to me. I've got some lyrics that I think will work with it."

"A song about driving a truck and drinking beer?"

"Nah." He let the strands unwind from his finger and drew her against his chest. "Better than that."

"This is the best place for you—songwriting—here in Highland Springs."

"And living here—yeah." As his hand stroked feather-light down her back, she braced herself for what was still unspoken. "And you want to practice law in DC." She released the breath she'd been holding and sagged deeper against him. He said the words she hadn't had the courage to say. Before she could stop them, large, angry tears streamed from her eyes. Why couldn't they be together? It wasn't fair.

He tightened his hold on her and ran his hand through her hair. "Come on sweetheart, don't cry. We both knew it was temporary."

"But it doesn't make it any easier. I knew this wouldn't end well."

"Do you regret our time together? Would you have preferred we stayed enemies?"

Kate swiped away her tears and rose onto her elbow, looking at the amusement on Brody's face.

"Enemies? I don't remember us being enemies…per se."

"Yeah, you only bit my head off the first time you met me."

"Well, that was different. You were breaking too many laws to mention." Brody chuckled as he enveloped her in his arms and planted a kiss against her temple. *The biggest crime of all was stealing my heart.*

"Look, we both held up our end of the bargain. You learned to relax." He pinched his thumb and finger together. "A little. And you've given me incredible inspiration. I'm writing again and you got your promotion."

"And you'd never consider moving—"

"To DC? I've got the farm, the brewery—"

"You're right. I know." She snuggled her head against his chest, drinking in the familiar scent of him, his soft hair tickling her cheek. Leaving him would be the hardest thing she'd ever done. "I'm going to miss you, that's all."

He rolled her onto her back and stopped her with that soul-deep gaze of his, the one she'd become so familiar with, the one that gave her a delicious shiver every time. "I'll never forget these past few weeks. They've changed my life. You've—"

"Changed me, too." An errant tear escaped down her temple and he brushed it away with the back of his hand.

"We're going to be okay," he said as his tender lips kissed her for the last time.

TWENTY-SIX

Kate snapped her laptop closed and spun her leather chair to face the floor-to-ceiling window in her new office. The illuminated Capitol dome glowed in the distance as DC commuters scurried home before the impending snow storm. They were calling for six to eight inches by midnight and she figured she had at least another hour before the flakes began to fall. The usual hum of activity outside her office door had died down when the support staff joined in the mass exodus back to the suburbs. Most of the time she liked the quiet that settled in after the office cleared out, but tonight she couldn't quiet her mind, couldn't focus on the brief she'd been writing. It had been a week since she'd last heard from Brody. With each day, there had been less and less contact. She arrived at the only verdict she could—they were officially over. Mindlessly, she swiped a tear and rotated back to the work strewn across her desk.

Her cell phone vibrated against the mahogany desk and she noticed an incoming call from Annie. "Hey, are you coming home early? I made vegetable soup, banana nut bread, and a batch of brownies. You know—get-snowed-in food."

"I wasn't going to, but since you made get-snowed-in brownies, I guess I better."

She wasn't getting any work done as it was, so why not join in the city stampede before the snow hit?

Stuffed beyond good sense after an expertly prepared comfort food dinner, Kate stretched out across the sofa, hearing the muffled sound of Annie on the phone in her room. There were equal benefits and disadvantages to having a roommate like Annie—she was an amazing cook who took all the burden of food preparation from Kate, but if it weren't for the fact that she rarely made it home for meals, Kate could easily grow to the size of a grizzly bear. The last time she felt this physically satiated was at Gram's.

She grabbed the pink photo album off the coffee table and flipped through the pages of her childhood. When she made it to the last page, she started again at the beginning with the eight-by-ten portrait of her father, mother, and herself as a baby. She rubbed her hand over the picture and found a thickness beneath it. "There's something behind this picture." She turned the page, but only found another eight-by-ten. Once more, Kate rubbed her hand over the photo, convinced something was behind the photos. She opened the clear sleeve, separating the back-to-back photos, and found a small envelope tucked between the pictures. She reached in and pinched it between two fingers.

To Katherine—on the day of your birth.

Shock waves racked her body when she recognized her father's hand-writing. She sat up and perched on the edge of the cushioned couch. "What is this?" Her hands quivered as she gently lifted the envelope flap, drawing the folded sheet from inside.

Dear Katherine (or maybe I'll call you Katie),

The nurse just took you back to the nursery and your momma is sound asleep. I'm supposed to be taking a nap, but I had the urge to write you a letter. I'm not sure how or if I'll ever give it to you, but I just wanted to say a few things before life gets crazy.

First, I want to tell you I love you. Seven months ago, when your momma told me she was pregnant, the last thing I thought I'd feel is love for you. But I do. By now you know we had you when we were young—too young—but the way I see it, God just hurried us along, that's all. I fell in love with your momma the first day of our senior year when she walked into our English class. She was the hot new girl in town and I swore I'd make her mine. Well,

I did and I got you in the bargain. That's okay though. As soon as I held you in my arms today, I was done for. I'm already wrapped around your pink little finger. I promised you then and there I would be the best daddy I could be and I'd love your momma until the day I die. That's the best I can offer under the circumstances.

I guess this is the part where I tell you all the things I wish for you as you grow up. My basketball coach used to tell us all the time: "Be your best self." I'm not sure what he meant by that because he sure yelled at us all the time no matter how hard we played. But I like that saying now that I'm a daddy. I think I'll use that line on you in the future. To me it means give everything you do your best effort, be kind to others, be satisfied with what the Lord gives you, and always follow your heart. I had big plans of going to WVU, majoring in engineering, and making a boatload of money. It didn't turn out that way, but I'm okay about it. Instead, I got you and your momma, and the two of you are more precious than gold to me.

More than anything I want you to grow up healthy, happy, and loved. Your momma and I will do the best we can to make all of that come true while you're young, but someday you'll be on your own. No matter what you choose to do with your life, I'll support you and be proud of you. Just remember to always be your best self and follow your heart. Everything will be just fine.

Love,

Your daddy

The blue ink blurred as tears flowed down her cheeks. She finally got through the letter and collapsed against the sofa pillow.

"Be my best self—not 'be the best.'" Kate hiccupped a sob into her fist. "That's what he always said."

Her dad had answered her—just like she'd asked him to at the cemetery. All she ever wanted was some kind of sign or message from her dad, and here it was, tucked behind a photo all these years. He said to follow her heart. He told her exactly what to do. Why did she feel like it was too late?

"Are you okay?" Annie placed her hand on Kate's back and leaned in close. "What's wrong?"

"It's that damned song. Why do they have to play it every Thursday night?" Kate had her elbows on the table and her hands pressed to her ears. It had been a week since she'd found her father's letter and she still hadn't done anything remotely close to "following her heart." And each time she met Annie and Derek for Trivia Night, the DJ played *Trivial* as the games began.

"I thought maybe you were sick." Derek leaned back in the booth and took a long draw of his beer. "You look like hell."

"Thanks, Derek," Kate mumbled toward the table.

"God, Derek, do you have to be so rude?" Annie rubbed her hand over Kate's back, bringing much needed calm to her jagged nerves. He was right; she did look like hell, felt like hell. Since being back she'd returned to her old fourteen-hour day schedule and high stress level, and couldn't remember the last time she'd had a full eight hours of sleep. When her head hit the pillow each night, instead of falling into a much-needed coma, she tossed and turned thinking about Brody and how much she missed him.

"Did he call today?" Annie's sweet, caring tone was like a knife in her chest.

"No." Kate barked. "He didn't call today or yesterday or the day before. In fact, Annie, I'm tired of you asking me if he called. He's not going to call. He hasn't called in a long time and I'm not expecting him to."

"Maybe you should call him," Annie said.

"Damn it, drop it, will you?" She turned to Annie and could see she'd hurt her, and felt terrible. Annie didn't deserve her wrath. "I'm sorry, but you have to let this go." She softened her harsh tone and squeezed Annie's hand. "Let's just play. Here's the first question."

Kate recited the first question flashed on the wall-mounted monitor.

"What legendary female country singer—" She slumped against the back of the booth and shook her head. "Really?"

"What legendary female country singer is known as the Pride of Butcher Hollow?" Derek finished the question and looked to Kate.

"Why are you looking at me?" she asked.

"Figured you might know something about it, seeing as you—"

"Banged a country songwriter? Is that what you were going to say?"

"Come on, Kate, it was more than that," Annie said.

She took a long drink from her lukewarm beer and slammed the mug on the thick, wooden table. "Well, it's not like we sat around talking about country singers."

"What did you talk about?" Derek pushed his beer aside and folded his arms on the table, drilling his crystal blue eyes into her. She'd known him long enough to recognize when he either had something to say or expected her to spill some information.

"Exactly what are you asking? Is there a specific answer you're looking for?" She pushed her beer aside and mimicked his posture, propping her crossed arms on the table.

"It's just you've been kind of vague about what drove you back to DC. The last time I was in Highland, you and Brody seemed kind of tight."

"My job, remember? Besides, it's none of your business."

"Wasn't it Loretta Lynn?" Annie suggested in a singsong voice. "Remember that old movie about her?" Her eyes sparkled and she looked expectantly at Kate and Derek, though neither one broke their stare. Her attempt to lighten the heavy mood wasn't working.

"So, you're telling me I'm only entitled to select information from you. Our long-standing friendship has its limits," Derek said.

"I guess I'll write down Loretta Lynn." Annie penciled in the answer as Kate stared at Derek.

"It does when it comes to my personal life," Kate said.

"Interesting. It's never stopped you or Annie from sticking your noses into my personal life, has it? Who needs nagging sisters when I've got you two?"

"How did I get dragged into this?" Annie looked from Derek to Kate. "If Kate doesn't want to talk about it, I think we should respect that."

"Thank you, Annie," Kate said.

"Every week I sit here with the two of you, listening to Annie whine about shit Kip did and listening to you whine about your boss or your client or how tired you are," Derek said.

"Kip hasn't done anything lately, I'll have you know." Annie drew herself up and lifted her chin. "He's just about perfect."

"Aren't you the least bit concerned? Look at her—" Derek directed his question to Annie, but threw his hand out in Kate's direction. "She's got dark circles under her eyes, looks like a stick figure, and is paler than my white shirt. How much weight have you lost?" He leaned across the table and glared at Kate.

She blinked back tears as she looked at Derek's face, only inches from hers. He was right. Theirs was not a typical guy-girl friendship, but more like brother-sister. He did listen to her problems and always offered sensible advice from his male perspective. Since she'd been back, she had avoided talking about Brody, finding it too painful to verbalize. Whenever Annie pressed for information as to what happened before she left, Kate did her best to explain it was a sensible, mutual decision, keeping the fact that she was hopelessly in love with him from entering the conversation. For all Annie or Derek knew, it was just a casual, non-committed relationship. In reality, that's exactly what it was—but not on her part.

"I'm sorry. I appreciate your concern." Kate grabbed Derek's hand but he didn't seem placated. "I am. It's hard to talk about Brody, that's all. It was hard leaving Highland Springs."

"Ah." Annie drew in a sharp breath and grabbed Kate's arm. "So, you did love him? I knew it. Why didn't you tell me? Why have you acted so nonchalant about it?"

"It was never supposed to get serious." She shrank into the corner of the booth and wrapped her arms around herself. "He didn't want me."

"Are you sure about that?" Derek asked, still leaning across the table. "That's not the vibe I got when I saw him on Tuesday."

"What?" Annie popped off the booth bench like a jack-in-the-box. "You saw Brody?"

Kate thought she was going to be sick. Her body started to quiver, afraid of what Derek was about to say. She had the same hopeful reaction as Annie, but couldn't bring herself to ask. Thank god Annie took over for her.

"Tell us everything," Annie said, settled back on the seat.

"Remember, I told you I had to go back to Clarksburg." He raised his brows at Kate, waiting for her recognition. She nodded, wishing he'd cut to the chase. "I got out of work a little early, so I decided to drive down to Highland Springs, have a drink at the Brass Rail."

Just hearing the name of that rustic bar where she had first kissed Brody made her yearn to be back there, back in his arms.

"I was there about fifteen minutes and Brody walked in."

"Was he with anyone?" Annie asked quietly, as if she were afraid of the answer.

"No, came in alone. I think maybe Liza had given him a call." Derek chuckled and lifted his beer mug to his lips. "He looks about as bad as you do. Has a shitty beard, hair brushing his collar." He flicked his hand below his closely cropped nape, showing them how long Brody's hair had grown. "Looks like he's been living out in the backwoods."

"Like he did when you first met him." Annie leaned against Kate and then wrapped her arm around her shoulders.

"Did he say anything?" Kate finally unlocked her vocal chords, praying Derek would give her a glimmer of hope.

"He asked about you. If I've seen you. How you're doing."

"And?" For once Kate was happy for Annie's impatient, inquisitive nature. Her voice had locked up again as tears threatened to fall.

"And I told him I haven't seen much of you except on Thursday nights, and that you were really tired and overworked."

"What did he say to that?" Annie asked.

"He said you're back in your element."

Kate's head sagged and she couldn't hold back the tears any longer. She grabbed the paper napkin on the table and pressed it to her nose, doing all she could not to let out a loud, embarrassing sob. Why couldn't he have said something like he wished she'd come back or he missed her or something, anything she could grab on to? She thought maybe after all these weeks apart, he would have come to realize he did love her after all. So much for wishful thinking.

"Listen to me." Derek reached across the table and pulled one of her hands free. "Listen. To. Me." He squeezed her hand tight, forcing her to look at him. "It's what he didn't say that I picked up on. The guy misses you. Wants you to come back."

"Stop it," she blurted between tears.

"I've been trained to read between the lines. Plus, I'm a guy. I know how we think." He tugged on her hand once again. "He's hurting. I can see it. Heard it in his voice. You need to talk to him."

"What could I possibly say that he'd want to hear?" She sniffled and wiped her eyes and nose with the napkin. "I wouldn't know where to start."

"Tell him you're miserable, that your job sucks, that you made the wrong decision. You'd move to Highland in a heartbeat if he'd just say the word."

"He's right, Kate." Annie went back to rubbing Kate's back and this time it actually started to work its magic. Her nurturing helped stop the flow of tears. Maybe Derek was right. She'd followed what she thought was the right path and she was miserable. The endless hours combing through evidence, depositions, testimony and constant research were making her crazy—and physically ill. Even now, thinking about going back into the office tomorrow morning at eight o'clock made her feel nauseated—a feeling she'd been having each morning for the past week. She had seriously considered quitting, regardless of the bonus and promotion.

"All I'm saying is—" Derek tipped up her chin with his knuckle, forcing her to look at him. "You look like you could use a little of Gram's home cooking and some rest. Why don't you go down to Highland Springs this weekend? And while you're there, why don't you go see him? You have nothing to lose."

She glanced over at Annie who replied with an enthusiastic nod and then she locked eyes with Derek once again. She drew strength from his confidence and agreed with a bob of her head. A weekend in Highland was exactly what she needed.

TWENTY-SEVEN

Gravel crunched under the rented Jeep's tires as Kate rolled slowly down the frost-covered lane. The sun's bright beam on the snowy field made it hard to see Brody's gray farmhouse ahead. A plume of smoke rose out of Liza's chimney, announcing she was home, as Kate drove past.

She had arrived in Highland Springs Friday evening, surprising Gram, and just as Derek had said, some of her grandmother's home cooking and a good night's sleep had made a world of difference. She had awoken this morning refreshed and relaxed, without the usual nausea she had been feeling for the past week. Just knowing she didn't have to go into the office had settled her nervous stomach. Gram had made a huge breakfast of eggs, pancakes, and sausage gravy, and Kate had eaten like it was her last meal. While sipping her second cup of coffee, Gram brought up the reason for her visit—something she'd kindly avoided the night before.

"Well, honey, it's time to spill it. What brought you back here so soon?"

"Gram, I'm hurt. Haven't you missed me?" She winked at her grandmother as she gathered their plates from the table.

"Of course, I've missed you, but whenever we talk you sound so busy. I didn't think you'd be able to get away."

"I missed you and that's why I'm here." She carried the coffee decanter to the table and refilled her grandmother's cup. "And I needed a little TLC." She went to the sink and filled it with hot soapy water. She looked out into the backyard and thought she'd seen Brody outside, stacking wood.

Of course, it had only been an apparition, one of many she was sure to have as she traveled around Highland Springs.

"You know you can always get that here." Gram patted Kate's chair. "Leave those dishes, honey. Come talk to me."

She wiped her hands on a towel and returned to the table, dropping with a heavy sigh onto her chair. She and her grandmother had always been close, even closer since her accident, and she so wanted to talk about the past two months. Her grandmother's wise counsel was what she needed.

"Gram." She shook her head, unable to speak. Her throat clogged with emotion and she was once again on the brink of tears—a condition which was becoming all too frequent.

"Take your time, honey. We've got all the time in the world."

She wadded a handful of tissues from the box always available on Gram's table and pressed them to her face. A steady stream of silent tears dampened her cheeks. After a few minutes, her vocal chords unlocked and she blurted out, "I'm miserable. I think I made a mistake."

"It's okay. Let it all out."

"I shouldn't have gone back to DC."

"You're not happy with your decision?"

With a vigorous shake of her head, she blurted, "I want to come home—I mean, come back—come back home."

"Oh, Katherine, honey." Gram climbed to her feet and pulled Kate against her soft belly, petting her hand through Kate's hair like she'd done since she was a child. "I hate seeing you so sad." Her grandmother's warm embrace and tender voice only made the tears fall harder. They stayed pressed to one another for several minutes until Kate was over the worst of her deluge.

"You can come home anytime you want. Your room is always made up for you."

"I don't know if I can come back. It will be too hard being in the same town as—"

"As Brody?" Gram stepped back and gathered Kate's face in her hands. "Have you talked to him lately?" She shook her head no and dabbed at a few stray tears. "Why don't you drive out to see him?"

"I don't know."

"I'm sure he'd like to see you."

"How do you know?" She sniffled and wiped her wet nose on the tissues.

"He's been by here a few times and always asks about you."

"Does he?"

"Every time."

When Kate had pulled out of her grandmother's drive ten minutes ago, she had been confident that this surprise visit with Brody would go well. Both Derek and Gram said he'd like to see her and when she left she was sure it was true. But the closer she got to his house, the more worried she became she was making a mistake. What if they had it wrong? What if he didn't want to see her or talk to her? What if he was happy with her gone? It wasn't like he'd begged her to stay. Would she have the nerve to tell him how she felt about him and her desire to move back to Highland Springs?

She pulled alongside the garage and cut the engine. She took a deep, steadying breath and climbed out of the truck, immediately hit with the cold, crisp wind blowing up from the valley. She walked toward the front porch, passing the window where she had so mischievously spied on Brody and chuckled at the memory. Walking across the porch, she quickly peered through the windows, but saw no one inside. The doorbell echoed throughout the house as she paced in a circle, waiting for him to answer. She rang again, but got the same unanswered reply.

As she rounded the corner to walk down the steps, she saw Loretta running up the lane, her brown speckled body streaking toward her, barking out a welcome with Liza following close behind. Her heart swelled against her ribs. She'd missed that dog so much—she didn't realize how much until now. And she'd missed Liza, too. In the short time she'd been in Highland Springs, she felt like they'd become real friends.

"Hey." Kate called out and waved to Liza, who was marching quickly up the drive. Loretta reached her first and jumped at Kate, landing her two front paws against her chest, nearly knocking her over. "Hey, Loretta. How're you doing, girl?" She rubbed the dog's ears with both hands and planted kisses on her long snout. "I've missed you, girl." Loretta's tail spun like a propeller at the end of her spine. Liza puffed white clouds of breath as she reached them.

"Liza, hey. It's so good to see you." She gently shoved Loretta's paws aside and stepped toward Liza.

"What are you doing here?" Kate dropped her outstretched arms when she realized Liza wasn't happy to see her. Liza planted her feet wide and crossed her arms, glaring at Kate in a noticeably unfriendly manner.

"I, um, stopped by to see Brody."

"Why?"

A worried shiver ran down Kate's back as she looked at Liza, standing ramrod straight, glaring at her as if she were her enemy. It was unlike Liza to be so antagonistic. Since the first time they met, Kate had felt an instant liking, a strong connection with her, but this angry woman standing in front of her was a stranger.

"I was in town for the weekend and thought I'd say hi." She steeled her nerves and took a step closer. "Is something wrong?"

"Oh, I don't know. How's Washington? Happy to be back?"

"Not particularly." Liza cocked one perfectly shaped eyebrow at Kate as her mouth twisted into a wry pout. "Did I do something to upset you?"

"Maybe." Liza still hadn't moved, hadn't changed expression, and Kate was becoming very uncomfortable.

"I'm sorry if I upset you somehow." She wasn't up for a confrontation today and had a feeling she couldn't win if she tried. "Just let Brody know I stopped by, will you, please? Maybe we can get together tonight at the Brass Rail."

"He won't be there."

"Is he out of town?"

"He's in Nashville." News that Brody had returned to Nashville knocked the wind out of her sails. What happened to him *needing* to live in Highland Springs?

"Oh? When's he coming back?" she asked.

"Who knows?" Liza struggled and pursed her lips. "Things are going really well for him down there, he might never come back."

"He's doing well?"

"Better than ever. He's recording, writing, having a great time. It's good for him to be back to his old life. He's in a much happier place."

"I'm, um, glad to hear it."

"Yeah, he's back hanging with his old friends." Liza took a step closer, keeping her trance-like stare locked on Kate. "He's been spending a lot of time with Callie Starr."

"Callie Starr? The singer?" Kate thought she was going to be sick. Her knees weakened and Liza's face blurred in front of her. Callie Starr was the hottest—in every sense of the word—female country singer in the world. Not only was she a platinum-selling recording artist, but she was drop dead gorgeous.

"Yep, the very same." With a satisfied smirk, Liza turned and started walking back toward her cottage. She looked over her shoulder and tossed out one more comment, just to make sure she'd driven the knife in deep enough. "She's all he talks about when he calls."

How stupid could she be? She honestly believed Derek when he said Brody missed her. Liza's announcement confirmed exactly what she had suspected before she left. They were just a casual thing to him—nothing more. All those weeks tangled up in his arms meant nothing to him, while she kept falling deeper and deeper in love with him—fooling herself into believing he felt the same. Well, at least he never lied to her.

"Good for him." A sizzling rage boiled up inside Kate, but she wasn't sure if she was angry at Brody or herself for being so blind. She stomped toward her car and mumbled as she passed Liza. "I hope he's happy," she sneered.

234 | LEIGH FLEMING

"What did you think he was going to do? Sit around here night after night alone?" Liza turned around, her fury pinning Kate against the door. "You didn't want him, so why should you care?"

"What?"

"You couldn't get out of town fast enough. You were the one who left him."

"I left him? Is that what he said?" She drew up straight, using her height advantage to hover over Liza.

"You're back in DC, aren't you?"

"Yeah, I went back to DC, but it's not like he wanted me to stay or was willing to move." She turned her back on Liza and threw open the car door. "I guess he wanted me out of the way though, so he could get back to Nashville."

"You asked him?" Liza grabbed the door, wrenching it out of her grasp. "You asked him to come with you?"

"Yes, actually I did."

"And he said no? That dumbass." Liza kicked a chip of gravel with her boot and stomped away, muttering under breath. "He's moped around here ever since you left."

"How was I supposed to know that? He hasn't called in a long while. And he never said anything when he did."

"But have you called him?"

"Well, no, but—"

"Uh huh, I thought so. I thought you were different. Boy, did I read you wrong."

"I don't know what you're talking about."

"If you really wanted him to move to Washington, you could've made a bigger effort."

"This is ridiculous." Kate climbed in the SUV, slammed the door closed, and reached for the seat belt. She wasn't going to listen to this garbage. She knew the truth. Brody made it perfectly clear his life was here and nowhere else. It wouldn't have made a difference if she'd begged him. And why should she? The reality was he was content to send her back to Washington so he could swim with the big fish in Nashville.

"Ridiculous?" Liza's words were muffled against the frosted window. Kate pressed the button to lower the window, knowing Liza wasn't quite finished. "You two should be together. Did you ever consider staying in Highland Springs?"

"Don't put this on me. He didn't ask me to stay." Kate thumped her hand on the open window and then drew back inside, turning the ignition key. "Besides I guess I'm a little old-fashioned. I always thought the man was supposed to make the grand gesture."

"What? Like ride in on his charger and carry you away? Storm into your office and carry you out of there like…like…that old movie?"

"*An Officer and a Gentleman?*"

"That one."

"Absolutely. Why the hell not?" She dropped her head against the steering wheel and let out a heavy sigh. Yes, that's exactly what she wanted. She wanted Brody to storm into her office, tell her he couldn't live without her, and take her back to Highland Springs. She wouldn't put up a fight. Crazy fairytale endings like that had always been just that to her—crazy. But since falling in love with Brody and missing him so badly, she'd often found herself daydreaming he'd walk into her office and tell her he loved her.

"I guess living down here in this small town has made you soft. I always thought you were the type to take what she wants," Liza said.

Kate's eyes welled, but damned if she'd let Liza gloat over her tears. "I've got to go."

Throwing the SUV in drive, Kate spun gravel as she pulled away, determined to keep her tears at bay until she was out of Liza's sight. She didn't need Liza reporting to Brody that she had melted into a puddle of tears over him. He had moved on and there was no way she'd give him the satisfaction of knowing she'd made the wrong decision.

As soon as she crested the knoll and passed Liza's house, she let go the dam of tears she'd been holding back. She stopped the truck at the end of the lane and sobbed against the steering wheel. All hopes of rekindling their relationship and moving back to Highland Springs washed away as she cried sad, angry tears. What should she do now?

TWENTY-EIGHT

"It's about time you got here." Derek pecked a customary kiss on Kate's cheek and then resumed his seat in their usual booth at the Old Towne Tavern. Trivia Night and once again it looked as though they were the only two coming. "Where's Annie?"

"She texted me as I was leaving the office. There was no way she'd make it." Kate raised her hand to get the server's attention and then shrugged her coat off her shoulders.

"Why do we even bother anymore? She's working in Annapolis, you're leaving DC as soon as you can, and—"

"Stop, we can't end it tonight. We've been coming here every Thursday for over two years." She reached across the table and gathered his hands in hers. "Annie promised she'd be here next week. Enough changes are coming as it is. Can't we just keep this one little thing going until Annie and I move out of our apartment?"

"Don't start crying again, for Christ's sake. I can't take it." He lifted her hands to his lips, giving reassurance he'd only been teasing. It was true Derek had taken the brunt of her tears over the past two weeks. Since Annie was spending most of her time across the Chesapeake Bay at Kip's cabin while starting her new job in Annapolis, it had been Derek who spent every evening with Kate, helping her decide on her future.

"I'm not crying. I'm done crying. Time to move on." She picked up her menu and pretended to study the choices as if she had never read them before. Lately, she'd had little appetite, but tonight she would force herself to eat. Her dramatic weight loss wasn't good for her and she was determined to take better care of herself.

"Hi, guys." Their usual waitress stepped up to the table carrying a tray of double shot glasses filled with amber liquid. "We're giving out samples of a new beer we've started carrying. It's called Cupid's Cherry Ale." She extended her tray toward Kate, who shook her head, and then the server handed a glass to Derek. "Cute name, huh, since it's almost Valentine's Day."

"Great." Derek took a sip and raised his brows as he nodded his head and took another. "Really good. What company makes this?"

"Um, I think it's called Misty Mountain Brewery." Kate's head popped up from the menu and she shot a look at Derek, who had nearly spit out the beer.

"I'll be back in a minute to get your order."

"No way. What are the chances?" He pushed the glass aside and pinned her with his crystal blue eyes.

"Tucker told me after he turned down that big offer they were going to connect with a new distributor. They must now distribute in the DC area." Just hearing the name Misty Mountain made Kate's eyes go misty, but she was happy they were doing so well. Having their beer sold in Washington was sure to double their sales. She'd grown so fond of Tucker and was pleased the company was becoming an even bigger success.

"Okay, so what are you having?" Derek slid his menu toward the edge of the table and settled back against the booth.

"Grilled chicken on a bed of mixed greens." She smiled and dropped her menu on top of his. "Just what the doctor ordered." She winked at him while leaning her elbows on the table.

At exactly six o'clock, the theme song announcing the beginning of trivia started, but it wasn't what she had expected. Two weeks ago, she had asked if they'd play a different song than *Trivial* to start out the game, and the manager agreed. But tonight, they had reverted to the same old song.

"Are they playing *Trivial*?" Derek sat up straight and cocked his head to the side. "It sounds different than the regular version."

"It sounds…live."

"You're right." He stood up and looked over the high back of their booth. He rested his folded arms on the wood railing and let out a slow whistle. "Well, I'll be damned."

"Who is it? Someone famous?"

"You could say that." He dropped back in his seat with a crooked grin on his face. "You definitely know this singer."

"Ooh, this is exciting. Someone famous singing at the tavern." Kate popped up, her eyes bright with anticipation as she glanced over the top of the booth. As soon as she focused on the performer, she felt the blood drain from her face. Like a flower wilting in the hot summer sun, she withered back into her seat and dropped her head in her hands. "Oh my god."

"How the hell did he find this place?"

"I don't know. I don't think I ever told him where we played trivia." Her heart was pounding in her ears, making it nearly impossible to hear Brody's sweet, soft voice. How was it possible he was singing in this bar on this particular night? She squeezed her head in her hands, hoping the applied pressure would somehow reduce the panic she was starting to feel. Was this a coincidence or had he sought her out, knowing she'd be here? She did her best to believe it was only a coincidence, even though she desperately hoped it was the latter.

"Are you going to go talk to him?" Derek asked, pulling her hands away from her face.

"I don't know." She stared at him while her heart continued to thump. "I don't know what to do."

The song came to an end and the regular crowd exploded with applause.

"How'd you like that surprise, folks?" The manager's voice boomed over the speaker system. "Give another big round of applause to Brody Fisk, award-winning writer of our theme song." The tavern erupted in even louder applause, drowning out the confusion in her mind.

"Thanks, everybody," Brody said.

She drew in a sudden breath as his silky, sexy voice came through the speakers. How long had it been since she'd last heard his voice? It felt like an eternity.

"I hope you've enjoyed the sample of Misty Mountain beer, proudly made in Paula's Creek, West Virginia." Wild applause rang out in the bar once again. "Sounds like it was a hit. That's great."

"So, he's just here singing to promote the beer?" Derek asked.

"Sounds like it," Kate said.

"I wonder if you'd indulge me again." Brody continued with a light strum of his guitar strings. "There's a song I've recently written I'd like to try out. Maybe you can critique it and let me know what you think." The crowd encouraged him to sing again, not seeming to mind he was delaying the start of the weekly trivia contest. "Okay, here it goes. It's called *First Love Song.*"

Kate sat up straight, squaring her shoulders, as her eyes locked on Derek's. Brody had told her he'd never written a love song and yet here he was about to sing one. Her heart resumed its thumping and she slowly rose to her feet to watch him sing.

You know how it goes,
I was in trouble from the start.
I knew it right away,
When you gone and stole my heart.
Tried to keep you at arm's length,
Thought I was too smart for your games.
That sexy walk, your tempting talks,
The way you said my name.

I never wrote a love song,
But said the words to one or two.
Thought I'd been in love before,
But now I know the truth.
This is my very first love song
Because I found you.

***

Brody had been in this bar for over fifteen minutes and had yet to see Kate. Her grandmother had told him the name of the place she played trivia every Thursday and in his mind, he thought he'd walk in and instantly find her. He hadn't been prepared for high-walled booths lining the perimeter as well as filling the center of the room. If he wanted to find her, he'd have to walk around and check every table. He hoped singing *First Love Song* would draw her out of the cocoon of her booth.

Toward the end of the first verse, he saw her. Across the bar, he saw her face above the wall surrounding her booth and noticed she was gripping the ledge as if she'd fall without its support. She was still as beautiful as he'd pictured in his dreams every night.

He did his best not to rush the song, even though he wanted to drop his guitar and run to her. He locked his gaze on her, so there would be no mistaking who the song was about.

Kept my guard up, the gates locked tight,
Afraid I'd lose myself in you.
Setting you free, only seemed right.
But now I'm drowning in your memory.
I'd take it back if I had the chance,
Tell you I love you so.
Ask to join me in life's dance.

I never wrote a love song,
But said the words to one or two.
Thought I'd been in love before,
But now I know the truth.
This is my very first love song
Because I found you.

He kept all his focus on Kate. The ting of barware, the murmur of the crowd, his own voice blurred into white noise as he watched her face go from pained shock to a pleasant half-smile. Was she hearing the words? Understanding he'd been a fool not to share his feelings back in December?

When I started writing this love song,
The words came out so fast.
Yes, this is my first love song,
and because of you, won't be my last.

He finished the song by running his fingers across the fret board, creating a flurry of notes, keeping his eyes on the strings. When he strummed one last chord, he looked up and she was gone. His chest tightened and his palms immediately started sweating. Several patrons rushed toward him, blocking any view he had of the bar. He shook some hands and accepted several pats on his back, and did his best to get away quickly while not appearing rude.

A sense of panic rippled through his body. If she had rushed out, he'd never be able to find her. Finally, pushing through the crowd, his eyes locked on her, leaning against a high-top table near the entrance. Immediately, his panic subsided, but a new fear coursed through his veins. What if Liza had been wrong?

He tucked his hands in his front pockets and walked slowly toward Kate, trying his best to remain calm. His future hinged on the next few minutes.

***

"That was a pretty clever marketing strategy, Brody." Doing her best to appear relaxed by leaning against the high-top, Kate prayed he didn't notice the quiver in her voice. "Free beer and a live performance. Should definitely boost sales." She forced herself to smile brightly, appearing cool while camouflaging the fact that her insides were doing somersaults.

"You liked that, huh?"

He stepped within inches of her and she felt dizzy. His spicy smell, his dark eyes, and his soft lips curled in a smile were knocking her off-kilter. Her fingers were itching to reach up and touch his soft beard, run through his longish hair. He looked exactly like he had the first day she'd met him in her grandmother's backyard.

"How've you been?" he asked, dragging her away from her reverie.

"Okay. You?"

He replied with a nod and pointed to the tall bar stools alongside the table. He pulled out her chair and held her arm as she climbed on. When he dropped into his chair he gave her a pressed-lip smile and sighed, resting his elbows on the table.

"I'm sorry I didn't get a chance to taste the beer, but Derek said it was really good. Was that recipe Tucker's idea? I like the name. Very apropos to the season. I'll have to order it next week." Kate was rambling, couldn't slow down, and was unable to stop herself. He was staring at her with those dark, arresting eyes. So why couldn't she stop? "I was surprised when I heard you singing—well, I didn't know it was you at first. They'd promised me they'd pick a new theme song and did play something different last week. Then, when Derek looked over—"

"Why?" Brody croaked. It was the first word he had uttered since sitting down.

"Why what?"

"Why did they—" he cleared his throat "—promise to play a different song?"

"Well." How could she tell him it was too painful to hear any of his songs—too painful to be reminded of what she'd lost? "I just couldn't… it was too…I thought it was time for a new theme song."

"Oh. So."

"So, you've grown your beard back. Still hunting season?" She tried to lighten the heavy cloud of trepidation hovering between them. She flashed a quick smile at him, but he didn't return the gesture.

"Nah, I'm done hunting." He looked down at his folded hands resting on the table and murmured, "I found what I've been hunting for." He raised his dark eyes and she was momentarily paralyzed, unable to form a thought. She snapped her gaze from his and cleared her throat.

"Did Liza tell you I stopped by a couple of weeks ago when I was visiting Gram?"

"Yeah. I'm sorry I missed you." He unclasped his hands and reached across the table toward her. "I was in Nashville."

"She told me." She pressed her back against the chair and looked down at her hands, resting in her lap. "She said it's been going well for you there. You've been spending a lot of time with Callie Starr."

"In the studio. We recorded a duet."

She drew her gaze back to Brody and found him leaning toward her, his hand outstretched on the table. "Just in the studio?"

"Yeah, I've known Callie since I first got to Nashville. She heard I was in town and asked me to sing with her on her new album. It's a song Kyle and I wrote a few years ago."

"So, you're not—" Placing her hands on the table, within grabbing distance of his, she leaned forward and looked closely at him. "You're not seeing her."

"No. Did Liza tell you that?"

She watched his tentative expression turn quickly to anger. "Sort of. Maybe I misunderstood. It's just that you stopped calling."

"You always seemed distracted."

"I'm sorry."

"Katherine." Eyes welling with emotion, she fought back a smile at the sound of him saying her formal name. "Did you listen to the words to my song? It was about you."

"I listened." Her fingers crept towards his and he smothered her hand under his.

"I really screwed up before you left. There was so much I wanted to tell you, but couldn't," he said.

"Why didn't you?"

"Because I saw how happy you were when you got the promotion. I knew how much it meant to you. It was your chance to shine. How could I ask you to give that up?"

"But, I—"

"And I was a coward. The last time I pushed someone to do what I wanted…well, you know what happened." He picked up her hand and threaded his fingers with hers. "Watching you drive away…I didn't know I could feel that bad."

"I didn't want to go. I was just…afraid not to. It was the hardest decision I've ever made."

Their eyes locked and they held hands across the table and for several moments neither one spoke. He still hadn't told her he loved her or wanted her to come back, but that couldn't stop her from sharing her feelings and future plans. She finally broke the silence.

"I gave notice the other day."

"You quit?"

"I'm working through next Friday, just finishing up some cases and turning over my work to the other associates."

"Sweetheart, you didn't have to do that."

"Do you have a better suggestion?"

"I could move here." He pressed his lips against her hand, letting his mouth linger against her skin.

"And what? Spend all your time alone while I work all day and night?" She inched to the edge of her seat and brushed his cheek with her free hand. "I miss Highland Springs…and you. I want to come back."

"You're sure about this?" He smiled as he nibbled her pinkie. Feeling his mouth on any part of her body made her pulse quicken and it was all she could do not to rush into his arms.

"I'm tired of killing myself for an illusion. I want to start living for something real." She watched the recognition on his face as he recalled those sage words he'd spoken by the river. "I'm coming back and helping Gram. I've convinced her to add a first-floor bedroom to her house so she can stay in it longer. They start construction as soon as the ground thaws. I want to be there to oversee it."

"How long do you plan to stay?" Without letting go of her hand, Brody slid off his stool and crossed to the other side of the table, wedging himself next to her. "I mean beyond the construction?" He brushed the back of his hand against her cheek, his brows arched and eyes hopeful. "Is there anything I can do to convince you stay indefinitely?"

"Well, maybe if you—"

"Tell you I love you? Would that do it? Because it's true, you know. I do love you."

She slipped her arms around his waist and pulled him between her knees. She rested her head against his beating heart and all the fear drained from her body. He had just said the words she'd been dying to hear, the words that would make all the difference. After a few moments with her face pressed against his chest, she pulled back and cupped his face in her hands.

"That's exactly what I needed to hear. I love you, Brody, so much. I've been so—"

Before she could finish her thought, his mouth covered hers, seeking her lips and tongue hungrily as if he needed her essence for his very survival. She didn't care if the whole tavern was watching, she was right where she wanted to be, with the man she loved and who loved her back. All at once, the heavy burden she'd held inside lifted and drifted away. She knew that as long as she had Brody's love and they were together, she'd be content. After a dizzying few minutes, their lips parted and they pressed their foreheads together while catching their breaths.

"Damn it, I've missed you so much." He gave her a quick kiss and then stepped back, but still kept her in his arms. "I guess this is the part where I pick you up and carry you out of here."

She chuckled and dropped her head against his chest. "Did Liza tell you to do that?"

"She might have said something to that effect." He tipped her chin up with his hand with a mischievous smirk. "As I recall, the last time I carried you somewhere I got real lucky."

How could she forget being slung over his shoulder and carried to his bedroom? That caveman move was the most erotic fantasy to have ever come true and resulted in the best sex of her life. Those first intimate moments had only confirmed what she had suspected all along: she was in love with Brody and wanted to be with him always.

"Well…" She covertly slipped her hand under his shirttail and ran her finger inside the waistband of his jeans. "This time you'll get doubly lucky."

"Doubly lucky, huh? I like the sound of that." He nuzzled his soft beard against her neck and took a playful tug on her earlobe. "Let's go."

"Um, before you go all prince charming on me," she pressed her hand on his chest. "you should know if you plan to carry me out of here, be prepared to carry two."

Time stood still. She was sure her heart had stopped beating as she watched Brody's playful grin melt into a thin line. He held her gaze, blinking away the confusion as his eyes darted from left to right. When he began to shake his head ever so slightly, she thought this would be the end. Her pregnancy would be the deal breaker to their future. Slowly his right hand glided from around her back and settled on her stomach.

"You're pregnant?" he whispered.

Emotion clogged her throat and, unable to speak, she replied with a tentative nod. She looked down at his hand still covering her abdomen and was afraid to look up at him again, afraid of what she'd see.

"We're having a baby." This time when he said the words, she could hear joy, wonder, even excitement. She looked up and found him smiling with every muscle in his face and his eyes dancing with happiness. "We're having a baby." He spoke loud enough this time that several people sitting nearby turned to look at them. Before she could say anything, he scooped her off the bar stool and spun her around, announcing to all within shouting distance, "We're having a baby!"

She collapsed against his shoulder, relieved he was sharing in her joy. As he held her in his arms, her feet dangled a few inches above the floor.

"I don't know how this happened. I thought we were careful." He dropped her gently to the floor and gathered her face in his hands. "But who cares? This is the best news ever."

"You're not upset? Worried? Angry?"

"Hell, no, sweetheart, we're having a baby…our baby."

"Yes, I'm having your baby." She leaned up and wrapped her hand around the back of his head, pulling him down for a long, loving kiss. "And I couldn't be happier." He gathered her close and smothered her lips with another kiss. When they pulled apart, her heart swelled to near bursting when she noticed dampness in his eyes and a beaming smile on his face. She wanted to freeze this moment in her memory. Brody pecked a kiss on her nose and then swiftly slid his hand behind her knees, gathering her in his arms.

"You were wrong, you know?"

"About what?" She draped her arms around his neck and raked her fingers through his hair.

"You said this wouldn't end well, and yet—"

"It has."

Brody pushed his back against the door, carrying Kate out into the crisp winter night as folks in the bar erupted in a loud round of applause.

ACKNOWLEDGEMENTS

The town of Highland Springs was inspired by my time spent as a student in Buckhannon, West Virginia, at West Virginia Wesleyan College. Located in the central part of the state, the area is surrounded by beautiful mountains that glow with color in the fall. Orange, red, and gold leaves dotting the hills will be forever etched in my memory.

The spring of my senior year, I was a social work intern, travelling with a caseworker into the surrounding counties to visit senior citizens in need. My most memorable client was a lady named Anna Linger, who lived in a one-room cabin deep in a "holler". *Cash's Holler* was Anna's holler: unpainted one-room cabins on cinderblock stilts, single-wide trailers, and junked cars. The gravel road was so steep going in and out of the holler that I feared my little Ford Pinto wouldn't make it. While visiting Anna one day, a bearded man silently unloaded a cord of wood and stacked it alongside her cabin. She told me he had recently moved to the area from New York City where he had given up his high-paying job on Wall Street, and now spent his days delivering wood to folks in the holler who needed it (at no charge).

I knew when I started writing that I would include this fascinating tale in a book someday, having wondered for over thirty years what made him give up that coveted career to live in the backwoods of West Virginia. That reflection is how Brody's story was born. So, thank you, Anna Linger and the mountain man for the inspiration.

Travis's conversation with Kate about pineapple tops growing well in a pot of soil actually happened to me—word for word. A blonde-dreadlocked man told me all about his experience working on a pineapple farm as I checked out of the grocery store. Thank you, pineapple man for sharing your expertise.

I had the pleasure of chatting with Christian Lopez at a local coffee shop to learn about his songwriting process. If you haven't listened to the Christian Lopez Band's amazing Americana sound, I encourage you to do so. I predict he'll be a household name someday. Thank you, Christian.

At the same coffee shop, I spent some time talking with physical therapist Dr. Emily Leonard Hockman about the best course of treatment for Gram's broken femur. When she told me about strapping patients into safety harnesses, I knew I had to include that in the story. Thank you, Emily.

Many of the character names from this book and *Whatever You Call Me* are actually names of my friends and family. I didn't ask their permission in advance. Hopefully they aren't mad at me but are happy to see their names in print, even though the characters are nothing like the actual people. Thank you, friends.

For the past five years, I've worked with an incredible editor whom I now call a friend. Thank you, Rebecca Faith Heyman for all your help and support.

I have to thank my husband and children for their patience, support, and love. Whenever I ask them to share a Facebook post or spread the word to friends, they always willingly oblige. Thank you, Pat, Tom, and Liza.

Finally, thank you, reader for taking the time to read *Whatever You Say*. There are thousands of romance novels and hundreds of talented romance authors, yet you took the time to read this one. Thank you from the bottom of my heart.

Thank you for reading *Whatever You Say*. If you enjoyed it, please help other readers find this book:

- Write a review on the site where you purchased the book.
- Share this copy with a friend.
- Keep up with news of upcoming releases by signing up for my newsletter at www.leighfleming.com.
- Like my Facebook page: www.facebook.com/leighhflemingauthor.
- Follow me on Twitter: www.twitter.com/leighhfleming1

ABOUT THE AUTHOR

Most days Leigh can be found in her windowless office, escaping to Highland Springs, a fictional town in the West Virginia mountains, as she continues writing her *Whatever* series. Look for *Whatever We Are* coming in late 2017.

Leigh is a member of Romance Writers of America and the Washington Romance Writers chapter. She lives in Martinsburg, West Virginia, with her husband, Patrick, and her deaf French Bulldog Napoleon, and is mom to adult children, Tom and Liza.